DETECTING
THE
FATAL CONNECTION

A MATT MALONE
MYSTERY

Marlene Chabot

Love,
Enjoy!
Marlene Micheil Chabot

Other Writings by Marlene Chabot

NOVELS
Detecting the Fatal Connection
(First published in 2003 as China Connection)
North Dakota Neighbor
Mayhem With A Capital M
Death At The Bar X Ranch
Death of the Naked Lady

Anthologies
Why Did Santa Leave A Body?
"A Visit From Santa"

Festival of Crime
"The Missing Groom"

SWF Stories and Poems
"The Gulper Eel"

DEDICATION

This novel is dedicated in loving memory to my father James Mc Neil and Sister Lois Wasielewski, O.S.F, who offered tremendous words of encouragement along the way. I wish they could've stayed a little while longer here on earth to celebrate the completion of this book with me.

~1~

December 10, 1999

Matt Malone's my name. Private investigation is my game. Irish blood courses through my forty-year-old veins, but you won't find me hankering for a shot of Jamison whiskey or even an invite to a so-called traditional Irish wake.

At present, this single self-employed guy takes up livable space in the Foley Apartment Complex situated near the heart of downtown Minneapolis, kitty-corner from the world renowned Guthrie Theater. Built in the mid '50's, when I was a wee lad, the Foley is on the cusp of its half-century anniversary, though you can't tell by its outward appearances.

The apartment's exterior, a classical-box-style enhanced with reddish-brown Chicago brick, is cleverly disguised with a thick growth of creeping-ivy covering everything above the first floor except the windows. If the ivy wasn't there, you'd definitely see how Minnesota's fluctuating temperatures has eaten away at the building.

The Foley's interior is a different story. Mr. Edward's, the elderly caretaker, swears time and the elements haven't affected it, only tenants. He should know; everyday between six a.m. and ten p.m., he tries his darndest to keep up with the trash-ladened hallways, snow-troddened stairwells, leaky toilets, and other emergencies that arise, to no avail.

Crazy as it may sound; I've found one grand job of Mr. Edward's that has remained untarnished. A couple weeks ago he scrubbed the hallways' soiled-yellow walls and they still glow. As a matter of fact, it's so bright now I have to don my Ray-Bans the second I step out in the hall. But fairly soon, I may have to switch to a welder's mask. That is of course if the halls actually get a fresh coat of paint like the building's owners have been promising for the past five years.

The Foley, which has an elevator and underground parking, loves to brag about its fifty apartment units that cover a four-floor radius.

I'd give you a run down on the various nationalities who reside here, but all one has to do is walk down our hallowed halls any afternoon or evening. One warning though, your stomach will beg to be fed.

I smacked my lips as tonight's delightful aromas flooded my nostrils. "Ah, yes—Pierogi, Stir-fry, Fettuccine, Falafel, Irish stew, and Southern Fried Chicken." Too bad I'm such a lousy cook. I sure would enjoy sampling one of those meals.

When relatives ask what drew me to this specific complex with such an assortment to choose from in Minneapolis, I usually give them the shortened version.

"My office is nearby." What I really refrain from saying is, "The easy access to the freeway systems, closeness to downtown Minneapolis, age differences of residents, and the Foley's cosmopolitan atmosphere make it the perfect place to live." So, keep it under your hat, okay. I don't want to find out all my friends and relatives are moving here next week. A guy needs to retain some semblance of privacy if you catch my drift.

In my line of work I run into scads of nosy people. If that label fits you, right about now you're probably yearning for info on the inhabitants who share the fourth floor with me. Well, I guess I can cough that up. As a PI, there's only two people I have time to communicate with; a thirty-year-old guy with Norwegian ancestry, Rodney Thompson, who dwells to the left of my pad, and an elderly woman originally from Italy, Margaret Grimshaw who lives directly across the hall from me.

Like I said earlier, I'm single, but if you get your kicks from knowing more, I'm a widower of two years, come April. No need to feel sorry for me. I do have a lovable live-in companion, a mutt, who comes running whenever the magic word *food* is mentioned.

Speaking of food, my business does keep me fed, but only because of a trusty little quirk passed unto me in a unique way from Great Aunt Fiona on my father's side, sixth sense or premonitions. The magical tool I had to graciously accept was terrific as a youngster, but once I reached teen years, it became a thorn in my side, a curse.

Sometimes my premonition level hits extreme heights and nearly explodes. I blame it on not tuning in. You know what they say about the gray matter between your ears, as you age, it goes south.

One such incident occurred a year ago December. The reason I remember is it was a warm day, a rarity for

3

the Midwest. According to the local newscaster, we hadn't had this kind of weather since 1885, right before the St. Paul Winter Carnival commenced.

~2~

December 13, 1998

In the wee hours of the morning, my sleepless body was being tormented. If I'd left the heat turned up too high before going to bed, I could've blamed it on that. But that wasn't it. Remember it was warmer than usual. No, my sleeplessness was caused by a conversation from the '50's that kept repeating itself in my mind like a spoiled kid over indulged on carnival rides. We all know what happened to him, right? Well, the dialogue bumming me out made me feel as nauseous.

The turbulent storm revolved around an article published in the Minneapolis Star Tribune. The unforgettable piece of journalism predicted that the constant battle for Number-One-Super-Power position, between the U.S.A. and Russia would soon end; a Third World country would acquire the rights to the title: China

My father's foghorn voice burst through the air first. I covered my ears but it didn't help. "I'm telling you Michael that writer has gone off the deep end. No country, including China, is capable of displacing the United States as leader of the Free World."

My sibling threw his arms in the air. "I'd prefer that you use my middle name Dad. Everyone at school calls me Sam."

"All right. All right. But you do agree with me, don't you?"

"Actually, Dad, I think Doug Sheer is on the right track. His article makes perfect sense. But it ain't China who will be running the show next. You'll see. When the timing's right, it'll be Australia who takes a swing at the title." He let loose with a recklessly upper-right cut that almost landed on my father's jaw.

It was at this juncture, Dad invited me into the foray. "Matt, what do you think?"

I shrugged my shoulders. "Gee, Dad, I'm only six. I don't know anything." Deep furrows settled on his forehead. He wasn't happy with my answer. So, I timidly added, "Okay, maybe China will become Number One." But off to the side I mumbled, "Or maybe not."

It took a sharp jolt to my chest to finally interrupt the constant rerun going on in the deep recesses of my head. My arms flew straight up. "Wa? What the heck?" The room was so dark I couldn't see a darn thing. Something began to lick my face. "Gracie, how many times do I have to tell you I sleep in on Sundays?" I pointed in the direction of the floor. "Get off the bed. Now!" The instant she shot to the floor I laid my head back on the feathered pillow.

What on earth triggered a long-ago discussion about China? And, why would I've thought it necessary to store it in my memory bank? I pulled the wool blanket up around my neck and stared at the ceiling, hoping for answers. None came. At least not yet.

A soft, "Woof, woof," apology came from the far corner of the room.

"Hush, Gracie." When the next whimper came, I ignored it and flipped over on my slightly bulging stomach. Changing to this position didn't help. I couldn't sleep if I tried. I sat up and turned the bedside lamp on. "You win. I'm getting out of bed."

Gracie inched her way forward to the double bed. When she reached it, she begged for me to rub her head.

I complied. But the minute I pressed a hand to massage Gracie's noggin, weird feelings generated through my entire body. Could it be the unusual weather conditions or the *gift?* "Nah." Minnesota's noted for strange weather occurrences throughout the year and I wasn't privy to anything of major significance about to happen in the world.

I shook the feeling aside as best I could and dropped my cold feet to the thick ugly pea-green carpeted floor.

Apparently, the dog didn't like my decision to dismiss what I'd experienced. Whenever she senses things aren't quite right, she does a sophisticated dance similar to the cha-cha.

Worried her fancy footwork might get out of control, I quickly intervened before the crappy bedroom carpet got destroyed and I'd be out mega bucks to repair it. "Settle down, Girl. The vibes you're picking up are nothing to worry about." She glared at me. "Honest. You don't see me sweating it." I ran a hand through my flattened hair. "A walk will clear your head, you'll see." *And hopefully mine too.*

"Woof. Woof."

I tossed on jeans, long-sleeved shirt, socks, and tennis shoes I'd left by the dresser last night after I had walked Gracie. I'm a little lazy about stashing clothes in the closet, but what the heck. I'm all for making things handy when you can't control what time your dog wants to flee the building to do her duty. Besides, one of the benefits of being a bachelor is I can do whatever I want in my pad. Finished dressing, I tugged on the dog's ear to let her know I was heading to the door.

When we got to the entrance closet, I grabbed a light jacket while Gracie plucked her leash off the floor with her teeth, something I taught her to do. "Good dog." I took the wet leash out of her mouth and hooked it to her collar. "Okay, let's blow this two-penny joint."

Once we reached the outside, Gracie did her dirty deed by a nearby tree on the boulevard and then we began our leisurely pace to Loring Park where we normally roam for at least a half hour. We've been following this predictable pattern in the mornings ever since I brought Gracie home from the animal shelter.

I regret to this day that I never got to know her as a pup. It would've been fun. Another family owned her for three years before disposing of her, one steamy summer day, along the Highway 100 corridor. Most drivers seeing the stray dog on the road probably thought she wouldn't see another day. But Gracie proved them wrong. A Good Samaritan pulled off the road, retrieved the mutt, and taxied her to the nearest shelter.

Since the Hennepin Humane Society found no dog tag or microchip implant on Gracie, they were forced to kennel her the allotted time, hoping a new master or old one would appear so she wouldn't have to be put down.

Luckily, I showed up right before her death sentence was sealed. But I didn't come to adopt. I needed to be cheered up. Animals always have this unique knack of lifting my spirits. And believe me; mine needed a major overhaul. It was the six-month anniversary of my wife's untimely death from cancer.

The second I walked through the entrance, I was instantly drawn to the medium-sized chocolate-colored mutt with huge soulful eyes sitting behind one of the many black barred metal jails. She looked as forlorn as I felt. Not the type of dog I needed to make me laugh. Little did I know this sad-looking dog's peanut brain had already sized me up and was about to manipulate this guy into becoming her new master.

As soon as I started towards the animal cages to select a rambunctious dog, she let out this ear-splitting howl and spun round and round. The act worked. I ignored the other dogs caged up and begged to take her for a walk. And as they say, "the rest is history."

Unfortunately, the walk around the park did nothing to quell the strange feelings I had earlier. Why couldn't I get the nonsense about China out of my head?

I eased my body on one of the many benches scattered throughout Loring Park. The sun's tic-tac-toe pattern displayed on the brown grass quickly conjured up pleasant memories of geese and ducks and kids passing out tidbits of bread. I glanced down to check on Gracie who had settled at my feet. She was chewing on a piece of paper clinging to the rungs of the bench.

"Silly mutt, that's not food." I bent over and grabbed the paper. It tore a little, but I still managed to read it. It was a complaint about keeping the pond clear of geese. I slapped my knee. "Dog gonnit! Geese are being eliminated. What next?" The geese issue had been bantered about at the Foley around the end of summer, but apparently, it had slipped my mind.

Gracie cocked her head after hearing my irritated tone and decided to remain a safe distance from me.

"I can't believe it." The park people think shrubs near the water's edge will deter the geese from polluting the air and water. Doesn't anyone besides me realize mankind is the biggest polluter of all? Just visit any landfill.

Grand weather or not this morning sucked. I felt crummy the moment I swung my legs over the edge of the bed to greet the mutt, and the stroll through the park did nada to perk me up. Instead, my stomach's flipping every which way. I yanked on Gracie's collar letting her know I'd had enough. She didn't budge. Maybe she was afraid I had more ranting to share. "Look," I said in a calmer voice, "I'm sorry my venting scared you," then I gently tugged on her leash again. "Come on, your favorite watering hole by the Guthrie is waiting."

"Aroooo."

~3~

The second I rounded the corner of the Foley Complex with Gracie I shortened her leash, causing her to stop so I could to get my daily fix of the <u>Star Tribune</u> for a pittance from the neighborhood's rusty battered newspaper stand. I detested home delivery and the constant forking out of tips for someone I've never met. Although, being a realist I knew one of these days I wouldn't have a choice in how I got the paper. The newspaper stand will simply fall by the wayside and become yet another legend like the pay phone.

I dropped the appropriate coins in the slot, opened the window, and withdrew a paper. When the door slammed, it startled the mutt so bad she spun around. "Come on, let's go inside," I said, as I tugged on her leash and sprinted up the steps leading to the Foley's main doors.

Mr. Edwards, the caretaker, was standing in the lobby with his back to the front door, holding a mop and pail. I gave Gracie a slowdown signal. She obeyed "It's sure a nice day, isn't it Mr. Edwards?"

"Yup." He set his metal pail down and then turned around. "Why Mr. Malone, I didn't realize it was you." The caretaker looked exhausted. It didn't help that his face was smudged with dirt and his glasses were askew. Mr. Edward's wiped his wet, calloused hands on his dark blue jeans before making a feeble attempt to adjust his brown plastic glasses.

Gracie treaded closer to him, making it easier to sniff his hands and feet.

The man kept an eye on the dog and allowed a tiny smile to crease his lips. "Well, Gracie, looks like you've taken your master for a Sunday morning walk.

"Woof. Woof."

The caretaker's hand swiped Gracie's back. "Got lots to catch up on," he shared with me. "Been gone two whole days. Had to see a sick brother who lives in Wisconsin."

"Oh? Sorry about your brother. I hope it's nothing serious."

"He had a cold he couldn't seem to shake, but he said he's feeling a bit better this morning."

"Glad to hear it."

Our conversation ended now as far as Mr. Edwards was concerned. He turned his back on us like we'd never been there and quickly dipped the mop into a pail of cleaning solution and water.

Knowing how much bleach bothered my eyes and lungs, I promptly escorted the mutt to the stairwell before the mop smacked the floor.

By the time we got to the fourth floor landing, both of us were huffing and puffing like idiots. Sure, I could've taken the elevator and been more comfortable, but taking the four flights kept the leg muscles and the ticker in shape. "You know, Gracie, maybe we need to rethink this extra workout routine. What do you think?"

The mutt didn't reply. She just pawed at the metal door leading to the hallway.

"Okay, I'll take that as a maybe." I flung the door open and continued on to the apartment.

The minute I reached the door, I noticed something was amiss across the hall from me. My neighbor, Mrs. Grimshaw, hadn't taken her Sunday newspaper in yet. *Lord, please don't let her be ill again,*" I prayed.

In the past five years, Margaret Grimshaw has had hip, foot, knee, and gall bladder surgery. The proud, feisty woman says she doesn't want anyone looking after her until she's six-feet under. With that kind of attitude, she'll probably outlive us all.

While I dug out the key and fidgeted with the lock, someone opened their door. I kind of hoped it was Margaret. But it wasn't. Off to the left of me I found FBI agent Rod Thompson scooping up his newspaper.

It was only after he straightened his tall frame that his deep-blue penetrating eyes caught a glimpse of me. He immediately rearranged his thick tousled blond hair. "I haven't seen you in a while, Malone. How's it going?"

"Keeping myself busy as usual," I lied. I hadn't had a new case in a while, but I added more fuel to the fire anyway. "As a matter of fact, I'm starting a huge case next week."

The Big Man upstairs hadn't come through for me yet and probably wouldn't after that remark. Although He knows how much I need the income: bills to pay, dog to feed, girlfriend to entertain.

Gracie broke loose of my grip and buzzed over to greet Rod. He lifted his heavily-robed arm and patted her back. "Great. Glad to hear it. You need to keep yourself out of trouble."

Keep myself out of trouble? What exactly is the guy insinuating? I inhaled deeply. *Relax.* This is not the day to let him get under your skin. There's plenty of other days for that. Shift to a safer topic. "Say Rod have you seen Mrs. Grimshaw lately?"

Rod yawned and rubbed his bleary eyes.

Must've been some hot date he had last night. Normally the guy's rip-roaring to go.

He lifted his sagging shoulders and then let them drop. "Yeah, I did. When I first checked to see if the paper had been delivered about an hour ago, she flew past me like a bat on fire."

Concerned Margaret might have been rushing to the emergency room at Hennepin County Medical Center; I inquired whether she said anything to Rod.

"It didn't quite make sense to me. She mumbled something about a nine o'clock service."

Church. Of course. Margaret attends Sunday services. Guilt riddled me. I used to attend church regularly when Irene was alive. But after she died, I kinda gave up on being saved by a higher power and the whole ball of wax.

Rod's eyes shifted to Margaret's doormat. "Her newspaper hasn't been retrieved. Ah, that's why you're inquiring about her."

I wonder if he used his fabulous FBI skills to deduce that. He's such a computer geek; common sense isn't even in his vocabulary.

Even though I hate running into Rod, something good came from our seeing each other today, I know Margaret's okay. Oh, don't get me wrong. I'm not the mushy sentimental type, but I do feel a certain responsibility for the elderly woman, like a guardian angel. It wasn't all that long ago that our roles were reversed. After Irene died, Margaret checked on me and freely shared bits of wisdom.

"You can sit in that easy-chair of yours the rest of your life, Matt," she said, "But if your wife could communicate with you, she'd tell you to get up, get moving. Start living again." And that's exactly what I've been doing — mixing with those who come into my life, whether they're good or bad.

"I worry about our elderly neighbor," I told Rod. "Margaret's no spring chicken. And she has no family, but I'm sure you know that." He nodded. "That's why I came up with this ingenious idea to use Margaret's newspaper like a health barometer. If the paper is outside her door at 9 a.m., I take action."

"What if you hadn't run into me? Would you have rushed in unannounced?" He didn't allow me to reply. Instead he droned on in that big brotherly fashion of his, forgetting once again I was a mere neighbor. "Did you ever hear of the phone? These days it's quite reliable."

My face felt like a well-stoked furnace. "Come on, my way is full proof," I snorted.

Rod shook his pale head. "I don't think so. Apparently you weren't listening to a word I said."

My head was getting hotter by the minute. "For your information, Margaret's told me many times that her daily routine involves rising precisely at six to greet whoever drops off the paper and then heading to the kitchen table to enjoy a cup of coffee while completing the daily crossword puzzle."

Rod had begun to retreat to his abode, but my last words stopped him cold. "What? Margaret Grimshaw works the crossword puzzle? Huh, I didn't realize she and I had anything in common. You know our age difference."

A chuckle escaped my lips. It was hard imagining Nordic Rod and petite Margaret sharing interests of any sort; the two of them are as different as steak and a pea. Rod Thompson stands over six feet without shoes. A muscular guy, he carries his two-hundred-pound frame exceptionally-well. Margaret, on the other hand, is thin as a snake and around five feet tall.

Feeling in a better frame of mind, I decided to question Rod about a matter not related to Mrs. Grimshaw. "Say Rod, you don't happen to have someone at your location who analyzes memories from childhood do you?"

He pulled his bathrobe belt tighter. "No. Why? What kind of memories?"

How do I tell him about the China conversation? I could be giving him too much ammunition to use on me later when he had a mind to. "I ahh..., I've been giving a lot of thought to something that happened in my early years of formation."

Rod's eyes glazed over. I could tell he wasn't interested in my childhood. He only wanted to know the latest scoop about me.

I loosely waved my hand in front of me. "Never mind. It's no big deal. See you later." I removed the key from the lock, grabbed Gracie by the collar, and went inside.

***

"What this?" My feet were greeted by a folded piece of typing paper as I glided across the threshold of my abode. Someone must've slid it under the door during my absence, more than likely the building manager. He probably thought he should remind those residents who park on the street about the odd-even parking regulations when the cities hit by a snow storm. I flipped the note open curious to see if there were new rules I needed to know about in case I had an overnight guest.

If you know what's good for you, you lousy deadbeat, you'll stay away from my cousin. P.S. I'm dead serious.

Well, it definitely isn't from management. "I can't believe one of Rita's cousins wants me to stay away from her." I pressed my fingers to my forehead. I thought I was on good terms with the few cousins she had. Who would do such a crazy thing? I snapped my fingers. "Cousin Arnie I bet." He's such a practical joker.

Clever guy I must admit. It takes smarts to get into a secure building without buzzing me. I can see why Rita's relatives worry about his jokes misfiring and him ending up in the slammer one day. Before going to the kitchen, I crumpled the stupid note and dropped it and the newspaper in the beefy-easy chair I frequent the most.

Seeing the direction I had chosen, Gracie trotted behind and whined her head off. Apparently breakfast was on her mind too.

"Be patient." While I waited for the coffee to brew, I pulled out the Alpo dog food I kept under the kitchen sink. Oh, boy. Not enough food left to keep the mutt's hunger pangs at bay for at least seven hours. Guess I'll be running to the grocery store later even though I hadn't planned to.

A few minutes later the coffee brew was ready. I filled a cup, grabbed a napkin and a four-day-old chocolate donut and returned to the living room to read the newspaper.

Gracie had already finished her food by then and stuck close to me. I'm thinking she kept a close eye on me because she expected me to share the donut with her too. Well, that wasn't going to happen.

I set the coffee and donut down on the end table by the La-Z-Boy and picked up the crumpled note and newspaper before plopping in the chair.

The mutt snuck up to the table, sniffed the donut, and whined.

"Donuts aren't good for you. Besides, I promised Rita I'd try to be a neater eater. Every time she heads home from a visit here she finds stains on her clothes."

My determination to stick to my plan didn't sit well with Gracie. She whined and then bolted straight to the other side of the room. Yup, the mutt's definitely a female. Every woman I know, including my sister, reacts the same way when they don't get their way. They stomp off in a huff.

I ignored the mutt and leafed through the various sections of the newspaper, leaving the front page till last. Most of the news in section A is national, but once in a while a local story slides in. It's the local news that piques my curiosity; probably because I'm always searching for the perfect case: one with tons of fringe benefits. Sometimes I luck out. I actually find a job.

Finding nothing of interest in the various sections, I went to the front page. "Hey? What's this?" In large bold letters a medium-sized article heralded the following: **Chinese Government Officials Call for Special Meeting.**

Interesting. My eyes rapidly scanned the flow of newsprint.

A special meeting is planned for mid-January. Nothing has been leaked to the media so far. Newsmen will be barred from the meeting. There has been speculation none the less. Most people living outside China believe the meeting will pertain to the harsh communist rules governing movement between other countries, freedom of speech, and the one child per married couple. All are issues the U.S. and other foreign countries say need to be addressed if China wants to join the United Nations.

I set the paper down and took a bite of donut. Gut instinct told me the news reporters were off base, on the meeting. I mean, come on, doesn't anyone besides myself remember Jiang Zemin telling the President no country was going to dictate how their country should be run.

Chapped chocolaty fingers danced on the edge of my chin. This darn article bugged me. "Couldn't China's government just be holding a meeting to discuss the drastic changes in their economy? We all know how secretive they are. They definitely wouldn't want the rest of the world to learn about their financial woes.

But hey, what do I know. My interpretation could be way off kilter. I'm certainly not privy to political problems and I'm no whiz on the economics of foreign countries. If I was, I'd have a nice cushy job with the White House and not be skimping on groceries to pay the rent. I guess I'll have to ride this one out like everyone else.

Goose bumps surfaced along my arms. Crap. Were the bumps the result of keeping the apartment temperature lower than the norm this time of year or due to the article? Surely the story was meant to leave the reader on an optimistic note. Oh, boy, trouble in the mid-section. The stomach feels queasy again. That eliminates the too cool room theory.

"What's wrong with you Malone? You've never met anyone from China."

When Gracie heard the tone of my voice, she charged over to the La-Z-Boy and rested her head on my lap.

"I'm fine. Thanks for checking." *Could I be having a premonition attack?* "Nah." It's been awhile since the curse has bothered me. I rubbed my arms and took a gulp of hot coffee. I suppose I should be thinking about work. I glanced at my watch. One o'clock. Oh, man. The heck with the queasiness, I've got to get over to the office and go through some files.

I dropped the newspaper on the carpet and went to the hall closet to retrieve an Air Force issued navy trench coat. At least Service clothes don't wear out after a person's discharged. Gracie watched as I put it on. "Sorry, Sergeant Gracie, you can't come with. Your duty is to guard our abode while I'm gone. And remember, no sleeping on the job like last time. Do you understand?"

The mutt posted herself by the door, raised her paw, and acknowledged what I said. "Woof."

Luckily, I have no trouble finding my white 1993 Mercury Topaz in the Foley's underground parking. It's the dirtiest one. I slid in the car, turned on the ignition and made a hasty retreat to Northeast Minneapolis.

The last time I used the car I had left the radio on. It was tuned to KRQT, a local "oldie" music station I enjoy listening to. The music being broadcast wasn't something I recognized, but I knew the radio personality would soon enlighten me. "That folks was the title song from the movie 'Road to Singapore'. One of the many Road movies Bing Crosby and Bob Hope appeared in.

There's something definitely going on here. First that old conversation about China tumbled around in my head, then I read the article on China, now a song about a city in China. I can't believe it's just a coincidence, but what else could it be.

~4~

This being a weekend versus a weekday my turnoff for Lowry Avenue came up sooner than I'd expected and I almost missed it. I flicked the blinker on, squeezed between two cars, hung a right at the corner, and then drove a mere three more blocks to my destination.

Years ago the Avenue and streets surrounding the building I work in overflowed with businesses. Then my generation grew up, got hungry for homes of their own out in the sticks, and a mass exodus from the inner-city occurred.

Yup, land development back then caused quite a stir not just for Minnesotans but for everyone. Old reliable corner stores disappeared to be replaced by massive strip malls. Deterioration's the only reminder of luxury left. A prime example is the stucco hole-in-the-wall building I use.

When I reached the office, I steered the Topaz off the street and onto a short gravel path where I always park the car, a stone's throw from the building which is also the only advantage to locating work here versus downtown Minneapolis.

As soon as I pulled the keys out of the ignition, I left the car behind, stepped up to the rotten office door that barely hangs on its hinges, and jiggled the key in the lock.

Darn! The inner-sanctum hadn't been magically transformed since I last visited. It's still messy and bleak. I eye-balled the thread-bare furniture and greedily hungered for a case that would bring in a sufficient amount of dough to replace the awful décor. Although, no matter how much extra cash started flowing into my bank account, I'd never part with the oak desk which is on Jubilee Junkyard's Top 10 Most Wanted List, too much history.

Unfortunately, the only history of interest to me today was the mail smothering the battered desk. *Yuck.* I spread my hands across the desk, shoved all the mail together and then shuffled through it. "Ah, ha, I was right," I said to the heavy stale air, "nothing important: bills and junk mail." I tossed the pile aside and punched in my voice-mail number.

Three lousy messages. Two were non-work related. The first was from my girlfriend, the lovely Rita Sinclair who has a soft sultry voice that pierces a man's heart like an arrow. "Hi, Matt. I figured the best place to leave this message was at your office. Sorry, Hon, our plans for this coming week are shot, too chaotic at work. Next Thursday for sure. Okay? Give me a jingle if that works." When Rita's call ended, my sensitive ears had the misfortune of hearing the harsh clunking sound of the phone receiver being set back in place.

I must admit I was disappointed that Rita wasn't available, but it didn't surprise me. Change of plans between the two of us happens all the time.

I gripped the top of the desk chair. "Delete or save the message?" a robotic voice inquired. *Delete.* I can recite the message from memory.

Message two, "Mr. Malone," a deep powerful voice said, "this is Neil Welch, President of Delight Bottling Company. We've never met, but a friend we have in common recommended I speak with you about a private matter. Give me a call at 1-800-DELIGHT Monday around nine if you're interested. Tell the secretary I'm expecting your call. She'll put you right through."

Whoa! Why would the owner of the world's number one soft drink company call me? It's got to be a mistake. The work I do is small meat and potatoes—nothing related to corporations. I raked my fingers through my hair. "My God, could my lie to Rod actually come true? I glanced at the message machine, one more to go. Maybe Welch called back to tell me he had phoned the wrong guy. Well, you won't know until you press the button.

As soon as the first few words were out of the person's mouth, I knew it wasn't the president of Delight Bottling. "Hey, Matt, what's cooking? Do you recognize this voice from the past?" the loud male asked. "In case you're having trouble, I'll save you the effort. It's Randy Williams. We spent time in the Air Force together, remember?"

Unfortunately, I do. Why was Randy reaching out to me after all these years? I've tried to stay as far away from him as possible.

"Say, I hope you don't mind, ol' buddy, but I passed your name on to a friend of mine, who shall we say is having a bit of a 'delicate problem' if you get my drift. I told him if a guy with your background couldn't help, no one could. I suppose you'd like his name in case he calls this weekend. It's Neil Welch."

"What?" Obnoxious Randy runs around in Neil Welch's circle? Unbelievable.

"Hey, Buddy, the next time I have a layover in Minneapolis let's play pool. I might even let you recoup your losses." There was a heavy snort. "Adios."

"Shoot pool with you, never." I haven't forgotten how you cheat, Randy. But then again, if your good deed turns into gold, I might have a change of heart.

Assuming Neil Welch would pop by here to meet with me, I scanned the office. Not a respectable place to do business with the likes of him. This pigsty has got to be squared away before he drops everything to see me. But where do I begin? I suppose the smallest things first. I grabbed an overflowing ashtray that a nervous client had filled up over a month ago and dumped it outside. With that done, I moved to the closet, took the Dirt Devil out, and gave the thinly carpeted floor the once over before brushing the dust off chairs and tables with my hand.

Finished with the cleaning chores, I surveyed the room and gave a nod of approval. It passed inspection. Cobwebs in the office had definitely been dispatched. Too bad one still clung to my brain, the strange call from Welch. I scratched my forehead. I couldn't fathom what a guy like him wanted with me. "It's personal," Randy said. Perhaps the wife is spending too much time shopping or with another guy on the sly. It doesn't matter. You'll have the answers soon enough, Malone. Now, where are those car keys?

~5~

After making a quick stop on the way home from the office and fighting my way through crowded aisles filled with grocery shoppers and their carts, I certainly didn't need to find an SUV, owned by the jerk in 413, parked over my line again. My anger meter escalated rapidly. How the heck did the SUV owner expect me to fit the Topaz in the assigned slot given me? I'm telling you he's treading deep water. We're going to have a serious chat real soon whether he likes it or not.

It took a significant amount of maneuvering to squeeze my bulk and the groceries between the two cars, but I finally managed and escaped to a noisy elevator anxiously awaiting me.

The moment I stepped on to the fourth floor, I directed my feet towards the apartment across from mine, number 402, Margaret Grimshaw's place, and knocked on the door with an elbow. She wasn't expecting me, but I'd hoped she was home. I had bought her a surprise.

A sweet melodious voice instantly responded from deep within. "Just a minute, I'm coming," then two deadbolts clicked and the door swung open. "My goodness, Matt, what are you doing here?"

"I thought you might like an addition to the Christmas decorations I figured you've already set out." I handed her the bouquet of red and green carnations I'd purchased at the store. The clerk told me carnations last longer than most other flowers.

Margaret's ever-twinkling green eyes dimmed slightly. Tears slipped down her pale cheeks. She took the flowers. "Come in, come in," she said and then looked beyond me. "Where are you hiding that sweet dog of yours, Matt?"

I entered her short hallway. "I left Gracie at home to guard our abode while I ran errands."

"Ah." She pressed the bouquet to her bosom. "These flowers will certainly add more color to my décor. I haven't had a chance to purchase a Poinsettia yet."

Darn. I knew I should've gotten that for her instead.

Margaret set the bouquet on her pine bookcase temporarily, to dab the tears from her face with a hanky.

I hate tears. I don't know how to react. Maybe it stems from being told at an early age *men don't cry*. I pretended not to notice the woman's emotional state and distracted myself with other things in the living room. So, where's Petey hiding today?" I asked. Petey scares the heck out of me. No, he's not a boyfriend of Margaret's, He happens to be a very protective thirty-year-old parrot.

"Petey is on loan for a couple days."

Out making whoopee, thank goodness. Ever since a parrot bit me on the arm, I've tried to stay as far away from them as possible.

The elderly woman finally collected her thoughts and found the perfect crystal vase for the flowers. "Wait here, Matt, while I get water for this lovely bouquet. I don't want the flowers to wilt."

"Take your time. I have nothing in my grocery bag that will melt."

Margaret returned to the living room and set the container of flowers on the end table closest to the entrance. "So, Matt, have you thought about what you're fixing for supper?"

"Not really. I might pop a TV dinner in the microwave."

She swished her wispy white hair off her forehead. "Well, how about joining me for supper? I always make too much spaghetti."

I hadn't anticipated a supper invite and didn't know what to say.

Margaret's eyes drifted to the brown shag carpet beneath our feet. "Of course, I understand if you'd rather eat a quick meal. You probably have tons of case paperwork to get caught up on."

"Nothing I can think of. Besides, I'd rather spend an evening with this good-looking mature woman who lives in the Foley. I've been told she makes the best darn spaghetti and meatballs. Supposedly the recipe has been passed down from generation to generation. Speaking with my hands, I mimicked Margaret's Italian heritage. "It's so delish."

She blushed like a new bride. You don't need to go overboard with your comments. I'll still feed you."

"Believe me, I'm not. I hadn't thought about what I was going to eat." I held my hand up in Boy Scout fashion. "Honest. I've been at the office all afternoon and I'm famished. But let me feed the mutt first, or she'll tear the place apart."

~6~

Twenty minutes later I returned to Margaret's domain and found the elderly woman standing next to the electric stove engulfed in a miniature fog, humming a tune from *Madame Butterfly*. Not wanting to give the ninety-year-old a heart attack in the middle of preparing a meal, I waited until she finished her chores to announce my presence.

"Ah, you're back, Matt, perfect timing. "Is Gracie all right?"

"Yup, she chowed down the Alpo in nothing flat."

"Poor thing. She must've been starving." Margaret took two serving bowls out of a cupboard by the sink, before returning to the stove, where a kettle of cooked noodles and another of meatballs with sauce waited to be carted off. She carefully filled the bowls and then handed them off to me. "Here, if you take these two dishes to the dining room I'll bring the French bread and teapot."

"Are you certain that's all I can grab for you?"

30

"*Si.* I already put the salads on the table."

As soon as Margaret joined me at the table, she offered a quick prayer over the meal in her native tongue. Even though I didn't know a speck of Italian I got the gist of what she was saying, thanks to my mother's teaching me the English version when I was a lad.

The wonderful meal Margaret had prepared began with a delicious salad, which consisted of head lettuce, pears, walnuts, and Parmesan cheese topped off with a smooth Italian dressing. It's definitely something I didn't remember tasting before. "I bet this is a new recipe, isn't it?"

Margaret speared a bit of lettuce and pear on her fork. "*Si.* I don't like making the same thing over and over. It's boring."

"I feel the same about the cases that come my way. When a really different one comes along, I'm truly thankful."

"Speaking of cases, are there any recent ones you'd care to share with this old woman?"

I borrowed the tongs sitting on the table and helped myself to a large portion of noodles. "Maybe. Let me think about it." I set the bowl of noodles down, picked up the meatballs with sauce and generously covered the noodles. "I've probably never mentioned this to you, but I've been working on the same case the past two months."

"You're right. I don't recall you telling me that." The old woman's fork continued to hover over the insignificant amount of salad left in her bowl. "Oh, dear. That's not a good sign, is it? From the tone of your voice, I get the impression you probably aren't going to make much on that job."

"Not really."

She poured me a cup of black tea and then shoved her empty salad bowl out of the way. "Is there anything else brewing?"

"A telephone message left on my office phone might prove lucrative. I'll know more tomorrow."

Margaret's nearly invisible eyebrows arched slightly. Tomorrow? How exciting. Let's hope it turns out the way you want."

I could tell Margaret was dying to know more, but I wasn't about to share anything else until I ate the terrific meal growing cold on the plate sitting in front of me.

The nonagenarian took what she wanted of the noodles and meatballs and placed what remained in the center of the table. Then she took a slice of French bread and passed the basket to me. "Matt, did you happen to read the article on the front page of today's newspaper?"

"I can't believe you asked me that. I assume you mean the one on China." Margaret nodded. "I don't know what's going on, but my mind's been distracted by China before I even crawled out of bed this morning."

"Do you think your sixth sense is trying to warn you about something?" Margaret's known about my *gift* for a long time. At least she's never made fun of me, like certain family members have.

"I haven't a clue. I don't know what the connection is to China."

Margaret patted my wrist. "Well, I'm sure you'll figure it out soon enough. Come on, eat up Matt. I've got plenty more on the stove." She stood and carried the serving bowls to the kitchen to refill.

The minute my elderly hostess returned I shared a bit more about the phone message that had me almost jumping out of my skin with excitement. "What would you say if I told you the guy who wants to meet with me is Neil Welch?"

The woman almost shot out of her seat. "Oh, my goodness. Neil Welch, the millionaire whose flavors of pop outsell every major soft drink competitor in the world actually called you? That's fantastic! Why, thanks to that man my stock portfolio is doing quite nicely." She pressed her hands against her hollow cheeks. "I can see it all now. Your name will be bantered about in every newspaper in the country."

"Slow down, Margaret. You're jumping the gun. He simply wants to talk. There was no mention of hiring anyone."

"Oh, you're too humble, dear boy. As soon as he meets you, he'll offer you a job. Mark my word. By the way, there's a rumor floating around about him and his wife," she flapped her hand, "but that's old news. You've probably already heard all about it."

"Uh, no. Actually, I haven't. I guess I don't listen to the right radio station."

Margaret leaned into the table a bit like she was preparing to share a secret. "Well, according to what I heard Mr. Welch and his wife are having marital problems. Why, I bet he wants you to dish up the dirt on her."

Did this sweet lady actually say that? I studied her small frame for a second. I guess there could be a ring of truth to what she said. "You know you could be right," I confessed, slightly tapping the table, "but that's enough shop talk for the evening. How about filling me on what you've been up to?"

She rested her elbow on the table. "Well, my hips giving me problems so I'll probably have to stop bowling."

"How do you feel about that?"

The light projecting off the ceiling fixture made her green eyes look even brighter. "I'm fine with it. There are so many other projects I can do with my hands."

I peeked at my watch and then stood. "Margaret, I hate to eat and run, but I've got to walk Gracie. Thanks so much for the home cooking." I patted my stomach. "Great meal. It's been a while since I've made a decent supper for myself."

"I'm glad you enjoyed it, dear, but you didn't get dessert."

"Don't worry about it. Next time you bake save me a slice of whatever it is."

Margaret followed me to the door. "I'll do that. I know you don't want to talk shop anymore, Matt, but I've been trying to remember the location of Neil Welch's bottling plants, and a couple came to mind: Colorado, Boston, St. Cloud, Germany, and Hong Kong."

"Hong Kong?" Did my voice really shoot up two octaves?

The elderly woman looked alarmed. "Matt, what is it? Your face is as white as my linens."

"Nothing," I mumbled, turning the door knob to leave. I didn't have the energy to explain. "Nothing at all."

~7~

December 14

The sun's early morning rays brutally bombarded the bedroom window. Gracie bellowed and then barreled off the bed like a cannonball. I opted to refrain from such nonsense and coiled up in a fetal position, enjoying the heat's intensity, until I noticed the time on the clock radio. "Seven?"

I scrambled out of bed and opened the window blind. "Time and tide wait for no man," according to St. Marher and Chaucer. And they're right. If I want to secure a decent job, I need to get cracking and put aside all thoughts of playing hooky with the mutt.

I turned my back to the window and almost tripped over Gracie. She was performing her morning stretch routine. "No stroll through Loring Park this morning," I warned. She pouted. "You can sulk all you want, but the only deal I'm offering is a quick jaunt around the block."

The mutt's paw shot up. I took it. "Okay, I've got a few things to do before we go." One of course to smooth out the sheets and blankets on the bed before heading to the bathroom to shave. A shower could wait till I got back, but there's no way anyone was going to see me leaving this apartment with a five o'clock shadow.

Too bad I didn't leave the shaving till later too. I'm so nervous about what I might hear when I speak with Neil Welch via the phone in a couple hours, I lost control over the razor. It's like someone suddenly turned back the clock and I was a teen shaving for the first time again. Unfortunately, the mirror did nothing to display the real me hidden under the brown Band-Aid dots decorating my face. The bright side of my condition, I wasn't meeting the man in person today, or so I thought.

Finally ready to meet the world head on, I grabbed the dog's leash and a cap and jacket for me. It might be sunny, but I didn't have a clue what the outside temperature was. I clapped my hands and Gracie came running. "All right. No fooling around outside, mutt. Do your thing, zip-zap."

The minute we got back I jumped in the shower, dressed, and went straight to the kitchen to look for something to eat. I don't know why I even bothered messing with breakfast. I was as nervous as a cat about to leap from one tall tree to another. I set the coffee maker first. Probably a mistake since a cup of java makes me even jitterier.

Gracie pawed my leg as I opened and closed each cupboard. "You've had your breakfast. Go lay down." She took a step back then made another feeble attempt to get me to change my mind. "No. There's nothing more for you."

I finally found the box of Cheerios and filled a glass bowl with the cereal. Then I added milk and a ripe banana to the mix and stood at the counter eating like I had all the time in the world. Of course, the whole while I questioned where I had stashed the number Welch had left on my answer machine. I remembered copying it down. But I sure couldn't recall where I'd put it before leaving the office. Did I put it in a pant pocket?

If I can't recall where I put it, this could end up being a huge disaster for me. I scratched my head. "Ah, yes." I set the dishes in the sink with yesterday's and scrambled to the hall closet. It was already 8:50. *Think, Matt. Did you wear your jacket or trench coat?* I recalled giving Gracie orders to stand guard. Okay, that means I wore the trench coat I'd left the service with. I thrust my hand in an inner pocket and came up empty handed. The note had to be in the coat somewhere. I tried the outer pockets and won the prize after the second try. With three minutes to spare, I rushed to the phone.

My sweaty fingers kept sliding off the digits. I swiped my hand on my jeans a couple times and tried again. The phone rang and rang on the other end. No one seemed to care one hoot that I was calling. Whatever happened to receptionist's sacred business creed of answering the phone in "three rings or less". No wonder so many businesses have gone down the toilet: irate customers.

"Good Morning. Delight Bottling Company," a sweet energetic voice said. "This is Carol, who do you wish to speak to?"

I picked a pencil off the desk in my bedroom and toyed with it. "Good morning, Carol. This is Matt Malone. Mr. Welch is expecting my call."

"One moment please."

I actually waited five minutes for Welch. "Mr. Malone, good to hear from you." Funny, he didn't sound like he meant it. Maybe he's having the kind of day I had yesterday. "I'd like to offer you a job, but I'd prefer to do it in person."

Yes. I curled my fist and thrust my hand into the air. I felt like I'd won a gold medal at the winter Olympics. I tried to sound calm. "Of course, I understand."

Neil Welch's baritone voice continued. "Could you possibly squeeze me into your busy schedule sometime today?"

Well, that's a new one. One of the busiest men around town wanted me to fit him into *my* schedule. Evidently he hasn't run a background check on me yet. "Ah, just a minute Mr. Welch while I take a look at my calendar. "Mmmm, it's pretty full." I held the phone near the desk while I flipped through a tablet of scratch paper with the tip of the pencil still gripped in the left hand. When I finished, I peered at my watch. That should do it. I placed the phone receiver near my mouth again. "Sir, it looks like I have an eleven o'clock cancellation. How's that time frame?"

Welch heaved a sigh of relief. "Perfect. Do you know where Delight's main headquarters is located, Mr. Malone?"

His office? Super. That means I don't have to flood my office with some exotic smelling air spray. Yay. "No, I don't." Shoot. I can't believe I just said that. That was the worst possible answer to spill out of a PI's mouth. As soon as I heard Welch's message, I should've learned everything about him, including where he runs his company from. Let's hope my dumb reply doesn't diminish any chance I have to work for the guy.

As it turned out, Welch didn't seem to be bothered by my response. "The main office is out on Industrial Boulevard, four blocks from Highway 35."

"It sounds like your building is fairly close to UPS and the Sheraton Hotel."

"Yes, exactly two blocks west of there."

"Mr. Welch..."

"Yes."

"Do you want to see a resume?"

A forceful, "No," stretched across the phone lines. Then Welch added, "See you at eleven," and ended our conversation without even as much as a good-bye.

I set the phone back in the cradle and ran my hand through my hair. What the heck is hanging in the closet that will impress Neil Welch? It's gotta be something real snazzy. I snapped my fingers—the navy-blue suit I bought at Dayton's a couple years back. Wait. Did I ever pick it up from the cleaners after I spilled salsa on it at a party?

I marched to the bedroom and looked for an outfit at the back of the closet covered in a plastic bag. It's there. All right I'm set. I'll wear a white dress shirt and a navy tie with it. I'll need to shine the black dress shoes though.

Before I bothered changing, I had one more important call to make. When Gracie and I walked past the Guthrie yesterday, I thought of a great Christmas present for Rita. "Hello. I'd like to purchase two tickets for the performance of the Christmas Carol on the 21st." This gift ought to surprise Rita. She thinks I have no imagination when it comes to planning a date.

"Hold please while I check the availability." When she came back on the line, she said the seating choices were slim. I told her to give me the best she had.

As soon as the tickets were squared away, I went to prepare for what might end up being the best day of my life. It didn't take long to change. I already knew what I planned to wear. And after I checked myself out in the mirror and splashed a dash of cologne on, I'd be ready to zoom out of here.

~8~

Traffic heading north was miniscule. Five more minutes and I'd be catching a glimpse of the buildings along Industrial Boulevard. I eased over to the right lane leading to the next exit ramp and the United Parcel Service building immediately came into view, then two blocks later Delight's tall lean reddish-brown brick building appeared. Delight's newer corporate office stuck out like a sore thumb. The neighboring buildings were squat, bland, and surrounded by twenty-foot oak trees.

The second I pulled into the parking lot reserved for visitors, my stomach lurched back and forth like someone had tied a bungee cord around it and then snapped it. *Grin and bear it, Matt. You've gotta make it through this meeting no matter what. You haven't much choice.*

I stretched across the passenger seat to open the glove compartment and remove a slim hand-held tape recorder plus a notepad and pen, items this PI tried never to leave home without. Once I had everything I needed, I shut the small compartment and stepped out of the Topaz.

The walk from the car to the Delight building was a short one, but there was enough time to study the building's architectural design. It was simple and appealing to the eye. The architect made a good choice when he included plenty of windows to cut down on artificial lighting. I bet the employees appreciate all the windows. I know I would. Instead of feeling cooped up in a cave you have a window on the world. When the weather turns crummy, you're aware of it before leaving for home.

My eyes drifted upwards to the sixth and final floor as I neared the entrance. Someone was looking down at me. Could it be Neil Welch? When I spoke with him, I got the impression he didn't tolerate tardiness. Luckily, I too think punctuality is an important trait.

The second I entered the glass enclosed atrium lobby a poker-faced sixtyish security guard greeted me. He was sitting behind a desk a few feet off to the left of the entrance. "Good morning, Sir. You'll need to sign in before heading to the elevators," he informed me, shoving a pen and clipboard across his small desk.

I read the plastic name tag attached to the pocket of his navy blue dress shirt. "Sure, Bob." I picked up the pen and began to scribble my name. As I did so, the man's probing eyes carefully studied each swirl and curlicue hitting the paper. Maybe Delight had problems with a certain individual recently. When finished, I slid the clipboard back to Bob's side of the desk. "There you go."

Bob immediately stashed the clipboard in the desk's top drawer and handed me a *visitor's* pass. It had a string attached so I slipped it over my head. "Okay Mr. Malone," the guard's tough as nails voce said, "what you wanta do is walk to the end of this here hall, hang a right, and then take the second elevator on the left to the sixth floor. When you get off you'll see a gal sitting directly in front of you. That should be Mr. Welch's secretary. She greets everyone with a quarter moon grin. Of course if she's gone to lunch, I don't know what kind of greeting you'll get." Some of those gals who fill in during breaks haven't a clue what a friendly smile is, if you get my drift."

Easing away from this guy's desk now, I followed the directions he had given me and found the elevator I needed. The ride was as smooth as silk, not jerky like the Foley's. And it had that new smell, plus classical music piped in. Personally, I'm a jazz lover. But since dating Rita, she's been slowly exposing me to music more in tune with her tastes. Thanks to her I recognized the piece entertaining me: Beethoven's Moonlight Sonata from 'Immortal Beloved'.

I know it sounds weird, but the elevator doors opened with reverence just as Beethoven's work finished and I found myself staring at the most knock-dead-gorgeous-redhead I've ever seen. If I wasn't so much older than her, I would've asked the young woman out on the spot. Rita and I aren't even close to being engaged.

Due to the monstrosity of an antique desk, circa about 1890's, the mid-twenties woman sat behind, I only got a partial view of her body, but I'm certain her lower portion fit extremely well with her heavily endowed upper half.

The minute I stepped off the elevator she lifted her head and gave me a generous grin, exposing her pearly white teeth in the process. "Good morning. May I help you?"

My usually tight smile widened as I gazed at her delightful greenish-brown orbs. "Pardon me, but are you

Carol? The security guard in the lobby mentioned she's Mr. Welch's secretary."

"Yes. I'm Carol Sims." The young woman's voice seemed a tad loud, but with her looks I didn't mind. "Welcome to Delight's headquarters," she continued, giving me another huge smile.

I extended my hand. "Nice to meet you, Carol. I have an eleven o'clock appointment with Mr. Welch."

"You must be Matt Malone. Mr. Welch said you'd be on time. It's a bit strange, but my boss always seems to know if someone he's meeting is going to be punctual or not."

Not so strange if the person working here has an office view of the parking lot.

"Please take a seat Mr. Malone and I'll let Mr. Welch know you're here."

When Carol moved away from her desk, I discovered I was totally off kilter concerning her proportions. The gal's tiny feet propelled her body across the carpeted floor fairly quickly, even though they carried a horrendous load thanks to her butt and legs.

Fascinated by Carol despite her body's discrepancies I watched as she placed her small hand on her employer's door, preparing to knock. Unfortunately, she never got the chance. A gray-haired man with small patches of coal-black hair walked out of the enclosed office. Could this be Welch? Or is he one of the other higher ups in the company.

"I'll take it from here, Carol," the man said in a fatherly fashion. "Mr. Malone, I'm so glad you could make it," he stretched out his darkly tanned hand, grasped mine, and pumped firmly. "Would you like Carol to get you a cup of coffee or perhaps you'd prefer a can of pop?"

"No thank you. I'm fine."

"Well, then let's step into my office, shall we?" Welch moved back a bit now, allowing ample room for me to pass through his office door.

I gotta admit I felt mighty jittery entering Welch's sanctuary. I didn't want to say or do anything to offend him, but after catching sight of his private surroundings I felt out of my league and almost told him he had called the wrong guy. Not one piece of furniture in the room came close to the contents in my humble inner sanctum. Today I'd had left my cave office behind to be entertained at the Taj Mahal.

Unaware of how I felt, Neil Welch lightly tapped the back of a low-cut leather chair positioned in front of his desk with his neatly-trimmed nails. "Have a seat Mr. Malone."

"Thanks." While I squeezed between the desk and chair, I took careful notice of what the wealthy man had on, a crisp, navy-blue suit which I perceived to be designed by Loro Piana. Whew. That suits too expensive for my line of work. But wouldn't it be worth it to wear even a borrowed one in front of Mr. Slick himself, Rod Thompson. He'd need my help prying his jaw off the hallway floor.

Neil Welch pulled his leather executive swivel chair away from the 56 inch darkly-stained L-shaped oak desk just enough to give himself room to sit. "Mr. Malone, before I lay out the reason I invited you here, I need to apologize for Carol's vociferous voice. When she's nervous, it gets out of hand."

I flicked my hand. "I hadn't noticed."

He set his hands, palms down, on the desk. "Well, I'm glad to hear it didn't bother you. She's such a great asset; I haven't the heart to mention it to her."

I felt like a mouse on holiday in the presence of this great man. Sitting so close to him I saw things on his body *Time* magazine has never captured. Of course magazines are noted for their touch-up techniques. His normal, broad smile splashed across magazine covers was non-existent at the moment. A stern look took its place instead. And the lower part of his heart-shaped face sported a new design too, a well-trimmed beard.

His body appeared in great shape for his sixty-one years. I've never read anything about him having a personal trainer, but perhaps he keeps that low key.

Neil Welch broke through my thoughts with gentle patter. "Did you have trouble finding us, Mr. Malone?"

"Ah, no. My office is only a stone's throw from here."

"So how long have you been at your location?" Why this particular question? Was he trying to figure out if I had enough PI experience?

"I've been there about five years."

Neil Welch straightened his blue-striped tie. It was the second time he had done it within the last five minutes. Was he nervous about sharing secrets with me? "Mr. Malone, do you mind if I call you Matt? I hate formality."

I turned my head slightly and caught sight of a Stairmaster against a far wall. Well, I guess I know how he keeps in shape. "Sure. Using my Christian name's better than some of the things I've been called in my line of work."

Welch laughed. "I like your spunky attitude. By the way, an Air Force buddy of yours, Randy Williams, steered me towards you."

"Ah, yes, Randy. That's one guy you don't soon forget. We finished up our four year hitch together in Grand Forks, North Dakota."

"According to Randy you worked in marketing and manufacturing before entering the PI business."

"That's true. My uncle who has a medium-sized sign shop took me under his wing while in high school and continued teaching me all through college. But after a four year stint with the service, a plastic molding company offered me a decent paying job I couldn't turn down."

"Interesting. Randy didn't tell me all that."

"I never shared the info with him. I don't make it a point to spread my history around."

"Smart man. No one needs to know everything about an individual." *Including him I'm sure.* The president of Delight settled an elbow on his desk and then pressed his fingers against his temple. "I appreciate your filling in the blanks for me, Matt. You see, I have a job in mind for you and it requires your particular qualifications. But before I discuss the details, you need to know considerable travel is involved."

"Travel?" I rubbed my sweaty hands on my pant legs. I haven't done much of that since leaving the service. "Where? Around North America? Or are you referring to places outside the U.S.?"

"A bit of both. I'd like you to take a look at three bottling plants here in North America and four overseas."

He's definitely piqued my interest. There's nothing keeping me around here. Well, okay, Gracie and Rita. But the job can't be that long, and it beats traipsing around town looking for deadbeat dads. I rubbed my chin. And the way Welch is acting, I rather doubt these travels have anything to do with a wayward wife, something that can be quite tricky. Perhaps Welch's problems are financial." *See if you can worm it out of him, Matt.* "Sir, it's none of my business, but do you plan to sell some of these plants off after the inspections?"

Mr. Welch surprised me with a clipped response. "Yes. A few may have to be put on the chopping list I'm afraid."

I guess it's really none of my business why the man needs to sell off plants. Maybe it has nothing to do with the wife or finances. Perhaps he has declining health. I listened to the ticking of our watches as we played the waiting game. Since this was Welch's turf, I figured he should make the first move.

He finally did. "Matt, I get the impression you're someone who calls a spade a spade. Am I right?"

I nodded.

Welch rubbed his smooth hands together. "Good. Trustworthiness and honesty are vital to this task."

"If I accepted the job, what would be expected of me at the seven plants?"

A wry smile enveloped Welch's face; he knew he had me. "You'd examine the equipment and conditions at each plant and write a detailed report explaining monetary losses or gains if a sale were to occur. Of course, I wouldn't mind you're observing the employees while you're at it. You know, be on the lookout for troublemakers. I can't afford to have anyone causing problems when it comes time to sell."

Holy cow. I had been hunched forward, but now I straightened my shoulders and backbone. What Welch described entails a ton of responsibility. Trying to spot troublemakers was a piece of cake. But soaking in all a pop bottling plant entailed and making recommendations, why that was way beyond the scope of what I do for a living. Could I handle it?

I glanced over Welch's sturdy shoulders and stared at a wall covered with twenty years' worth of pop industry awards. I'd never catch up in the awards category. I have one measly plaque the Northeast Chamber of Commerce gave me a couple years back. "Sir, pardon my bluntness, but why aren't you giving this task to one of your employees? It seems a bit strange to ask an outsider, a PI at that."

I know what you're thinking. Here I was being offered a chance of a lifetime to make some decent wages and what do I do? I question the head honcho about his decisions. My gut told me I wouldn't be blown off quite yet.

Neil Welch's chocolate chip colored eyes almost popped out of their sockets. "Mr. Malone." *Oh, oh.* We were back to being formal. Maybe I did screw up. "You of all people should understand why an outsider is necessary. Let's face it; an associate would have difficulty being brutally honest. Plus the job assignment wouldn't be a secret for long."

I crossed my arms. "Probably not. So, what's stopping *you* from touring the plants?"

The man tightened his throat. He was probably asking himself why he ever contacted me. "It's been years since I've visited most of the plants. If I showed up at any of them now, the men would wonder what the heck I was up to. Can't afford that—too risky. Rumors spread like wild fires. Once the union gets in the thick of things, boom it ends up on the evening news and becomes headline fodder for the newspapers."

Headlines! Yesterday's news article about China jarred my cranium. Stomach turbulence soon followed. I hugged my arms. "Sadly, that scenario you painted occurs a lot in the business world, Mr. Welch. But no matter who takes the job, employees will be suspicious, especially if the person is examining the plant with a fine tooth comb, unless you've got a great plan up your sleeve."

"I do," he smugly replied. "Before you arrive at each plant, a fax will be sent to the manager in charge stating that their plant has been selected for an upcoming ad campaign. I believe you'll find that notice sufficient. If they're a good plant manager, they'll jump over backwards to facilitate you in any way they can." Welch took a breather and studied my face.

I'm glad he's so confident.

"Don't worry, Matt." Darn he must've caught a glimpse of my famous skeptic frown. "They'll buy the story. Delight's releasing a new line of pop the end of January which means a huge marketing blitz."

"Ah?"

"There's one other thing you need to know. None of the managers at these plants will have knowledge about your visits to the other sites. And that's the way it has to be played out. Do you understand?"

"Yes, Sir."

Welch cleared his throat. "Well, I think I've given you enough meat to chew on, don't you? Why don't you give my job offer some serious thought tonight and we can discuss your answer back here tomorrow, say the same time, if that works for you of course?"

I stood. "I think that time frame should be all right."

Delight's owner smiled broadly, came around his desk, and slapped me on the shoulder. "Great, Matt. I look forward to seeing you tomorrow then."

~9~

December 15

Neil Welch was comfortably seated at his desk, head bent, sorting through paperwork spread out before him when Carol ushered me into his office and promptly stated, "Sir, Mr. Malone is here to see you."

His head shot up. "Thank you, Carol. Please hold all my calls."

Carol beamed. "Yes, Mr. Welch," and then she paraded back to the outer office.

Receiving no direction from Delight's president myself, I said, "Good morning, Mr. Welch. It's another terrific day isn't it?"

"You bet, Matt. Shall we get to it?" and then he shoved all his paperwork to one side of his long desk.

"Sure." I strolled the short distance to the chair I used yesterday and sat.

Now that his desk was cleared, Neil Welch steepled his fingers and rested his bearded chin on top. "I hope you've come to tell me you'll take the job."

My dry mouth remained tightly clamped. To be honest I hadn't made a decision yet, but I wasn't dumb enough to tell that to this wealthy businessman. It all came down to how much time I'd be expected to devout to this particular job.

"You're not talking. What's holding you back, Matt? I figured you'd jump at this golden opportunity." He became silent for a second. "Say, if you're worried danger might be involved with the job, forget it. I can promise you there's none."

"To be honest I wasn't thinking about the risks involved."

"Then what's the problem?" Welch dropped his hands to the desk. "Oh, I get it. I haven't mentioned the pay yet, smart move, Malone. Don't accept a job until you know the fee. Believe me it will be quite adequate. Plus I'll throw in free travel. How's that sound?"

I rubbed my hands back and forth on my dress pants. "More than generous, Mr. Welch." *His offer was too good to pass up*. Remain calm, Matt. Remember what your first rule is for a PI? *Never let a client know how hard up you are for a job*. I cleared my throat. "The job offer is appealing, sir, but you've never said how much time this huge project would entail and I do have other commitments to think about." Hey all the tea in China ain't gonna sway me, if it means being away from Rita and the mutt for more than a couple weeks.

Neil Welch opened his top desk drawer, pulled out a calendar, and flipped past December. "A month and a half if everything goes smoothly," he said, and then shoved the calendar back in its respective drawer.

"And when would I be expected to leave, the day after Christmas?" I secretly hoped it wouldn't be. My family and Rita would never forgive me. Spending time with them during the holidays is a major event.

"No. No. After New Year's day, the bottling plants will have quieted down by then." He reached in another side drawer and brought out a black appointment book and a pair of metal half-eyes, reader glasses. He opened the book and perched the glasses on his nose. "Let's see, it looks like there's nothing scheduled for the private jet on Friday January eighth." He closed the book and tilted his head back. "Okay, Matt. It's up to you. I believe I've given you sufficient facts to make up your mind."

Hmm. The time frame should work. I just hope Rita doesn't throw a fit. I thrust my hand across Welch's desk. "Mr. Welch, I accept your offer."

"Wonderful. You know as long as you're here maybe you'd like to see a few photos of my bottling plants. Just so you have a notion of what to expect."

"That would be helpful."

Welch scooted his swivel chair to the L part of his desk which held two deep file drawers, opened the bottom drawer and took out what appeared to be a leather bound photo album.

I started to get up to go around to Welch's side of the desk but he motioned for me to remain where I was. "I'll come over there, Matt. It'll be easier to view the pictures sitting alongside each other."

"I guess I might as well start with the plant here in St. Cloud," Welch said, "You'll be going there when you get back from your overseas business. It's off Division near Industrial Park. Perhaps that area is familiar to you."

"It is."

After studying the interior photos of the Delight plant in St. Cloud, Welch moved on to Colorado and then flipped to another section of the album.

"Wait," I said. "Do you mind if we back up a few pages? I caught a glimpse of an intriguing photo."

Welch complied. He slowly paged back until I dropped my hand on the page. "You sure this is what caught your eye?"

"Yes. The landscaping is quite unusual. Where's it located? I've never seen anything like that around here."

"It's on the grounds of our Hong Kong bottling operations."

China again. My stomach stung. I felt like a bee had somehow made its way down to the pit of it. I crossed my legs hoping Neil Welch hadn't noticed how uncomfortable I had become. With China in the mix, I had to find out once and for all if this was the reason my stomach continued to give me discomfort. "Will I be visiting this plant, Sir?"

"No," he emphatically assured me.

I poked my hand in a pocket, drew out a Tum that had been slumbering there, and discreetly popped it in my mouth. Hmm. That crazy curse I inherited must not be playing with my body like I thought. Maybe I picked up a flu bug. It is that time of year after all. I glanced at the photo again hoping my stomach didn't have a repeat performance. It didn't. Good, the Tum must've helped. "I must say Mr. Welch the landscaper you used has an eye for beauty."

"Actually, our employees did the work," his eyes lingered on one spot in particular. "The area to the right is a meditation garden. Ten years ago I would've frowned on setting aside greenspace for that type of project. But if a business in today's world wants to survive in the global market, they have to be supportive of local customs and mores. The employees at this plant also designated a corner of the lunch area for a tea room."

Neil closed the album. "By the way, Matt, I never asked if you have a decent camera. If not, I'll throw in extra Ben Franklins for you to spend on the right equipment so you look legit."

"Thanks for the offer, but the Minolta I have does a fantastic job. If it's all right, though, I'd like to use a video camera too. More area can be covered."

"Video cameras are so clumsy and a hassle to keep track of." Welch rubbed his beard. "I don't know, Matt. I sure wouldn't want an employee or a competitor to get ahold of it."

"Oh, you wouldn't believe the sizes video cameras come in today. The one I recently purchased is so tiny it clips right on a tie."

Welch's bushy eyebrows became quite pronounced. "What? You need to give me the name of the business you purchased it at so I can pass the info on to my security people."

"Sure, if you promise not to share it with them until I finish my assignment."

"Why of course, Mr. Malone. I wouldn't think of interfering with your work."

***

The minute I left Delight's headquarters and started cruising at a steady rate on the Central Avenue corridor leading north to my hole-in-the-wall office, I began to think about a slew of things, most of which needed to be jotted down before I forgot them, but since I was driving it was impossible to do so. *Too bad I don't have a passenger tagging along with me to play secretary*. The mini tape recorder I used yesterday suddenly came to mind. Yes, of course, the recorder works just as well. And it's still on the passenger seat.

My fingers fumbled around until they latched on to the recorder. Once I had it in hand, I set it against the steering wheels midsection, clicked the ON button, and began to dictate. "Look for passport, buy traveler's checks, purchase another suit, arrange for Gracie's care, stock up on blank video tapes and 35mm film, and notify post office to hold mail." That ought to cover it. I flicked the recorder off and gave the road my full attention once again.

By the time I arrived at the office it was lunch time. Unfortunately, there were no food machines in my cave or even a fast food place within a mile radius of it. I guess I'd have to suffer a while longer. I quickly glanced at the message machine on my desk. It wasn't indicating anyone needed my services. For once I was glad. "All right, quit stalling Matt. You need to get down to serious business."

I snatched the glass coffee pot off the shelf, filled it with cold, cloudy water, carried it over to the coffee maker stand, and deposited the water in the reservoir. Then I scooped a generous amount of Folger's ground coffee out of a half empty can, dumped it into the filter basket, and flipped the switch to ON.

Travel plans swirled in my head again. I grabbed a pen to jot down more stuff. Get travel books for the Philippine Islands, Brazil and Germany. Check what their monetary rates are. Pack good walking shoes—

Darn. Leave it to the phone to interrupt me while I'm in the middle of something. I tossed the pen on the table and waited for the message machine to kick in. After six rings, I gave up and picked up. "This is the office of Matt Malone. How may I help you?"

"It's me," a female warmly purred. It was Rita. When I didn't chime in as soon as she expected, she became curious. "Did I catch you at a bad time?"

"Huh? Ah, no. I was just making a list."

"What kind? A grocery list?"

"Nope. Work related. So, how are you?" I picked up the pen I'd thrown on the desk and twirled it. "I've been thinking about you a lot."

"I'm fine. I'm glad to hear you've been thinking about me, Matt, cuz I've been thinking about you too. Did you get the message I left at your office this weekend."

"Yeah, I did. Thanks. As a matter of fact, I planned to call you this eve…"

Rita cut me off before I had a chance to finish. "I'm sorry. I really wanted to do something this week with you, but with the new computer system just getting hooked up and then transferring all our work to it, office life has gotten nuts. Talk about a huge nightmare. Then, to make matters worse, a few minutes ago my boss confided to me that important documents may have been lost."

"Honey, don't get so stressed out. If it turns out you're missing some stuff, I'm sure my neighbor Rod Thompson could squeeze in a little moonlighting. He's the computer nerd I've told you about."

"Thanks for reminding me but I'm sure our boss wouldn't want someone outside this office realm looking at our stuff."

"I don't think he'd have a thing to worry about. Rod works for the FBI."

"Oh? I don't remember you telling me that." She sighed. "Anyway, I'm really sorry our plans fell through."

I ran my hand through my hair. "I understand. Your job pays the bills. Say, do you think you might be able to squeeze in a phone chat later this week? I've got a new assignment I'm taking on."

Someone yelled Rita's name. "I'll be right there, Mr. Carpenter," then it sounded like she took a quick swallow of something, probably coffee. "I've got to go, Matt. That's my boss. Congrats on your new assignment whatever it is."

Squeezing the phone, I mercifully begged, "Don't hang up yet, Rita. I want to tell you about our plans for next Thursday." I got no response except a dial tone.

~10~

December 22

Another mysterious note showed up on my doorstep when I was out this afternoon. The same words were used as the last one. *Stay away from their cousin.* I set the note aside. No dumb message was going to deter this guy tonight. Rita and I were going to dinner and taking in a Christmas production at our world-renowned theatre, the Guthrie, and nobody, but nobody was going to interfere with those plans, period.

It took me quite a while to decide what to wear for my date, but once I did I rolled on all six engines. My final preparations took place in front of the bathroom mirror of course where I combed my hair and splashed musk cologne on my face, a gift from Rita on my last birthday. I must admit I lingered in front of the mirror longer than normal. You would've too if you looked as sharp as I did, all decked out in my Sunday finest and no thick red hair flying off in every direction.

Ten days had already flown by and believe it or not I never had the chance to give Rita the details about my job offer from Welch. The only other time she touched base with me all I managed to squeeze out was about tonight's date. Oh, well, this evening I'll have plenty of opportunity to share the news. But should I surprise her with it before or after dinner?

I spotted Rita the instant I strolled through the double oak doors of Fu Yu's Restaurant, my favorite Chinese eatery. Rita didn't notice my appearance. Her nose was stuck in the menu. Excited to see her, my heart pounded wildly.

Right before my feet took off in her direction though, I searched the room to see if I recognized anyone I've ever helped put behind bars. It's a cautious habit this PI practices religiously. I swallowed hard. The coast was clear. But apparently my feet didn't care. They wouldn't propel me forward.

"What …the?" I actually felt suspended in time. The ugly foreboding I felt earlier in December slid over me. The ornate Chinese furnishings surrounding the diners must have something to do with it. But why did things pertaining to China affect me so? No surprise, queasiness came next. Dang it! Of all the nights for my dumb curse to act up. *Forget about your stomach, Matt. Focus on Rita.*

Rita lowered her menu and glanced towards the entrance as if I willed her to. The minute she became aware of me she stood and waved her petite hand in the air. I bet she thought I'd just arrived. Which was okay, I didn't want her knowing about my problem.

Barely energized, I forced my size eleven feet to move one foot forward and then the other. At the rate I was going it would be a while before I reached the corner table at the far end of the restaurant where customers can spy on Loring Park. This time of year the view is spectacular. Miniature lights adorn snow sprinkled trees.

Slow as my steps were I was pleased when I finally managed to reach the halfway point and even displayed a smile for Rita's benefit. But then wham, a tiny light-brown hand flew out in front of me and stopped me cold. "Excuse, sir," the owner of the hand said, "Need to wait for table like other customers, please."

"But I do have one," I pointed to Rita who was still standing, "I'm with her."

"Ah, so sorry. Big mistake." The restaurant's tiny hostess bowed and placed her hands in steeple fashion. "I wish you much happiness in your work next year."

Why on earth did she mention work to me? Could she read my inner most thoughts? Or was it simply a well-worn comment she dished out close to the New Year. I guess it didn't really matter. I tossed the comment aside and continued on to our table.

Fortunately, the lights of Loring Park didn't distract me as much as the shining star waiting for me. Whew. I have a feeling all eyes will be focused on my lovely lady friend tonight. And I don't blame them. Rita's long, curly dark-chocolate hair had been braided and pinned to the back of her head. Pearl earrings dangled from each ear and the matching pendant necklace encircled her neck, both a gift from me the previous Christmas. Her slender shoulders held the black-velvet spaghetti strapped evening gown close to her medium frame.

"Hi, I was hoping to get here before you." As I leaned over to peck Rita on the cheek, my nostrils received a hint of rose perfume. "Did you order yet?"

Rita clenched her napkin. "I did. Why didn't you wave back?"

I pulled out a chair and sat. "Hon, I didn't ignore you intentionally. The waitress caught me off guard. She wasn't happy. According to her a person couldn't just walk in and take whatever table they wanted. They needed to follow protocol."

"Oooo. In that case I guess you're forgiven." She wagged her finger at me. "But don't let it happen again, fella," she warned, placing her hands in her lap. "I suppose I'd better be nice and tell you what I ordered, huh?" I nodded. "Your favorite of course, Moo Goo Gai Pan for two."

"Should be good. I haven't had it in a while. By the way, thanks for ordering this beer too. I was ready to tell the hostess to give me a free one after the hard time she gave me."

Rita clasped her hand around a glass of wine, probably Zinfandel, and lifted it to meet mine. Our glasses clinked. "Cheers."

"Cheers," I repeated. Then I took a sip of beer and cautiously studied Rita's fine features. I wonder if I looked as tired as she does. What my sweetie could use is an uplifting remark. But what should I say? I'm not good at dishing out snappy or sappy comments and I sure don't want to mention her face."

Rita's eyebrows rose slightly. "Don't say a word. I know there are bags under my eyes. And yes, that's not normal for me. But extended working hours and a zoo like atmosphere aren't a girl's best bed partners."

I hadn't had a decent amount of sleep in a week either. Too much jammed into my head concerning the bottling plants. Would I be ready to do a decent job for Welch? Hmm? Rita has to know she always looks drop dead gorgeous in my eyes, no matter her routine. *That's it.* But before I could spill my guts, the girlfriend took over.

"On the other hand, you Mr. Malone look simply spiffy." She entwined our hands. "I fear I may have to fight off other women trying to vie for your attention tonight."

"Funny, that's exactly what I was thinking I'd have to do with the men who stared you down. You're gorgeous."

Rita purred. "Mmm. Isn't it nice to relax and simply forget about work for once."

"Yup."

"But you will tell me about your job offer, won't you?"

I swiftly retracted my hands from hers and clamped them around the damp glass of Bud Light still waiting to be finished. "Why of course," I bravely replied, "Right after we finish our fabulous meal the waiter has brought us."

Seeing that we had moved our hands out of his way, the waiter swooped in and set the tray of food in front of us. As soon as he left, Rita and I took possession of our chopsticks and sampled the food. "Very tasty, don't you think?" I said.

Rita nodded in agreement.

"Is it just me or did it seem like it took longer than normal for our order to come?"

"Uh huh. I think you might be right."

I finished my beer "Oh, well, it was definitely worth the wait," I said, taking another mouthful of food with the chopsticks. "Rita would you like another glass of wine? I'm going to order another beer."

"Sure. I don't think it'll make me too sleepy."

After our waiter cleared our table and brought another round of drinks, I proceeded to tell Rita about my new job. "Honey, what I'm about to tell you is going to blow your mind. Neil Welch, owner of Delight Bottling, hired me."

Rita got so excited she almost spilled her wine. "That's great news, Matt."

Obviously the girlfriend's wild reaction was a good sign. "I know. And get this; he merely wants me to inspect a few of his bottling plants. Nothing dangerous involved at all." The sweat on my hands intensified. I rushed on before I lost my nerve. "Of course, it does mean I'd be gone about a month and a half."

What? No outburst. I'd been prepared for one. Maybe I don't know Rita's emotions as well as I thought.

"Where in the Midwest will you be going?"

Oops. Clearly I didn't state my job assignment quite right. Nothing new for us guys. I took a short detour. Call it stalling. "Hey, you know what we've forgotten to do?"

Rita's beautiful orbs stared back at me. "What? Pray? We don't usually do that when we're out in public."

I shook my head. "I wasn't referring to prayer. We didn't open our fortune cookies yet."

"Oh?" She peered at the table. "Apparently we've had too much other stuff on our minds."

"Why don't you go first," I suggested.

"Okay, if you insist. Mine says, 'A big surprise is in store for you.' Hmm? I wonder what that means. Hint. Hint. Christmas is just around the corner, if I'm not mistaken. Hey, did I ever give you any suggestions yet?"

"Nope."

"I was thinking maybe I should. Some gals at work have been sharing details of the crazy things their significant others have given them for Christmas. And they weren't too happy about it."

"Like what?"

"Oh, you know a vacuum cleaner, frying pans, stuff like that."

"In other words items related to housework."

"Exactly."

"Well, honey, you don't have to worry about that," I said. And I meant it. The show at the Guthrie was my gift to her.

"Glad to hear it. All right Matt, it's your turn. Here," she handed me the other fortune cookie.

I pulled the clear wrapper off, cracked the crisp cookie in half, took the secret fortune out, and placed it in front of me. "Your long journey is just beginning."

Rita touched the top of my hand still holding the cookie. "Well, you're certainly going to be traveling soon. But what states exactly? You never said."

"I can share where I'm going, but you have to keep it under your hat," I confided, and then I popped the two-halves of the fortune cookie into my mouth.

Rita raised one delicate hand in the air. "I solemnly promise to keep my lips sealed until I'm told otherwise."

Satisfied with her oath, I permitted my travel itinerary to roll thickly off my tongue. "I'm going overseas and to various sections of North America."

Rita's high C range reaction startled me to the core as well as the diners surrounding us. "You're leaving the country? Is that why we're doing all this fun stuff tonight?"

I objected. "Of course not. I had all this planned way before I met with Mr. Welch." *Well, at least a half a day anyway.*

Deeply upset, Rita drifted away from the conversation for a while, turning to the window and watching what was happening outside in Loring Park instead.

Good grief. How am I supposed to remedy this if she doesn't believe me? I told her the truth. What more can I do? I placed a hand on top of hers. "Listen, we can keep in touch via e-mail or phone. The same as we usually do."

Rita tilted her head towards me again. "You're right. I'm sorry I reacted so strongly to your news. You've had a rough time lately with lack of work and this job with Welch is extremely important to you."

Thank you Lord! I strolled over to help Rita out of her seat. "First thing tomorrow I'll call Welch's secretary and ask for an e-mail address where friends and family can contact me. How does that sound?"

"Fine. Where to now? You want to finish the evening with drinks at my place?"

I took Rita's coat off the back of her chair and helped her slip it on. "Not yet. How about the theater?"

Her eyes sparkled. "Really? Which one?"

"It's a surprise. You'll see soon enough."

A few minutes later, we waltzed into the lobby of the theater. "Matt, you've really blown me away tonight with dinner and a live stage production. How did you ever manage front row seats at the Guthrie?"

I knew she'd be impressed. I'm sure glad I accepted the tickets Neil Welch offered me. The only seats I managed to get for *A Christmas Carol* were with a partial view in the upper balcony. "Does it really matter?"

"Well… ah, oh, Matt, I forgot to tell you I can't make it to your parents' home on Christmas. My family is expecting me at their house."

Crap. I was truly disappointed, but at least Rita wouldn't notice since the theater lights were dimming. I patted her hand. "Well, don't worry we'll think of something. Now enjoy the show."

~11~

December 25

Celebrating Christmas at the Malone homestead is considered a command performance—be there or be written out of the will. But this year I had an additional reason for being there, to speak with my parents about the job I'd be undertaking and to drop off the dog. I didn't really want to leave Gracie with them this soon, but they insisted. Supposedly I'd be too busy preparing for the trip to have time for her.

Since it had been snowing heavily for the past two hours, I expected to find at least five inches of fresh stuff covering Dad's driveway but that wasn't the case. When I pulled up, I found only a half-inch of powdery white snow hiding the blacktop. Apparently someone had plowed the driveway "Well, Gracie, you lucked out. I won't have to rub snow clumps off your legs before you can be deposited on Mom's clean entrance floor."

"Woof. Woof."

"Yes, I know you're happy to be here." Even though the driveway was cleared, I parked the Topaz at its outer edges, giving me easy access to an early retreat if I so desired. "All right, girl, let's go see them." I took the mutt out of the car, let her sniff around a bit, do her duty, and then led her up to the house.

Dad must've been looking out the window when I arrived because he suddenly appeared at the front entrance holding the storm door ajar. "Hurry up and get inside. It's freezing out there."

"Tell me about it," I grumbled," yanking up the parka's zipper closer to my chin as if it would help. I don't know why I bothered. I'd be in the house in two more seconds.

I stamped my feet before stepping inside my folks' well-heated home and said, "Merry Christmas, Dad."

"Merry Christmas, Son."

My arms were full of gifts when I crossed the threshold, so I hinted for Dad to close the door. "No sense in letting all the warm air escape. I seem to remember that was one of your favorite mantras, wasn't it?"

"Yup," he stepped behind me and shut the door, "that's what I told you kids. It's nice to hear you remembered something from your childhood.

Oh, I remember a lot more, especially from when I was six. "Hey, is that cinnamon I smell?"

"Yup. Your nose is working fine. Mom's warming up the cider."

"Great. That'll take the chill off."

Dad turned his attention to Gracie. "Well, hi, girl. How have you been?"

The mutt spun around. "Woof. Woof."

"Settle down, girl," I ordered, "We're not outside."

"Oh, leave her be, Matt, she's okay."

"All right. It's your home. Say, do you mind taking these packages so I can take my coat off?"

"Of course not," he cheerily replied, taking the wrapped presents from me. "By the way, your timing couldn't be better."

"Why's that?" I asked as I opened the hall closet and hung my coat.

"Your mother has been running back and forth from the kitchen to the living room window every five minutes searching for your car."

"Geez. Sorry I'm late. If I'd known she was going to fret so much, I wouldn't have told her what time to expect me. Most of the roads haven't been plowed yet."

"Don't feel guilty, Matt. Mom wasn't anxious about you. She was thinking about Gracie. The last couple days she's been scurrying around here like she was preparing to babysit one of the grandkids. She even bought special dog treats. Heck she never buys me special sweets."

I glanced at my father's protruding gut. No sweater can hide that. "She doesn't have to. You eat everything she sets in front of you including goodies she's baked."

"Very funny. I notice you've put on a few extra pounds too."

I patted my stomach. "Oh, this? I'm just slouching. When I stand nice and tall, my stomach's flat." Watch. I sucked in my stomach and raised my shoulders. "See."

Dad tried to copy me. "I guess it doesn't work for everyone. So where's your lovely girlfriend? Coming a little later I suppose?"

"Afraid not. Her family wanted her with them this year. I guess her eighty-year-old grandmother's not doing too well."

"Darn. We rarely see her."

"Ditto for me."

"Well, maybe you can get her over here on New Year's."

"I'll see what I can do."

"Is that Matt's voice I hear?"

"Yup," Dad readily replied.

Gracie took off to look for the person inquiring about her master.

"There you two are," my mother said a few minutes later, skirting into view wearing black dress pants, a bright-red sequined top and a Christmas apron. "Merry Christmas, Matt." She moved in close to me and kissed me on the cheek.

She smelled like stuffing. I threw my arms around her and she quickly pressed hers against me. "The same to you." Gracie got jealous and tried to squeeze between the two of us. "Hey, mutt, you don't need to barge in on this. It's a private moment. Besides, you'll have plenty of time to spend with my mother when I leave here."

"Arooooo."

"Come on Gracie," Dad said, "We know when we're not wanted." Then he carried the gifts I brought into the living room and set the gifts under their seven foot Christmas tree.

Mom released her hold on me. "Matt, go join your father. I have to check on the ham. It's almost ready to come out of the oven."

I obeyed, taking a chair by the gas fireplace. "I'm surprised no one else is here yet. I thought dinner was set for two."

"You mean to say you've forgotten how the rest of the gang always shows up late."

"Of course not. I just thought maybe they'd surprise you for once."

Dad looked at me quizzically. "You look like you're not getting enough sleep, son. What's troubling you? Is it the new job?"

I rubbed my forehead. "Nope. A crazy dream has been interfering with my sleep the last week or so. I don't know what to think of it."

Dad folded his thick hands. "Maybe I can help. What's it about?"

"Do you remember the article about China dominating the world in the near future?"

Dad chuckled. "Don't tell me you're losing sleep over that? "The reporter who wrote the story was way off track in the '50's. A new century is almost at our door and no such thing has occurred. The U.S. is still on top where it should be. Maybe you need to watch a good movie or read a book before going to bed so it takes your mind in a different direction. You can't afford to be falling asleep on your new job. Your faculties need to be alert at all times."

"Your right," I yawned, "I'll try one of your suggestions. Maybe the dream is bugging me because I'm going to be working on a job involving China at a later date. At least I know the task I'm taking on in a couple days doesn't have anything to do with China."

Mom stepped into the living room, as if on cue, carrying a tray with three mugs of hot cider and a plate of Russian Tea cookies, both my favorites since a tyke. "Whatever you two men were talking about sounded serious."

I grinned. "Nope, nothing serious. We're just discussing a little of this and that. You know men stuff."

"In other words things I'm not interested in, like football or wrestling." Mother set the tray down on the coffee table and then joined Dad on the leather couch.

Gracie raised her head and stared at my Mom. "Don't worry, Gracie, I've got a treat for you too." She picked a Milkbone off the tray and tossed it on the carpet.

"Mom, I've got a small request."

"What's that, dear?"

"Please don't overdo the spoiling while I'm gone. I won't know how to handle Gracie when I get back." After I collected a mug and a couple cookies, I returned to the chair I had been occupying.

Mom flapped her hand. "Don't you worry about a thing. She'll be fine."

I leaned back in the chair. "I know Gracie will. I'm just giving you a hard time. You know, I'm really glad the gangs not here yet."

"Why, Matt? Is it because of all the kids?"

"No. The nieces and nephews don't bother me. It's just easier to explain my trip without others eavesdropping." I set my empty mug back on the tray and moved it to left side of the coffee table before pulling out the map stashed in my shirt pocket. "I've circled the towns I'll be going to and jotted my itinerary on the back. The info is highly confidential, so make sure it's safely tucked away."

Gracie rushed to the living room window and whined.

"Oh, oh," Mom said, "You know what that means."

"Yup, the gangs all here," I replied.

"Matt, hurry up and fold the map. I'll shove it in one of my apron pockets."

Two seconds later car doors slammed and Mom rushed to the door.

~12~

January 8, 1999

The alarm on the clock radio buzzed at 5 a.m. on the nose, but I didn't care. I felt like a drunken sailor. No, I didn't party hardy for the last several days if that's what you're thinking. I felt the way I did due to loss of slumber again. That darn China issue from the '50's played a major part in it, but so did thoughts of what awaited me at Delight's German bottling plant. I threw the covers over my head and secretly wished a blizzard was pounding at the Foley's front doors.

Ten minutes later, on auto-pilot, I dragged my weary body to the window and pulled the dusty lime-green foam-backed curtains aside. You know, to see if my wish actually came true. Foiled again. A corner street lamp illuminated the ground below. Only a mere dusting of snow covered the boulevard and walkway. "Well, Malone, you'd better get your rear in gear if you don't want to miss your ride to the airport.

The limo driver, hired to take me to the airport, patiently waited his turn to drop me off at the Minneapolis/St. Paul International Airport. When space was finally made available for him, he parked, opened the passenger door, and then scrambled to retrieve my luggage from the trunk.

I handed him a tip. "Thanks." Then I rolled my luggage over to another car and hopped in. This one took me to Delight's private hangar where the pilot was supposed to be already waiting for me.

When I arrived I found a neatly dressed middle-aged guy leaning against a card table sipping a cup of java. *Oh, great. I hope he's not as tired as I am. We may end up in the ocean.*

"Perfect timing, Mr. Malone. The co-pilot and I just completed our flight check."

"Great." I set the suitcase down next to me and stretched out my hand.

"David Good," he said, reaching for my hand, "nice to meet you, sir. You couldn't have ordered a better day for flying. Is this your first flight overseas?"

"Not really. When I was in the Air Force, they flew me to Pakistan."

"I bet it was on a C-141, am I right?"

"Yup, you nailed it. So, are you ready for me to board?"

"Not quite. Grab a cup of coffee. You'll find the freshly brewed stuff on the counter behind you."

"No thanks. I can wait until I'm on the plane."

David shrugged. "Suit yourself. We're still waiting on the stewardess assigned to this flight. Hopefully she'll be here any minute." He placed the foam coffee cup he'd been holding on the table, pulled his crisp white dress sleeve back, and glanced at his watch. As soon as his sleeve fell back in place, we heard the click, click, click of heels smacking the cement floor.

David's eyes shot to the back of the hangar. "Speaking of the devil, there she is. Come on and meet our passenger, Candy."

The tall Cindy Crawford look alike immediately joined us. "Sorry, I made you wait. I got stuck in traffic of all mornings."

"Its fine, Candy," the pilot assured her. "Mr. Malone arrived about two minutes ago." He grabbed his cup off the table, finished his coffee, and tossed the empty cup in the trash. "I'll take care of Mr. Malone's luggage while you get him settled, okay?"

"Yup." Candy looked at me and winked, "You heard the pilot, Mr. Malone. Let's get on board, shall we?"

The gorgeous woman with long thick eyelashes and lavender lip gloss would get no argument from me. As a matter of fact, I think this flight with Candy is going to be just dandy.

While the private jet taxied down the runway to get in position for takeoff, Candy sat next to me and chatted. "I recently retired from one of the major airlines," she explained. "So, when I heard about a part time flight attendant opening for Delight, I figured what have I got to lose."

I grinned. "Nothing."

The instant the plane lifted off the runway Candy stopped small talk and stared at her long, finely filed lavender painted nails. No rings. Perhaps she's unattached. "Well. I bet you're famished Mr. Malone. How about I round up some grub for you?"

The thought of food caused my stomach to let loose with a loud growl. "You know that's a great idea. I was kinda rushed this morning and didn't even have my first cup of coffee yet."

"All righty. I'll be back in a few minutes." Candy pushed herself out of the seat she had been occupying and made her way to the galley area located at the front of the plane.

Luckily for this male her departure was slow. I enjoyed watching the woman's lightly gyrating hips. Talk about being mesmerized. I could feel heat rising to my neck. Darn. Something had to break the spell before too much damage occurred on this flight. I unzipped the small black carry-on bag sitting in the seat next to me and took out a magazine.

Fifteen minutes later, Candy returned carrying a tray loaded with a huge breakfast consisting of orange juice, pork sausages, Belgian waffles topped with blueberries, and a cup of hot coffee. "There, Mr. Malone, that ought to hold you over for a couple hours."

"More like eight hours," I joked. What a meal. Too bad somebody couldn't rustle this up for me every morning. I grabbed the fork and dug right in.

Satisfied that she'd pleased me with such a scrumptious breakfast, Candy went back to the galley.

After breakfast, I returned to my magazine, but soon tired of it. There's got to be other reading material floating around here somewhere, I thought. I stood and looked around.

When Candy saw me staring off into space, she immediately jumped out of her seat and came to my assistance. "Is there something I can help you with, Mr. Malone?"

"Ahh, yeah, I was wondering if there might be books or magazines onboard I could read."

She pursed her lips. "The only magazine I've seen is on the seat next to mine. Would you like me to get it?"

"Sure, if it's not too much bother."

"No problem. That's why I'm here, to make your flight as enjoyable as possible." Candy did a hundred and eighty degree turn, went back to where she had been sitting, and plucked the magazine up. "Here you go. Is there anything else I can get you, water, coffee, pop, juice or maybe a snack?"

I waved the magazine in front of me. "No thanks. This is all I need."

"Well, if you change your mind, let me know."

I grinned. "I will." I stared at the cover of the magazine I held in my hand. It wasn't what I'd expected. Good thing Candy wasn't around to see how disappointed I was. The reading material she gave me wasn't *Sports Illustrated*. Darn. Well, I guess learning a bit about the pop bottling industry would put me ahead of the curve so to speak.

Unfortunately, it only took me ten minutes to realize the thick trade magazine was dry as expected. Although, I must say I did glean an enormous amount of information concerning the soft-drink business.

"790 gallons of soda pop are consumed every second. In the U.S. alone, each person consumes fifty gallons of soft drinks per year."

Whew! No wonder Mrs. Grimshaw's stocks are doing so well. I continued reading.

"The cans themselves are coded on the bottom with the time of day, date, and initials of the city the plant is located in." Huh? For tracking purposes I suppose, in case the pop doesn't taste right.

"The concentrate used for flavoring tastes and smells terrible, but one gallon of the finished mixture makes enough syrup to flavor 4,500 cans of pop."

"Wow."

Candy cleared her throat. "Excuse me Mr. Malone, did you want something?"

"Sorry, I didn't realize I had reacted aloud to one of the articles in this magazine."

"No problem." Candy stood and stretched. "I'm going to prepare lunch for the pilots in a few minutes. Would you like me to get yours ready too?"

"I guess I'd better. We'll be landing at Frankfurt in an hour."

~13~

Frankfurt

Carl Von Hoff, a robust German with out-of-control thick white eyebrows and a bushy mustache to boot, met me as soon as I disembarked. "It's a privilege to chauffeur an employee from Delight Bottling, sir. A great company to work for, *ja?*

I played along. "Yes, it sure is."

Carl collected my luggage, quickly ushered me to his stretch limo, opened the back door for me, and placed my belongings in the trunk. Then after checking to make sure I was comfortable, he slid behind the wheel and took off. "The hotel is an hour from here, *Herr* Malone," he informed me, "but I'm sure you won't mind the drive with all the provisions at your disposal."

I examined the well-stocked goodies and simply yawned. Nothing appealed to me, including a bottle of

Riesling and Pinot noir. "A guy couldn't go wrong with all the stuff stashed back here," I said, "but I think I'll catch a little shut eye. The long flight wiped me out." Here's hoping Carl caught the hint and won't keep up the chatter.

He'd gotten the message. Ten seconds later the window dividing the front and back section of the car went up and peace reigned until we arrived at the first leg of my trip, a large stoic building known as the Hotel Ebert.

The minute we walked into the tiny lobby, Carl set my luggage down next to me and stepped up to the reception counter to have a short conversation in German with the check-in clerk. When he finished, he pointed to me and said, *"Guten Tag.* Here *ist Herr Malone."*

The stern clerk immediately greeted me. *"Guten Tag,"* and then waved his hand, signifying I should come forward and sign the guest book. As soon as that was taken care of, the clerk dinged a bell notifying the bellhop someone needed assistance.

Seeing that his presence wasn't required anymore, Carl prepared to leave. *"Herr* Malone, I'll be back in two days. Get some rest, *ja. "*

"I'll try. *Auf Wiedersehen."*

"Auf Wiedersehen, " Carl repeated.

~14~

January 11

Well rested after taking a few days of leisurely down time to do whatever I wished in Frankfurt, it was finally time for this guy to earn his fee. I glanced over at the clock on the nightstand while I fixed my tie one last time. Carl's probably wondering where the heck I am. Finished with the tie, I threw on my suit coat, locked up, and hustled down the stairs instead of waiting for the elevator.

Out of breath when I reached the lobby, I barely managed to offer Carl an amiable smile before rushing outside to the waiting limo.

The second we left the Hotel Ebert and the little German roads behind, Carl became a speed demon on wheels. He floored the gas pedal and the car took off down the autobahn like we were Indy 500 race car participants.

With no hand strap to hold on to, I dug my short nails into the leather seat and prayed I'd make it to the plant alive. To think some people back home in Minnesota believe driving 70 m.p.h. is crazy. I took a quick peek at the speed odometer. Carl was doing at least 120 m.p.h. No wonder my breakfast was about to jump ship.

Unfortunately, my driver's fast and furious driving wasn't the only thing that almost left me lifeless.

After being alone on the autobahn for a good ten minutes, a mustard-colored VW whizzed past, skimming the limo as it did so. The near collision didn't seem to faze Carl, but it left me shaken. So shaken that I had to question whether someone was trying to keep me away from Delight's plant or if the childish game of tag was merely a consequence of the nasty hairpin-turn both cars had taken at the same time. Hopefully it's the latter and not the former so nothing serious crops up while I'm in town.

Twenty minutes after our near mishap, Carl rolled us into Delight's parking lot, drove straight to the front of the massive white brick plant covering at least two square blocks, and dropped me off at the front entrance.

A rosy cheeked, portly gentleman dressed in a dark suit, standing on the sidewalk running alongside the building, quickly dropped his unfinished cigarette and crushed my hand. *"Guten Morgen. Willkommen.* I'm Gustav Schmidt, Delight's manager. You are *Herr* Malone, *ja?"*

Gustav's hand pumping was relentless. If I didn't speak up soon, I'd end up with a broken hand. Okay, remember what Margaret told you. Press your mouth together like a bird and you'll be fine. *"Guten Morgen, Gustav. Ja,* I'm *Herr* Malone." There. I hoped that impressed him.

Gustav shared a token smile. With polite greetings out of the way now, he released his grip on my hand. "For someone living in the States your German sounds pretty good. Do your parents speak German?"

"*Nien.*"

"I understand you're from the corporate location, *ja?*" I nodded. "I have not been there in ten years. So, do you like *da* new headquarters?"

"Yes." *How do I describe a place I've only been to twice and which only included the lobby and Neil Welch's floor?* I stretched my arms out as far as they'd go. "The offices are huge. Really huge."

One of the hefty man's suit coat buttons was about to launch into orbit any second, but it would be rude of me to warn him. Heck, I just met the guy. "*Herr* Malone, I don't mean to offend you, but you may want to consider speaking slower while you're here. Believe me, the employees will appreciate it."

I tapped my forehead. "*Jawohl.* I wasn't thinking." I drew out the next words escaping my lips. "There- are- four- large- conference- rooms. The walls are decorated with employee art. The building has many, many windows. Mr. Welch's office is on the top floor."

Gustav presented a wide grin, reminding me of Santa. "Ah. I should visit my brother in Minnesota. Then I could see for myself." He clapped his hands unexpectedly. "So, what do you say, shall we begin the tour?"

"Sounds good to me."

My tour guide, for the duration, held the entrance door open and then followed me in. "Would you like a cup of our strong German coffee before we stroll through the building?"

"*Nein.* I had plenty at breakfast."

Gustav rested his hand on his stomach. "Ah, *ja,* *Frühstück* A meal I never miss if I can help it."

I grinned. Looking at his generous girth I'd figured as much.

"Let us start then with the storage room where the empty bottles and cans hideout." He opened the door directly behind me so I could take a peek inside.

Whoa! How the heck do they manage to move anything out of the room? The containers had taken over every nook and cranny. I'm no whiz contractor, but even I knew this area definitely needed to be enlarged. "Looks like you don't have to worry about running out of containers anytime soon, huh?"

Delight's manager viewed the room as if for the first time. "*Nein,*" he replied, quietly shutting the door behind us and then clapping his thick hand on my shoulder. "Come, Mr. Malone, there is so much more to see." Then Gustav aimed a chubby finger at a machine next to the storage room. "*Das ist* the depallitizer."

"What does it do?"

"It sets the empty bottles and cans on the conveyor belt." He raised his voice a couple notches now since it was so noisy. "Watch the operation," he suggested. "You'll be surprised how quickly the cans get loaded."

Gustav wasn't exaggerating the machine's swiftness in getting the task done. The cans whizzed by so fast on their way to other equipment further down on the belt, I barely recognized their shape. Before they made it to where I stood though, the cans had to pass under special equipment to de static them; any foreign objects in the can, including metal filings, get removed at that point.

"From here the cans go on to the *rinser.*" Gustav shouted, taking my arm and leading me closer to the equipment. "This *ist* where our cans get sprayed inside and out with warm water before being filled with soda."

On cue warm water shot out and my upper body received a fine mist similar to what the fresh vegetables settled in bins at your local grocery store are treated too. I pulled out a hankie and swiped the droplets off my face. "That's one way of waking up sleepy employees," I commented.

Amused, Gustav released a barrel laugh. "*Ja* it is. So, after the containers have their nice shower, they enter another room where da *filler* machine works its magic."

Since the trade magazine I perused on the flight discussed various *filler* machines and how they put pop into the cans, I decided to head off any explanation in that regard and inquired about the pop mixture instead.

"*Ja*, the pop mixture *ist* kept in the carbo-cooler until bottling time."

Unfortunately, Gustav's reply didn't quite answer my question. I wanted to know exactly where the good stuff was stashed in case I had the urge to whip up a batch of soda for myself while I was here. Just kidding. There's no way a *supposed* marketing guy would be allowed to touch anything. But on the plane I had read the carbo-cooler, syrup supplies, and concentrate were all kept in the same room and the PI in me wondered if there were tight controls for this room or if anyone from the plant could wander in and out whenever they darn well pleased. "Do you mind showing me where the carbo cooler is next?"

"Come. Follow me."

The minute we turned to go in the opposite direction, a forklift careened around the corner and almost struck me in the back. If it wouldn't have been for Gustav's fast reaction, I would've been a goner. I swallowed hard. Two close calls the first day on the job made me wonder whether Welch was telling me the truth when he said there'd be no danger involved.

Gustav made a fist and shook his head. "Dat Peter. Da crazy fool. I been telling dat young man to slow down. This isn't a race course. He does not listen. Another incident like this one and he will be gone. I promise you."

Remembering my own wild youth I didn't comment, but I'd definitely keep a close eye on Peter while here. At the moment though a strong wave of urgency swept over me and I felt the need to visit the computer room. Perhaps it was a wake-up call to reach out to Rita, especially after my close call with death. "Gustav, would you mind showing me your computer control room sometime today?"

"*Ja.*"

After taking a couple breaks and a long lunch hour, the plant tour ended around five, leaving the computer room unseen as of yet. Being a patient man, I decided to let Gustav remember what I requested earlier in his own good time. As the manager of the plant, I'm sure he had a lot on his mind.

So far I was impressed with Frankfurt's manager. He seemed to have a good solid relationship with the employees. Plus he had done an excellent job of introducing me to those in charge of the various departments. Of course, I hadn't run into the maintenance guys yet, but it didn't matter. They didn't factor into my assignment. The main thing is I had gleaned plenty from the walk around the building today and it was tightly stashed in my memory bank, making it easier for me to waltz in tomorrow and go right to the spots I needed to examine and photograph.

Gustav nudged me in the elbow. "*Herr* Malone, don't worry I haven't forgotten to show you our computer room. It's on the next floor. But first, I make an important phone call, *ja*. Then we go up the steps and I'll introduce you to Li Qizheng, the department supervisor."

Hmm? A *Chinese* fellow oversees all the inflow and outflow of company info. Could this be what my curse tried to warn me about?

Five minutes later Gustav strolled out of his office and led me upstairs to the computer room. To my disappointment we found it empty.

"He must be on break," I said.

Gustav glanced at his watch. "*Nein*. Too late for that. He's gone for the day. We meet with him tomorrow when you come again, *ja*?"

"Okay." In no rush to exit the room, I slowly examined the many computers surrounding me, trying to decide whether I should risk letting Rita know I had arrived safely. I didn't know a soul at this facility or how secure the computer system was without a password.

The plant manager must've noticed how deep in thought I was. "Would you like to send an e-mail?" he asked.

"Ja, if you don't mind."

~15~

January 12

"You are early, *Herr* Malone," Katarina, the perky middle-aged receptionist said as she unlocked Gustav's office door.

I swung the strap of my regular camera over my shoulder. "*Ja.*"

The brunette plunked her stylish purse on her desk and then trotted over to a closet at the back wall to retrieve a few items. *Herr* Schmidt isn't in the building yet. Perhaps you'd like a cup of coffee while you wait."

"*Danke.* Black, no milk, *bitte.*"

When Katarina finished what she was doing, she closed the closet door and headed in the direction of the break room.

During her absence, I swiped a piece of scratch paper off her desk and scribbled a quick note to myself to leave the building a half hour earlier than I did last night, allowing ample time for me to examine the building's exterior before Carl picked me up. The excuse I'd offer Gustav would be a fib of course.

Five minutes later Katarina returned with a steaming cup of strong black coffee.

I hurriedly stuffed the note in my shirt pocket, stood, and took the coffee. "*Danke schoen, Katarina*. I think I'll get going. I've got tons of pictures to take. When Gustav arrives, please tell him I'll talk to him later." Then I left the office and slowly wandered the corridors trying to remember exactly where the backstairs were. I planned to start in the computer room with or without Gustav.

The second I entered the computer area I ran into a hornet's nest. Gustav was standing by one of the computers wringing his thick hands. Apparently he had arrived earlier too and had come straight here. But why? "Gustav, what's going on?"

Hearing his name, he straightened his shoulders. "The computer control panel started acting strange last evening. Today the capper machine *ist* stubborn. It won't seal the lids on the cans right." He wrung his hands again. "If the shipments are delayed, whoosh we lose money."

Computer problems? Hmm? Luckily no one knows I've just been given great info for someone secretly spying on a company. "Do these problems occur frequently, Gustav?"

"Nein! Li usually finds the glitches before the machinery goes loco."

"How long do you think it'll take to get things running smoothly again?"

The plant manager frowned. "At least a day if not longer. Do you think you can find your way around the plant without me, *Herr* Malone?"

"*Ja*. I showed him my camera. If I get lost, I'll ask for directions."

"*Sehr gut*. I'm going to stay here until Li decides if I need to call other support people in."

"By the way, I'll be departing earlier tonight." Since the computer room was crawling with employees, I didn't offer a reason for the different schedule. Instead, I quickly backed out of the room and returned to the stairwell where I checked the mini video camera, making certain it was safely secured to my tie before I went any further. If this little bugger picked up only half of what my eyes caught yesterday, Welch will be convinced what a profit potential plant he has here in Germany.

After leaving the computer area behind, I casually moved from department to department snapping photos of workers and machinery. The gathering of info took place separately. Whenever I felt the urge to take a break and get recharged with coffee, I'd seek out an employee willing to talk about work.

The day went by swiftly. It was already four-thirty. Gustav had never sought me out the entire day so I assumed the problems in the computer room were still being smoothed out. I placed the camera back in its carrying case, slung it over my shoulder, and retraced my steps to the lobby.

I had already covered eleven feet of the fifteen foot lobby floor that led outside when I heard what I'd been waiting to hear all day. "*Herr* Malone, wait. I brought Li down to meet you."

I spun around and studied the small man alongside Gustav. He appeared friendly enough. I thrust my hand out to him. "*Guten Abend*."

The young man from China bowed before taking my hand. "*Guten Abend, Herr* Malone." Well, I'll be. The connection didn't produce goose bumps along my arms like I'd expected: a good omen perhaps. Is it possible the curse that haunts me is way off the beam, simply running amuck?

"Li, did you get the machine working again?" I asked.

"*Ja.*"

"Good. I'm sorry I didn't get to chat with you earlier." I glanced at my wristwatch. "Perhaps another time. My driver will be here any second." I turned to Gustav. "I'd better get outside. Thank you for the grand tour. *Auf Wedersehen.*"

Gustaf gripped my hand tightly. "Have a safe trip to Minnesota. *Auf Wedersehen.*"

One plant inspection completed and six to go. Okay, so I still have to look at the exterior of the building, but that won't take all night.

I pushed the front door open, stepped out into the cool night air, and looked around to see if anyone was lurking about. No. "Rio de Janeiro here I come," I yelled, and then I drew silent as I walked briskly to the corner of the building.

As far as I could tell, the back of the building required no repairs, but the parking definitely needed a face lift to continue being filled to capacity. After I snapped pictures of the worst sections, I stared out at the sea of cars covering the rest of the blacktop. Many weren't German brands which surprised me. I figured most people living here drove German made cars.

In the midst of all those many vehicles one stood out from the pack, a brightly mustard-colored car. Could it be the same VW that scraped the limo on the autobahn yesterday? I decided to investigate. Before I could do so though, the whistle blew for the first shift to end and employees converged on the parking lot. So, I kept my feet planted where they were, like any other good PI would do, and watched to see who owned the car. Hmm? The plot thickens. Remember the young guy who almost killed me with the forklift? Guess what? Apparently the car belongs to him.

Talk about bad timing. How can I figure out what the guy might be up to when I'm expecting Carl any second? Speak of the devil. Carl's limo just cut through the parking lot and was headed for the building entrance. That's it. I'm out of here. Info on Peter will have to be put in the notes for Welch.

~16~

January 13
RIO

Twelve forty-five a.m. was an unsavory hour to go through customs inspection, but that's exactly what the Frankfurt Airport personnel expected me to do. Thankfully I only had two small pieces of luggage and hadn't gone beyond my limit, money wise, on items purchased at the market for friends and family.

As soon as I finished with the custom agent, I rejoined the three flight crew members by the door leading to the airstrip. David and Brian seemed chipper and raring to go, but Candy wasn't the charming gal I met on the flight coming over. She could barely keep her eyes focused and her speech was a bit fuzzy. *Somebody didn't get enough rest today.*

Ten minutes later, Captain Good's calm voice boomed over the intercom, "Please fasten your seat belts. We're about to take off for Rio. Barring any weather complications we should reach Galeao International Airport about two-fifteen this afternoon, German time. For those of you who have changed your watches before leaving this evening that's ten a.m. You'll be happy to hear the corporate office has allotted us exactly twelve hours to explore the fantastic beaches in Rio or hit the shops before continuing on to the business portion of the trip, Sao Paulo. See you when we land."

Candy finally came alive when she heard the captain's last sentence. "Imagine, all that time to do what you want Mr. Malone. That's what I call a real vacation." She gave me a quick high five.

Surprised I smacked her hand back. "That's wonderful." Shopping wasn't in my vocabulary, but hanging out at the beach sure was. Unfortunately, this fair-skinned, blue-eyed redheaded PI burns easily.

I shut my eyes and tried to recall whether I'd tossed a tube of sunscreen with a SPF rating of 15 or 30 in my suitcase. Depending on which one I brought, I'd either look like a boiled lobster or tan slacks at the end of the day.

Deciding not to fret about it, I opened my eyes and found Candy carrying on her flight attendant duties despite her lack of sleep. Lucky me. The curvature of her body was enough to drive any man crazy, including this guy. *Ooo la la.*

Oh, don't get all hot and bothered. Rita doesn't mind her cat looking as long as the cat doesn't stray too far. *Watch out, Malone, incoming. The foxy lady's turning around and is headed your way with a tray.*

I yawned. It was way too early to think about digesting food, but I politely accepted the tray filled with cheese, crackers, pop, and set it down. "Maybe I'll nibble on it in a couple hours after I've had a nap," I told Candy.

"If you like, I can take it back to the galley."

I stretched my feet out. "No. It's fine where it is."

Candy offered a tiny smile. "Would you like a pillow and a blanket, Mr. Malone?"

"Sure."

She went over to one of the cabinets, retrieved two pillows and blankets, and brought them back. "I like your idea about getting some sleep. Since you don't need anything, I thought I'd do the same."

Talk about cozy. "Might as well." When I took a blanket and pillow from her, I noticed the wedding ring. She didn't wear one when we flew to Frankfurt. I was sure of that. Why did she feel she had to have it on now? "Do you know anything about the hotel we're booked into in Sao Paulo?"

Candy sat down and draped the blanket over the front of her. "Why, no. Didn't you like the accommodations you had in Frankfurt?"

"Ah, yeah they were terrific. I was just curious."

The flight attendant began to yawn and covered her mouth. "Well, maybe you want to ask the guys. I'm not going to Sao Paulo."

"You're not?"

"Nope."

I tucked the pillow behind my head. "How about Rio's beaches, you ever been there?"

Candy licked her bright pink lips. "Yup. Dozens of times. Copacabana Beach is terrific for sunning or beach volleyball. Plus it's got beautiful views and perfect spots for people watching."

Ah, that explains the ring being dusted off.

"But if you want to swim in a good spot," she continued, "Leme is the place to go. It can't be beat. There's a tiny, quiet cove where you can rest between swimming."

Her eyes started to flutter, but she didn't get to drift off to sleep. Captain Good turned on the intercom again. "Candy, you're wanted in the cockpit."

She sighed, "A flight attendant's job is never done. Sleep tight."

I leaned back and pressed my head against the pillow. "I plan to," and the next thing I knew I was in dreamland for eight hours.

***

I was reluctant to travel alone in such a heavily populated foreign country. I didn't know squat about the people, their customs or languages, but thanks to Candy's tips in regards to which bus to get on and the cost to ride one, I figured how could a guy like me mess up. Before I hopped on any bus though, I needed to find the nearest men's room at the airport terminal. There's no way I'm wearing wool pants and a heavy sweater to the beach.

Ten minutes later I exited the Galeao terminal having donned new items: a white short-sleeve shirt, new black el' cheapo tennis shoes, blue denim shorts, a Panama hat, and tons of sun lotion. *Oh, my, God. They dropped me in Hell not Rio.*

The summer outfit I packed didn't help. An intense combination of heat and humidity was too much for this Minnesotan to handle. My hand flew to my sweaty forehead. Maybe going to the beach shouldn't be part of the agenda. "Nah." How could I skip the beach when people back home just got bombarded with twelve inches of snow?

While waiting for the bus, I tried a remedy for fighting the heat. I pictured myself covered with a mound of snow in minus twenty-five degree temperatures. Unfortunately it didn't work.

Murphy's Law seemed to prevail and appeared it would continue to do so with my mode of transportation. When the bus arrived, it was full. I'd have to wait for another one no matter how long it took. But luck intervened. The determined bus driver didn't plan to leave without me. He laid on his horn and then motioned for me to hop on. I stalled. He honked again. I gave up. I wiped the sweat from my brow and jumped on.

With my body extending partially out the door, I had a good view of the passengers. They were a potpourri of ethnic groups similar to residents at the Foley: Italian, French, Chinese, Japanese, and American. Fortunately, there were other advantages to standing half in and half out of the bus too: the refreshing breeze cooling me when the bus swerved, and no one blocking my vision of Rio's breathtaking scenery.

On one side of the magnificent Atlantic Avenue the teal sea lapped at the white sandy shoreline and on the other a mass of hotels reached towards the sky. Too bad the bus is so crowded. I'd happily forgo the beach for a ride up and down the avenue.

A couple miles later the bus screeched to a halt and the driver signaled to me. It was my stop apparently. I jumped off and ran across the street to meld with the sand and begin a two mile trek to Leme and seclusion.

After forty-five minutes of treading non-stop in scorching sand, a rocky outcrop appeared. That's got to be the spot Candy mentioned. I checked the area. No one seemed to be around. I set my knapsack down, shed my outer clothes, spread a towel on the ground, slathered more lotion on, and then sat. *This is what I call real solitude.* I'd better not share this little luxury with Rita when I get home. She'll be jealous. All she's got going while I'm traveling abroad is her struggles with a new-fangled computer system at work.

Still thinking about Rita back in Minnesota slaving away at her desk with office equipment while I sat in my own private corner of the world, I was surprised when someone tried to get my attention. "Sorry. What did you say?"

"*Boa Tarde.* Do you mind if I share this spot with you, *Senor?*"

Ruffled by the stranger's intrusion, I cupped my hand over my brow and looked up. "*Boa Tarde.* Drop your towel where ever you like."

The thin Chinese gentleman set his blanket about four feet from me. "*Obrigado.* Thanks. American on vacation, I assume."

I glanced at my pale skin. "Guilty. How about you? Do you call Rio home?"

The thin man took a book out of a cloth bag and plopped down. "Nope. I live in Sao Paulo. I'm on a mini vacation."

"Oh? I have to catch a work related flight to Sao Paulo later tonight," I shared.

The stranger stretched out on his blanket and opened his book. "I go back home tonight too. A visitor from our corporate headquarters is arriving tomorrow, and I must be there."

The younger man's last statement ended the brief discussion between the two of us, leaving this PI guessing what he possibly did for a living. After tossing a few ideas around in my head, I gave up. I didn't come to Leme to uncover what job some guy had. I came to chill out. Little did I know I'd discover the stranger's talent soon enough.

~17~

January 14
Sao Paulo

The torrential rain in Sao Paulo had been coming down for over an hour and I hadn't thought to pack rain gear, even though Carol, Welch's secretary, had forewarned me about being here during the rainy season. I'm sure the driver scheduled to pick me up in front of the Sheraton Mafarrej Hotel and Towers was growing impatient with me. According to the clock in the opulent lobby, he had been already waiting twenty minutes for me to pass through the hotel's front doors. It's now or never.

I bolted through the door wearing a nylon windbreaker over my suitcoat, the only protection I could find, and attempted to dodge as many marble-sized raindrops as possible on the way to the limo.

Juan, my designated driver for Sao Paulo, greeted me in a somber fashion. "Good morning, *Senor*. Plenty of rain, *si*?"

"*Si.*" Not wanting to soak the car's seat, I removed the windbreaker and tossed it on the floor.

"It's the rainy season," he explained for my benefit. "It will let up soon, you will see."

He was right. Once we drove a few miles from the hotel, the rain miraculously stopped. Impressed by Juan's prediction, I wondered how much money it would take to lure him to Minnesota. WCCO or KARE 11 would do cartwheels for a forecaster like him. Why, I bet the offer of a home on Lake Harriet or even my uncle's log home on Crow Wing Lake would suffice.

Not too long after Juan shared his weather prediction with me, I discovered he was also a speed demon on wheels like Carl in Frankfurt. He got us to the bottling plant thirty minutes ahead of schedule. I didn't mind. Extra minutes to survey the exterior of the building worked to my advantage. I could take care of it now and scratch it off my list.

I dug a pen and notepad out of the camera bag right before leaving the car and slipped them into a suit coat pocket so they'd be within easy reach.

Prepared to explore now, I started my venture around the outer shell of the building with the front left side and continued clockwise from there, carefully examining the walls of the structure, windows and roof as I went.

The mortar securing the hand-made bricks nestled snugly between joints. A good sign. The few windows surrounding the building looked sound too. Finishing up at the front right side, I found spots where the sheeted tin didn't rest properly on the roof and immediately made note of minimal repairs required on the roof. There might be necessary repairs required for the ceiling inside as well, right below this area, if water seeped through. I quickly jotted a reminder to myself to check for water damage later.

I peered at my watch. Almost time to meet with the plant manager. *Better get inside, Matt.* I stepped up to the heavy steel door and tugged on the handle. Going from the brightness outside to the dimness indoors took several minutes for my eyes to adjust, but once they did they worked overtime to locate the reception area.

When the spot finally got pinned down, I discovered a thin, dark-haired man, approximately five-five sitting on the front edge of the reception desk having a serious conversation with a beautiful young woman sitting on the opposite side of the desk.

The receptionist's long flowing black hair bounced back and forth as she acknowledged me and then hurriedly interrupted the man who had his back to me. He immediately stopped talking and spun around. *"Bom Dia,"* the man of seemingly Spanish origins said. *"Senor* Malone, we've been looking forward to your visit." A broad smile crept across his face exposing gleaming white teeth.

"Sergio."

He extended his hand. *"Si."*

The guy's sincere gregariousness was contagious. I stretched my mouth to the limit, clutched his calloused hand, and returned his greeting. *"Bom Dia."* At least Sergio's soft hand grip ensured me my hand would remain intact while touring his plant.

The plant manager's jet-black eyes left me for a second and swept the lobby. "You travel alone?"

"Si."

With great urgency and no explanation, he locked arms with me and whisked us down a long well-lit corridor.

The fast paced clip caused shortness of breath for me, which brought to mind the most recent walks I had with Gracie before this trip overseas. But Gracie's speed comes naturally, she's a dog. Why would this South American man, who lives in a country where people are known for being laid back, be in such a rush? I'm sure he's been told I'll be here two whole days.

Sergio must've read my mind. The blur of motion halted abruptly. He released my arm. "*Senor* Malone, I must apologize for dragging you through the building so quickly, but I wanted you to see a bottling procedure that will occur in a few minutes." He pointed to an area about two feet from us. "The men, they are preparing to release the soda from the carbo-cooler and send it to the *filler*, the machine which looks like a huge circular hopper."

"Ah, I wondered where you were taking me." I wish I could've told him not to worry about anything. That I'd just completed a thorough tour of Delight's German plant. But my trip had to be kept secret, unless I wanted to be canned.

"Come, let us join the workers," Sergio suggested.

I slipped my camera out of its carrying case, adjusted a few buttons, nestled the camera between my hands just so and aimed. Show time.

The employees were so engrossed in the *filler* process that they never noticed what I was actually taking pictures of. Click. Click.

When the Minolta finally required adjustments, it offered me the opportunity to examine the equipment from a closer perspective and from different angles. Ah, the machine was much older than the one in Germany. I wonder how frequently it breaks down. Hopefully someone around here besides Sergio speaks English.

I tuned into the conversation going on between various employees and caught a few English words being bantered about. The culprits seemed to be employees standing furthest from the machinery. I decided to mingle with them.

Tucking the camera away, I left Sergio's side and wandered over to the group using my language. An easy ice breaker should gain their trust: ask their names and how long they've worked there. "Hello. I'm Matt Malone. I'm visiting your plant for a couple days. Do you mind telling me your names?" My plan worked like a charm. Since I had them eating out of my hand, I probed deeper. "Does the *filler* machine always run so smoothly or does it act up sometimes?"

One of the men spoke for the rest. "It can be fickle."

"Like once a year, once a month?"

Utter silence. Shoot. I ran my hand through my hair. I should've waited till tomorrow to inquire about such things. I hope I haven't opened a can of worms. Sao Paulo's attitude towards me could change drastically overnight.

Sergio was busy speaking with a few employees, so I stayed where I was for the time being. Maybe these people simply need more time to think about my question.

"Er…, *Senor* Malone," a soft spoken woman around forty-five said. I believe she said her name was Maria.

"Yes."

She pushed a stray strand of hair behind her ear before stepping to the front of the group. "I've been here the longest, so I speak for the rest. The machine gives us trouble two to five times a year. We don't count." The others in her group shook their heads in agreement. This produced a grin on her face. "What's important to us is that we never get behind in our work." Her peers patted her on the back.

Bingo. That was the type of information I was sent to extract.

Sergio left the employees he had been speaking with and rejoined me.

The group mingling with me acknowledged their manager and then hurriedly dispersed to their various departments.

"Those people are great workers," he shared with pride. "They watch the clock. They don't take more breaks than allowed or go beyond their break time." He pointed to the corridor straight ahead. "Come, we can go at a slower pace now. So, did anyone tell you why Mr. Welch built a plant here in Sao Paulo?"

I responded in a cautious manner. "No. I don't believe so."

"Sao Paulo is the largest industrialized state in all of Brazil, many large corporations especially those heavily involved in the international market locate here." Sergio grew solemn. "You see, it's a big mistake not to have a business in this town," he swiped his index finger across his neck. "You understand, Amigo?"

I smiled meekly. Whoa! Was he sending a mafia style warning to Welch via me? If he was, the rest of my stay here could be quite awkward or mighty dangerous. Awkward I could handle, danger was another matter.

~18~

Unaware of my internal turmoil, Sergio went into teacher mode yet again. "We store all the caps for cans and bottles here in this room. Each package contains 400 lids. Now if we take a few steps to the right, you can see the capper machine in action."

I bit my tongue. I wanted to shout, "Enough, already. I don't need to know how the darn machine operates."

"See the cans moving towards us?" I nodded politely. "They've come from the "filler" room and are ready to be capped."

Good for them.

He pointed to one of the employees in the capper machine room. "Once he opens a package of caps, he'll stack them in that chute on the capper machine so the lids can slide down onto the cans."

I watched the process even though I wasn't a bit interested. Maybe the machine would malfunction while I was standing here. One could only hope.

Sergio went on. "As many years as I've worked here, I'm still amazed at how fast those caps go on. The process takes less than a second. If it was any slower, the fizz would be gone and you would taste flat pop."

"It sounds like this is one machine you can't do without."

"*Si*. A human can't cap cans that fast."

Since we were by the capper machine, I asked Sergio to pose leaning against the glass window separating us from the equipment and then I snapped about five pictures.

"Would you like to see the control room next?"

"Sure."

The second we entered the room, déjà vu swept over me. The room was set up exactly the same as the German plant.

"*Senor* Yang, I'm sorry to interrupt you, but our guest from Minnesota has arrived. Is it possible to break away from the computers or is this a bad time for you?"

Yang didn't look up. "Just give me a minute." He typed a few more phrases on his keyboard then stopped and twirled his office chair around to face us.

I had no idea what my face looked like when I saw Yang, but I had a feeling it looked similar to his, one of bewilderment.

"So, we meet again," Yang Quing said.

"But in a business setting this time," I pointed out.

Sergio scratched his head. "You two met already? How? Where?"

"I went to Leme yesterday," I explained, "and our paths crossed."

"All we mentioned to each other was we were on holiday," Yang added.

"Well," Sergio said, resting an arm on his hip, "since you've already met, I'll leave you two alone for a while, and go back to my office to take care of some paperwork I've been neglecting."

"Do you want me to notify you when Mr. Malone and I are finished?"

Sergio stood in the doorway for a moment. "*Si,* please do."

The door closed and Yang quickly offered me a chair. "I still can't believe you're our visitor."

"I know. Some coincidence, huh?"

"As long as my boss isn't here, I'd like to share something with you."

Oh, oh. What could Yang possibly want to divulge? He barely knows me. "Does it happen to be work related or personal?"

"Personal."

Darn. I was hoping it was work related. The more info I can gather the better decisions Welch can make. "I see. Well, no matter what it is, I want you to know you can trust me. I won't share anything with your boss."

Yang Quing scooted his office chair closer to mine and lowered his voice. "Mr. Malone, for a long time I've been considering moving to the U.S. The air quality in Sao Paulo is suffocating me." He folded his hands in prayer. "I need to... no, I have to live where the air is clean. My lungs can't take much more."

"According to reports on the news, the heavy smog in China, Mexico and California are already causing serious health issues, but I had no idea it had reached South America too." I plucked a Bic pen out of my pocket. I really didn't know what else to say. I didn't have the power to transfer someone from this plant to one Stateside. I wasn't even a Delight employee.

"You could put in a word for me, yes?"

Was this the China connection my curse was warning me about? I didn't see how it could be. The curse usually flairs up to alert me to danger. So far, Yang Quing has only asked me to say something nice about him. There's no crime in that.

"Sorry, it doesn't work that way. I'm only involved with the marketing department. I'd suggest you send an e-mail request to Delight's HR department at the corporate headquarters. I'm sure they keep a list of openings in your field. Of course, you'll want to find out what the pollution levels for each town are prior to applying for any available position."

"Thank you. I appreciate your suggestions. I will think about them. Now, before I get fired, I'd better share what I do for this plant."

Late afternoon I felt compelled to return to the computer control room again. What exactly was drawing me into its web? Earlier, Yang had told me the managers for this department had to be fluent in the Chinese language since the complex system had been built in Singapore. Could that tidbit be clawing at my heels?

Yang was busy pressing buttons on the computer enhanced control panel when I entered. Not wanting to disturb him, I remained silent. When he finally realized someone was standing behind him, he turned towards me. "Ah, I'm glad you're here. Are you free for dinner tonight? I'd like to talk to you about Minnesota."

I hadn't expected that, but what good fortune. I'd been given the opportunity to chat about the Sao Paulo plant without anyone else eavesdropping. "*Si.* I'd enjoy that."

"Do you like fish?"

I laughed. "I'd better. Minnesota's known for its ten thousand plus lakes."

***

Tell me about Minnesota," Yang said, when we finally sat down around seven to eat at Trout at Truta Rosa's Restaurant.

"Well, as I mentioned earlier, we've plenty of lakes. So, if you like fishing or water sports it's a terrific place to live. Plus we have plenty of outdoor sports: hunting, tennis, skating, baseball, golfing—"

"What's this Vikings I hear so much of?"

"That's our football team. Some years they do better than others." I picked up my glass of beer and took a couple sips. "Yang, do you mind if I ask a work related question?"

Yang braced his head with his hand. "What would you like to know?"

I broke open a bread roll the waiter had offered a few seconds before "Actually I was wondering how long the pop stays in the plant once it's ready for shipment?"

"Ten days is the longest a load can sit there. Each truck driver is assigned a certain day to pick up his load. Depending on the season, a driver may be expected to make four or five runs in a day."

"When Sergio showed me where they stack the finished product, I couldn't believe how many cases of pop were ready to go out the door. I imagine some of the drivers picked up their loads after I'd seen the area. Is there some sort of marking on the cans to prevent a mix up concerning which load goes out the door first?" Sure the trade magazine Candy gave me explained the procedure, but it never hurts to hear from someone who actually works in the field.

Yang set his glass of wine aside. "Tomorrow when you pass by where the loads are sitting, pick up a can and turn it over. Numbers are stamped on the bottom. One set of numbers represents the date the pop was canned."

"Really? Perhaps I'd better do that as soon as I arrive in the morning before all the stacked cans disappear."

Our fish dinner finally came. The waiter asked if we'd like anything else. "Another drink for you gentlemen perhaps?"

"Yes. How about you, Yang? My treat."

"No, thanks. One glass is my limit."

"Speaking of liquids," I said nonchalantly, as I squeezed the tiny portion of lemon allotted me over the deliciously prepared fish, "do you know how many cans get bottled in an hour?" Gustav had informed me that a plant in full operation fills 2000 cans an hour. If Yang's answer is considerably lower, I'll know his plant has problems.

"About 1,500."

~19~

January 15

I rolled out of bed at the crack of dawn with an excruciating headache, determined to call my folks and ask how Gracie was handling my long absence. But before my fingers could play with the buttons on the phone, someone else was reaching out to me. *Could it be Rita?*

I stifled a yawn before answering. "Hello?"

"Matt, I'm so glad I caught you."

"Good morning Mr. Welch. I didn't expect to speak with you until I got back to the States. I suppose you're wondering how it's going over here. You'll be pleased to hear the digging is paying off."

"Excellent. Listen, Matt, there's been a slight change in plans. I want you to postpone the other plant inspections for the time being."

"Oh? Has something happened back there I don't know about?"

"No. Nothing like that. According to an insider friend of mine who works at Delight's bottling franchise in Boston, the owner is about to approach our corporate office to see if we'd consider buying him out. I guess he wants to retire."

"What does that have to do with me?"

"I'd like you to accompany our CFO and one of our department supervisors when they go there in a couple days. You can chat it up with the employees, snoop around, and snap photos of the machinery while they're kept busy with other things."

"Do you want me to contact David about the change?"

"No need to, I've already spoken with him. He's making flight arrangements as we speak."

"Sir, do you want me to at least finish up what I started here in Sao Paulo?"

Welch cleared his throat. "I'm not sure. Just stay put until David contacts you. I'll see you at the corporate headquarters when you get back. Have a safe trip."

~20~

January 18

Traffic was still snarled due to the huge snowfall that had covered most of Minnesota the evening of the sixteenth, but I managed to arrive at the Delight headquarters ten minutes before nine. I remembered what Carol told me my first trip there. Her boss liked people to be punctual.

I found an empty spot in the parking lot close to the entrance, despite the mounds of snow that waited for removal yet. The sidewalk leading to the main entrance had been cleared, so I took it instead of a shorter path which would've left my feet covered in snow. The minute I strolled in the building I signed in, picked up a pass, and pinned it on.

The security guard scratched his face. It wasn't Bob. "Is this your first visit here, Mr. Malone?" he asked.

I shook my head. "Nope. Been here a couple times."

"Visiting the same person again?"

"Yup."

"I guess you don't need directions then. Go on up."

When the elevator opened on the sixth floor, perky Carol glanced up. What's this? She's blowing bubbles. Sure hope Neil Welch doesn't catch her.

Caught in her indiscretion, she immediately grabbed a tissue, spit the gum into it, and tossed it in the trash.

I pretended not to notice. "Hello, Carol."

Her quarter moon grin came off a tad lopsided. "Oh, Mr. Malone. What a pleasant surprise. I didn't expect you back in Minnesota for quite some time." Apparently the boss was too busy to keep her in the loop. "How did it go overseas?"

I offered her a smile. "Fine. By the way, the drivers you hired did an outstanding job. And I was mighty impressed with the rooms you reserved for me, especially the Sheraton in Sao Paulo. You knocked it out of the park with that one. I sure didn't expect butler service."

Carol tilted her head higher and batted her long, thick lashes at me. "We aim to please."

Remembering the small gift I'd brought back for her, I pulled a tiny, square white box from my inner suit coat pocket and deposited it on her desk. "A little trinket I picked up for you in Sao Paulo. I hope you like it."

Carol acted shocked. "Why, why, thanks, Mr. Malone. That's so thoughtful of you." She took the lid off the box and peeked inside. "Oh, my, gosh! What a gorgeous pin. I love it." She lifted the jeweled jaguar out of the box and pinned it to the collar of her blouse.

"It goes good with what you have on," I said.

"Is he here yet?" Neil Welch asked, popping out of his inner sanctum unexpectedly. The man probably had seen me when I drove into the parking lot and wondered what happened to me. "There you are Matt." He threw his arm around my shoulder, treating me like a soldier returning from the war. "Glad you made it back safely," he said, leading me to his office and quickly closing the door. "Considering you're probably suffering from jet lag, Matt, you look well-rested."

"Sleeping in my own bed helped I'm sure."

A tiny smile erupted on Welch's lips. "I understand you had to spend the night in Boston because of the blizzard that blew through. I hope George Olson showed you a good time. He's been managing the Boston plant for many years."

"He did a great job. By the way, he said to tell you one of these summers he's going to make it back here to do a little Muskie fishing on Leech Lake."

Welch fingered the papers on his desk. "Did he tell you he and I went to the same high school and college, way back when?"

"No, but he did give me a commemorative package of pop to take home with me. I thought that was a nice touch."

"Don't be too impressed, Matt. When cans don't pass inspection, they're set aside and employees can take them from what we refer to as the *toss pile*."

"Oh?"

"You know, I'm kind of glad you had a chance to meet George. At least he won't question what you're doing at the Boston plant when you show up." He flipped open his black schedule book and stared at the calendar. "I suppose you'd like some idea when you might be flying back to Boston."

Thinking of my limited income, I said, "That would be helpful."

Welch picked a pen off his desk and tapped a couple dates on the calendar. "Here's what I think, Matt. Today's Monday. If the owner is as serious about selling as I've heard, he'll call me by Friday. When he does, I'll tell him I can have my guys out there by Monday the twenty-fifth, weather permitting of course. Does that work for you?"

"Yup. I'm wide open. If you can't reach me, just have Carol leave a message."

Welch closed his black book, slid it into a side drawer, and then leaned back in his chair, making himself more comfortable.

Since I assumed he'd want to hear my assessment of the two plants I'd already visited, I opened a folder I'd brought with which contained my written notes and rifled through them. "I apologize for not having my notes typed up yet, but I didn't expect the trip to be cut short. I hope you don't mind."

He didn't respond. He appeared to be off in his own corner of the world.

Geez, I hope I didn't say something to upset him.

A few seconds passed, and then Welch said, "News of the plants can wait, Matt. There's something I think you should be made aware of. Before you left, you asked me if I planned to sell some of the plants you'd be inspecting."

I closed the folder and set it aside. "Yes, I remember. You told me a few may have to be."

"Well, if I'm going to have a PI working for me, I should've told you the whole story up front. You see my wife and I have been having marital problems for a couple months now. I don't think our relationship's going to end in divorce, but you never know. That's why I hired you to look at the plants."

The truth finally comes out. "I see. Well, I'm glad you told me. If rumors start flying at any of the plants I'm visiting, I'll make sure to straighten everyone out."

"It's too late for that."

I scooted to the edge of the chair. "What do you mean?"

He slammed his fist on the desk.

The unexpected noise caused me to react accordingly. I threw my back against the chair; if it wouldn't have been cushioned I would've cracked my vertebrate. Something tells me this morning isn't going to end so great.

"A damn European tabloid got wind of my marital problems."

"But who would've shared that information with them?"

"I don't know, Matt. But that's only half of it. The guys at the German plant don't believe your visit had anything to do with marketing either."

I stuffed my hands in my pockets. "What? I swear I did everything I could while I was there to convince the employees I was creating a new ad campaign. Is it possible to squelch things before it gets out of hand?"

Welch toyed with the Montblanc writing pen on his desk. "I had a long discussion with Gustav and assured him what was written in the tabloid was utter nonsense. They only wrote it to increase sales."

"How did he react?"

"Gustav seemed to agree with me. He said he knew I wouldn't lie to him."

"Hmm? Do you think he meant what he said?"

Welch behaved like violin wires tightened to the limit. "If he didn't I'm in for one hell of a ride, especially if he shares what he knows with our other plants."

"I'm sure messages are sent back and forth, but do you think they'd be related to things outside of work."

"It's hard to say. But with the Internet word travels fast, be it good or bad."

If I didn't calm Neil down soon, we'd never discuss the condition of the Frankfurt and Sao Paulo plants like I planned. "Look, Mr. Welch, I think you took the right steps with Gustav. Things will blow over, you'll see."

Welch looked directly into my eyes. "Let's hope you're right, Matt. I can't afford a mess at the plants, not when a new brand of pop is about to be released."

~**21**~

My brain was on information overload after leaving Neil Welch's office. I needed to chill out big time and only one lone mutt could help.

I steered the Topaz onto the cleaned side of my folk's driveway and scrambled up to the front door, looking forward to Gracie knocking me over. No such luck. When my mother opened the door, she told me Dad had taken her to the veterinary office about five miles away.

Seeing the concern on my face, Mom squeezed my hand. "Gracie must have eaten something she found in the yard. There's no way she could've digested anything in the trash, the basket was always kept out of bounds."

I wrung my hands. *She'd better be all right.* If Welch's calculations were correct, I'd be leaving for Boston in eight days. "When did Dad takeoff?"

"About an hour ago." Mom continued to study my face. "I wouldn't start worrying yet. If the vet's office is as busy with pets as a regular doctor's clinic is with humans, it could be a while before they get back. Why don't you come in the kitchen and I'll make you something. I bet you didn't bother with breakfast, did you?"

I followed her down the hallway to the back of the house and sat. "Good guess. You can't make anything without food."

Mom's eyebrows arched. "Oh, Matt, I'm sorry. We didn't know you were that strapped for cash. You never told us."

Even though I was worried to death about Gracie, Mom's comment made me chuckle. "My income is fine. There's no food in my apartment because I emptied the fridge and cupboards before I took off for Germany."

"A sound idea. No one wants to come back to a house full of spoiled food." Mother moved in between the stove and the fridge. "Would you like scrambled eggs and bacon, or do you prefer something else?"

I pressed my hands to my forehead. "Eggs and bacon I guess." I held my left wrist at an angle and glanced at my watch, trying to figure out when Gracie and Dad might walk through the back door. Hopefully it would be any minute. The mutt loves scrambled eggs.

Mom cracked a few eggs, added milk and poured the mixture into a medium-sized frying pan and then she placed bacon in another frying pan. "So, what's the scoop on your travel plans? Are you flying out again tomorrow?"

"No. Probably not till the twenty-fifth." I folded my hands and rested them on the table. "That's the reason I came by to get Gracie. I figured you didn't need to watch her while I'm in town."

Mom flipped the bacon and eggs over. "She's no bother, Matt."

When the garage door went up five minutes later, I rushed to the side door connected to the garage. "Son, what are you doing here?" Dad asked. "Your mother didn't get you too riled up about Gracie I hope."

"I stopped by to get Gracie." I glanced over his shoulder. The dog wasn't there. "Did you leave her in the car or with the vet?"

He took his jacket off and hung it on a peg. "Heck, no. I didn't leave her anywhere. She's out back letting off steam."

"Are you sure that's okay?"

Noticing the cooked breakfast sitting on the stove, Dad said, "She's fine. Sit down, eat, and I'll tell you what the doctor said."

Mom set my breakfast in front of me and then poured coffee for the three of us. "Okay, Archie, tell us what happened."

Dad took a sip of coffee first. "Well, according to Doc Mallard your mutt ate something that didn't agree with her."

Mother interrupted. "You and I suspected that much. But didn't they tell you what she might have eaten?"

"Nope. She threw up too much this morning before I took her in. The main thing is she's her old self again."

I sighed. "That's a relief. I've got enough on my plate, including several problems that have recently cropped up for Neil Welch, without having to leave a sick dog behind while I'm jetting all over the world."

Mom, who I get my Sherlock Holmes genes from, threw out a few questions. "Meaning problems that have arisen since you left for Frankfurt? You didn't create them did you?"

"More like after I left Germany and before I took off from Sao Paulo. And no, I don't think I'm responsible for either one."

She put her hand over mine. "Please tell me these new problems that have arisen don't entail danger."

"I can't say."

Mother rested her hand on her cheek. "But Matt…"

"Now, Mother," Dad said, "leave the boy be. He chose the profession he's in. We didn't." Dad pushed his chair back. "Come on, Matt. Get your coat on. I know someone who's anxious to see you."

~22~

January 25
Boston

"Is Mr. Olson in? Delight's CFO asked the plant security guard. "I believe he's been informed of our visit."

Manny, a department supervisor, and I, dressed in similar neatly pressed suits, stood in the lobby with Dwight patiently waiting for a brief response from the man.

"Afraid I haven't seen him yet," the sixty-something guard replied, pushing the visor of his cap up higher resulting in exposure of his forehead's deep furrows. "But then, one never seems to inform me of anything, including visitors from the corporate office." He grabbed the phone on his desk and almost tore the wire from its connection. "Jennie, have you seen Mr. Olson? He's where?" When he ended the call, he punched in more numbers. "Yeah, this is Gene, the security guard in the lobby. Three people from corporate are here to see you Mr. Olson. Ah huh. All right, I'll do that." He placed the receiver back in its cradle. "He says he'll be right with you."

Ten minutes lapsed before George Olson showed up to get us. His appearance was a little disheveled compared to the night he showed me around Boston. I suppose when a person's running here and there in the plant they can't look like a Ken doll. "Sorry I wasn't here when you arrived. A little emergency cropped up in the *filler* room, but all's fine now." Without wasting anymore words, he raised his hand to indicate we should proceed to the left side of the building.

"Dwight, all the financial books are laid out for you in my office in the next room. There's a big pot of brewed coffee waiting for you and a plate of Danish pastries. If you need anything else, Jennie my secretary will know where to reach me."

"Thanks. I guess I'll catch you two later then."

Both Manny and I peeked at our watches. "Yeah, around lunch time," we said.

"Matt," George said, "You might as well tour the plant with us this morning."

"Sure. Just let me use the facilities first. I overdosed on coffee." What I really needed to do was make sure the camera attached to my tie was working.

When I rejoined Manny and George in the hallway leading to one of the sections of the plant a few seconds later, George was already discussing the age of the building. "This building has been standing thirty-five years. It used to house one of our competitor's products up until fifteen years ago. That's when Owen Sinclair purchased everything and made it into a Delight bottling operation."

"Perfect location and setup," I said, "He's lucky no one else snapped it up."

George rubbed his bald head. "Yup, he sure was. Say, do you guys mind if we start where the finished product is stored? I get so dang tired of walking around the plant in the same direction every day."

"It doesn't matter to me." Actually I couldn't be happier with the plant manager's decision. It's possible I overlooked a few things at the other plants and by touring this operation from finished product to the start I might spot something I missed.

"I don't care either," Manny added, "Whatever works best for you."

When I rejoined Manny and George in the hallway leading to one of the sections of the plant a few seconds later, George was already discussing the age of the building. "This here building has been standing in this spot for thirty-five years. It used to house one of our competitor's products up until fifteen years ago. That's when Owen Sinclair purchased everything and made it into a Delight bottling operation."

"Perfect location and setup," I said, "He's lucky no one else snapped it up."

George rubbed his bald head. "Yup, he sure was. Say, do you guys mind if we start where the finished product is stored? I get so dang tired of walking around the plant in the same direction every day."

"It doesn't matter to me." Actually I couldn't be happier with the plant manager's decision. It's possible I overlooked a few things at the other plants and by touring this operation from finished product to the start I might spot something I missed.

"I don't care either," Manny added, "Whatever works best for you."

Once we neared our destination, George shared a bit of info regarding the huge garage style area buzzing with forklift activity. "Until Delight's fleet of trucks comes in and swoops up what they need for their delivery routes, our forklift drivers are continuously loading packaged cans and bottles on pallets and then stacking and storing them. So, watch your step."

After the near fatal incident with the forklift driver in Frankfurt, I didn't need any warnings. I planned to be on high alert all the time. "Hey, George, do you mind if I get a shot of you and Manny here among the stacks of pop. It would make a great ad," I lied again. You and I both know I don't need a photo for an ad. But the photo op would document a water damaged ceiling and extra wide loading dock doors. The two men were happy to oblige. "Thanks."

"Packaging department next," George said, waving us on. "We'll catch some excitement there." Just as he began to lead us into this department, he changed his mind and almost stomped on my foot. "Hu," he said in a surprised tone, "I didn't see you."

A young Chinese man with coal-black hair came into view. "I didn't see you either. Sorry," he said, continuing on his way.

"Hu, come back. I'd like to introduce you to these men from Delight's corporate headquarters."

Hu spun around.

"Manny and Matt this is Hu Ping, our computer wizard. Without him we'd be lost."

When I took Hu's stiffly extended hand, queasiness engulfed me. I disconnected as fast as I could.

"I imagine you'd like to see our state-of-the-art computer system while you're here," he said.

"Of course, they would," George replied. "We'll stop by after we check out the packaging department."

***

As soon as the three of us entered Hu Ping's domain, a fax came in via the regular computer set-up. Being a PI, I was curious to know if the message contained anything regarding Neil Welch's possible divorce or sale of some of his plants.

While Manny and George were distracted, I edged to within a few centimeters of the equipment receiving the fax. The message appeared to be gibberish, although it could be some type of code. Here's hoping the mini video camera caught it.

Hu noticed me by the fax machine and rushed over to retrieve the message. "It is from my brother in Hong Kong," he softly commented, glancing down at the floor.

"Is this the brother you told me works for the Hong Kong plant," George inquired.

Hu held the fax close to his chest. "Yes," he then proceeded to share what information the message contained. "My brother's family is already making plans for the Chinese New Year and they wonder if I can join them in Las Vegas." He lifted his eyes off the paper and gazed directly at me. "It's the *Year of the Rat*."

"So, I've heard." But the only rat I smell is you. Either Hu has extrasensory perception or he's up to his eyeballs in no good. To lighten the somber mood in the room I said, "I never can remember if I was born in the year of the boar or the monkey, but whenever I'm asked to share my sign, everyone hanging out with me laughs so loud people around us complain." No one reacted to my dripple, including Hu, so I threw an icy stare back at him.

Besides the dirty look Hu continued to give me, I noticed he seemed more aloof since the fax came and his thin face displayed sweat, even though the room seemed mighty cool. "Ah, George," Hu said, finally breaking his contact with me, "is there anything specifically you'd like me share about my work?"

George glanced at Manny and me for a second. "Nope. A brief rundown is all that's necessary."

"All right." Hu swiftly drew our attention to the computer control panel to explain what he did and I immediately lost interest. I had bigger fish to fry, like looking into his background. Perhaps Carol can help me with that.

Determined to leave the building behind and dig up dirt on Hu as quickly as possible, I made a lame excuse about my stomach bothering me. "Probably something I ate for breakfast," I complained.

"Do you think you can hang on a few more minutes, Matt? I've got Tums back at my desk."

"I'll try but Tums don't usually work for me."

"Hu, do you mind if we put off your little talk till later? There's one more thing I wanted to show the guys while we're in this area of the building."

Hu's face suddenly took on an air of satisfaction. "No, of course not."

He's acting too darn smug. I'm positive the guy's hiding something, but what?

"Okay, Matt and Manny since we've seen the back end of the plant, I thought I'd show you a process we don't usually talk about, the purification of the water that comes into our building."

Purification of water? Apparently the two managers I already visited with missed sharing this step with me.

"Why is that necessary? The cities we live in take care of that process."

George nodded. "They do, but if Delight didn't treat the water with chemicals again at each of our plants to remove any taste of chlorine or minerals, the pop wouldn't always taste the same."

"And then the consumer would get disgusted and turn to a competitor's product," Manny added.

"So, approximately how many gallons of water do you use per day?" I inquired."

"About 250,000."

I leaned against the door. "I imagine the water gets tested too."

"Yes," George replied, "our quality control technicians test and taste the water, making certain it's extremely pure. If something seems wrong with the water, they'll write up an order to have it purified again."

All right, Matt. You need to cut loose. I clutched my stomach like I was in severe pain. "George, I'm sorry, but I think I'm going to have to return to the hotel and lie down for a while."

George patted me on the shoulder. "Maybe it's not your breakfast bothering you. I bet you picked up a bug on the plane."

"I suppose. It is the flu season."

"Well, hopefully you'll feel better by tomorrow. Come on, Manny, let's go check on Dwight."

When I left the plant, I kept up the pretense of being ill and slowly dragged my body to the rental car in case an employee inside or outside caught sight of me.

Unfortunately, it wasn't until I got in the car that I noticed a red Toyota Corolla lazily driving up and down the parking lanes. Could the driver be a news reporter hot on the trail of a messy story? If so, they'd get nada from this guy.

I continued to keep an eye on the car as it inched ever closer to where I sat, making sure to allow myself enough time to slouch down in the seat. PI's use this procedure at plenty of stakeouts, hoping to catch a glimpse of a person of interest without them seeing us.

Three car lengths from me the driver slowed to a crawl. He wore a baseball cap low over his eyes. Smart move, but something about him looked vaguely familiar. What was it? Could it be the shape of his face or the length of his hair? When he finally moved on past, it dawned on me where I'd seen him before. Why was Peter, the forklift operator from Frankfurt in Boston? He sure wasn't here on holiday. Who the heck was he looking for?

I whipped out my cell phone and pressed the saved number for Delight's corporate office. "Yeah, Carol, this is Matt Malone. I've got a huge favor to ask."

~23~

January 28

Remember those sayings that rolled off your grandparents' lips when growing up, like 'When it rains it pours' and 'Things come in threes.' Well, that about sums up Neil Welch's escalating problems on the home front.

It started off with the private jet not being able to leave Boston Wednesday evening due to fog, stranding us at Logan till early Thursday morning. Of course, Welch had expected us to report to him at nine sharp and when we didn't, he threw a fit.

Being an outsider, I didn't receive the brunt of Welch's displeasure, thankfully, which left me on the sidelines watching how his employees reacted to his flare up.

"Sir, it couldn't be helped," his cool, in control CFO said, dangling a thin black leather briefcase from his hand. "Fog closed down the airport."

Nervous Manny, on the other hand acted like he had been overpowered by a super hero. He kept running his trembling hand through his thick dark brown hair. Apparently, he didn't enjoy being cross-examined. Maybe he's never irritated Welch before.

Welch stepped away from his desk. The mood he was in, I expected his employees to be lambasted further, but I was dead wrong. "Sorry, men, I didn't mean to come down on you so hard." He ran his fingers across his forehead. "You can't control the weather. Look, I need to discuss a few issues with Matt first. Why don't you two grab a cup of coffee in the outer office and I'll have Carol let you know when I'm ready for you."

The second the two men walked out, Neil and I sat side by side in the comfortable leather chairs arranged at the front of his huge executive desk. I spoke first. "Mr. Welch, I believe something sneaky is going on at the Boston plant. I can't put my finger on it, but I suspect it may be connected to another plant."

The millionaire tapped his well-manicured nails on his pants. "Yes, Carol informed me you had inquired about an employee who has worked there for some time."

Since Welch assumed I was speaking of only one person, Hu Ping, I left Peter out of the picture for now. "Yes. Unfortunately, your human resource department has hit a brick wall. All they can find is proof of his attending school for the type of position he holds."

He looked at me thoughtfully. "That's a little unusual, isn't it?" I kept silent. I had the feeling the man was just expressing himself out loud. "Maybe I'd better have George keep a closer eye on Hu Ping's activities in and out of the computer room."

"I agree. If I wasn't on this secret mission for you, I'd ask you to have George keep me in the loop."

"Don't worry, Matt, whatever I learn I'll pass on to you. So, what did you think of the plant as a whole?"

"From my perspective the machines were working properly, but see what Manny has to say. He took copious notes. I did notice water damage to a ceiling in one of the areas. It doesn't look like much. But since George mentioned the building has been around thirty-five years, I'd recommend hiring a roofer to inspect the roof too. The exterior and interior of the building look sound. And unless you're going to change the departments around, I don't foresee any other concerns. On a positive note, the loading area has wider doors than the Frankfurt and Sao Paulo plants. And as a side bar, I thought you'd like to know the employees speak highly of George."

Welch beamed. "Well, if the other two men give me as glowing a report as yours, I'd say this corporate office will be running another plant soon." He leaned over and patted me on the back. "I suppose I should explain what I really was upset about a few minutes ago."

Not wanting to appear too curious, I said, "Mr. Welch you don't owe me an explanation."

"No, you need to hear it, Matt," he stammered. "My anger had nothing to do with you men arriving here late." He stood, went around to his side of the desk, plucked a note off it, and waved it in my face. "I was saving this till after you finished your report."

"What is it?" I asked dreading his reply.

His hand shook. "You know the problem we were worried about?"

I stared at the vibrating paper. "Which one are you referring to, the news article or the sale of some plants?"

"I called it wrong regarding Gustav," he said sourly. "He went and sent faxes to some key managers here in the U.S. Joe West, from the St. Cloud plant happened to be one of them. You're scheduled for St. Cloud next and I'm afraid you're going to be walking into a hornet's nest. The men are gathering steam, Matt. There's talk of a walkout. And on top of that Joe just informed me someone broke into the plant during the night." Welch took a gulp of air. "The scary part is whoever the perpetrator was they knew enough about the plant to work around the security guard's schedule."

I pressed my hand against my cheek. "Did they do any serious damage?"

"Joe said a machine looked like it had been tampered with and tons of paperwork was strewn on the computer room floor. But that's the extent of it."

What would they want from the computer room? "Did Joe report the break-in to St. Cloud's police department?"

Welch sat down. "No, and I'll tell you why. Nothing was stolen and I didn't want the break-in to be covered on the five o'clock news."

My legs cramped up. I stood and walked around Welch's office. "I guess I can understand that. So, when would you like me to investigate?" Hopefully, it wasn't today. I had planned to get my taxes in order and then take Rita out on a date after she got off work.

"Safety wise, I think the sooner the better."

In other words today. "Any chance your competitor Big Top Soda is behind the break-in?"

Welch looked shocked. "What would they have to gain?"

"I'd say being concerned about the release of your new pop and how it will affect their sales is reason enough to create havoc at one of your plants."

"Nah. They wouldn't do that."

"What if an informer told them about a possible strike? If I was your competitor, this would be the perfect time to infiltrate your plant and have the misdeeds attributed to a disgruntled employee. A competitor loves turmoil when it's not on their home turf."

Welch frowned. "I still say it wasn't Big Top. They would've attempted other crazy things long before this."

I set my hands on my hips. "Okay. What about Mary?"

Talk about a hornet's nest. At the mere mention of Welch's spouse, the man looked like he could destroy me with his bare hands. "Mary wouldn't dream of doing this," he snapped. "so, don't you go blaming her. It's not her style."

I didn't want to be rough on Welch. The man could destroy me. But he needed a jolt of bluntness. "Sir, in order to do a decent investigation, I have to take into consideration who might want to cause harm to you or your business. No matter if it's your wife or a close confidant. So, if you don't want me to handle this case, tell me and I'll hand over all the photos and notes I've taken thus far."

~24~

St. Cloud

Welch's words tumbled around in my head like rare rocks found in a quarry. "That won't be necessary," he said. Meaning, I still had a job to finish for him, including discovering who broke into the St. Cloud plant. But whether he was giving me a long or short leash to obtain the objectives still remained to be seen.

I don't usually mind cruising around town on Minnesota's Interstates, but after an hour of driving on slick snow-packed roads I was anxious to get off them and be where I was supposed to be.

As soon as passed Waite Park's welcome sign, I eased off of Division Street, drove east until I caught sight of Delight's huge plant, and took the first left into the parking lot. The second I found an empty *visitor* slot I turned the ignition off and headed in.

Knowing the owner of this business totally backed my investigative endeavors meant I could play the game any way I desired. So, lookout whoever's tampered with this plant, I'm coming at you with two full barrels of ammunition. That's figuratively speaking of course. This PI doesn't pack a gun. I had enough of that in the Air Force.

Half expecting someone to be mulling around just inside the front door and not finding anyone I walked further into the building and popped my head in the first room I came to. A guy, a couple years younger than me, sat behind a solid wood desk half hidden by a pile of paperwork and several thick manuals. He was so wrapped up in his work he wasn't even aware of me. "Hi. Sorry to disturb you but I'm supposed to check in with Joe West. Do you have any idea where I might find him?"

The light sandy-haired fellow with grey-blue eyes lifted his head. "That would be me. What can I do for you?"

Looking at his dressed down appearance of jeans and plaid shirt, I was glad I'd left my suit hanging in the closet and switched to jeans. I'd blend in better. "I'm Matt Malone. Mr. Welch asked me to look into the break-in that took place here."

Joe brushed his thick tousled hair off his forehead. "Oh, yeah, that's right. Welch told me he'd be sending someone around who has worked with cops. I've been so busy this morning I completely forgot." He reached across his desk and clasped my hand, pumping away unenthusiastically until I let go. "So, how was the drive from the cities?" he questioned, lifting the mound of paperwork off his desk, seeking a place to deposit it, and finally opting for his incoming basket.

I lightly leaned against his desk. "Pretty slick after the three inches of new snow we had last night. But with the efficiency of the highway crews around here, I'm sure the roads will be in great shape by the time I leave."

"I'm guessing one of your friends told you how quickly snow around these parts gets removed, am I right?"

"Nope. I attended college at St. Cloud State."

"Ah, a Huskie fan. What was your major?"

"Business."

"Well, Matt, pull up a chair and I'll give you a quick rundown of what's happened here before you go out on the floor."

"Mind if I use your desk?"

"Go right ahead."

I opened the valise I brought with and took out pen, notepad, mini recorder, and set them on the desk in front of me. "I'll be taking notes," I explained to Joe, "but I like using the recorder too. It captures information I might miss while writing."

"If you think about it, shorthand probably should've been mandatory for all of us when we were in high school," Joe kidded, as he leaned back in his swivel chair and stretched his arms on the desk. "No, on second thought maybe not. Most days I'm so rushed I can't even read what I've scribbled down for myself in longhand."

"I'm glad to hear I'm not the only one who has that problem." I picked up my pen and clicked the recorder on. "All right, I'm ready for you."

"First off Matt, I think you can save yourself quite a bit of time if you don't go looking for a disgruntled employee."

"Why not? That's the most logical place to start."

"You're absolutely right, but whoever tampered with the *filler* machine didn't know squat about how it operates. They only removed nuts and bolts from the bottom of the machine. If an employee wanted to do serious damage, they would've messed with the tubes that fill the pop cans. Once those babies are damaged, the whole production line shuts down for at least a week if not longer."

Crap. If he's right, I might have to rethink Big Top Pops involvement too, which leaves only Mary Welch. *Don't even go that route yet, Matt.* "I appreciate your insight, Joe, and I'll definitely take it into consideration, but I still want to speak with various employees around the plant. Did Mr. Welch tell you I wanted to question the security guard who works third shift?"

"Yup. We're in luck. Steve Mc Guire doesn't have any classes today." Joe looked at the silver watch wrapped around his wrist. "He should be here within the hour."

"Good. What else have you got for me?"

Joe picked up a pen and tapped on his desk. "There's one more thing I wanted you to know. Wang Feng and I left the computer room just the way we found it. Not a single thing has been touched."

"I'm glad you did that. It makes my work a lot easier." With Joe's debriefing over with, I collected the mini-recorder, pen and notepad, and stuffed everything of mine back in the valise. "Okay," I said, picking up the valise, "I think I'll start in the computer room. Wang would probably like the mess in his area taken care of right away."

"I would imagine so. As much moving around as he does in the computer room, he could slip and fall. And we certainly don't want any accidents. It would spoil this plant's accident free rating we've held the last three years." Anxious to get back to his paperwork, Joe grabbed what he'd set in the IN basket and spread them on his desk again.

As I stepped away from Joe's work area, my stomach loudly complained that it was empty. Too bad lunch would have to wait till possibly two o'clock. Maybe I can speed it up a bit. "Hey, Joe, let me know the minute Steve shows up. I'd like to get his interview out of the way as soon as possible. "

"Yup, will do. I understand how fickle this weather can be."

"Thanks."

I didn't know what to think of Wang Feng, the plant's computer guru, when I met him. He was as jumpy as a kangaroo the second I entered his domain. I suppose having a stranger in the control room, one who is at least a foot taller than him, grilling him about every minute detail didn't help especially if he's a nervous geek to begin with. "You're sure nothing is missing, Wang?"

He shook his small head. "Not completely. I do know none of my manuals I keep on the desk are gone. And none of the special notes I've jotted in them since becoming a Delight employee have been torn out. But I can't answer about the mess on the floor until I can gather everything up and put it in order."

"Okay, well let's get to it then." I set a foot next to a piece of standard white paper used with computer printers. "What type of information would you say is contained in these papers strewn about, Wang, anything pertaining to pop formulas?"

"No," he adamantly replied, gripping his oval chin. "I have nothing to do with formulas. Some notes are from a recent manager meeting others pertain to the new pop being released."

I set my valise on a clean surface of the floor, opened it, and pulled out a fingerprinting kit.

"What are you doing?" Wang inquired in a high-pitched voice. "I thought we were cleaning up this mess."

"Not quite yet," I replied. "First, I'm going to try and lift fingerprints off a sampling of what's down here and then I'll take your prints."

Wang trembled. "Why mine?"

"So I can dismiss yours from others I might find."

~25~

Wang wasn't the most cooperative person this PI's ever fingerprinted on this planet, but in the end I wore him down and got what I wanted.

Once I lifted a reasonable amount of fingerprints off the bonded papers tossed helter skelter on the computer room floor, I signaled Wang that he could join me in clearing the mess.

Starting at opposite corners, in crouched positions, we eventually met in the middle. "You're right about the info I just fingerprinted, Wang," I said, clutching the final stack of papers I'd gathered up, "I didn't see anything worth stealing. Of course, I don't know the first thing about how a pop bottling plant operates," I lied.

Having squatted far too long already, my legs began to complain bitterly about being constricted. I hastily shoved the papers still in my hand behind me, thinking they were joining the rest of the collected papers sitting on the floor, unaware a few missed the mark and went in my valise. After I snapped the valise closed, I picked up my pile of papers, handed them to Wang, and stood.

The computer room supervisor added the papers he'd gathered up to mine, set them on his desk, and then pulled his body up to full height too. "Is there anything else you want to examine in here, Mr. Malone?" he nervously queried.

"No, I believe that's it." Since there was nothing else to keep me prisoner in the computer tech's little fiefdom, I decided to wander to the other side of the building next. But before I could follow through, Wang's phone shrilled. Remembering that I told Joe to contact me when Steve Mc Guire arrived, I waited to see if it was him.

Wang picked up on the second ring. "Hello. Yes, sir, I'll tell him." He tilted his head back a few inches. "Joe said the person you wanted to see just arrived."

I offered no explanation just a casual smile. "Well, at least we've finished in here. I won't have to intrude on you any longer." I walked towards the door giving every indication of leaving, and then bam I spun around to face Wang again. Joe expressed his thoughts about the tampered machine but would this computer wizard be willing to share his theory. There's only one way to find out, ask him. "Wang, do you think one of the employees was mad enough to destroy company property?"

His tinged face turned ghostly. His mouth appeared stuck. "I ah, I don't think it wise to comment."

"Don't worry, the thoughts you express with me won't go any further. I swear."

Wang remained silent for a moment. "I ah feel someone may have um wanted to stir the pot, but not necessarily cause harm. Do you understand?"

I nodded. "I think so." Unfortunately, that wasn't the truth. My brain wasn't functioning at full speed. "Wang, will you be around the rest of the day if I need to discuss anything else concerning your area?"

"I'm here until five," he replied with a tremor to his voice which wasn't apparent before.

Something definitely wasn't jiving with this guy, if I could only put my finger on it. Maybe Steve has the answers I need.

As I exited the computer room, a few employees gave me the once over. Afraid they might think I was from the corporate office sent to squelch talk of a walk-out, I swiftly spouted, "I'm new here. I got a little turned around and can't figure out where to go. Can someone point me in the direction of Joe West's office? He needs me to fill out more forms."

"Down the hall and to the right," they shared.

"Hi, Steve," I said, as I walked into Joe west's office and left my valise by the door. "I'm Matt Malone. Sorry, to keep you guys waiting." I quickly pulled up a chair next to Steve's. "I ran into a few employees down the hall by the computer room and had to cook up a plausible reason for being in the building."

"I hope you came up with a good one," Joe said.

"Yeah, I hate to tell you this but you've got a new employee on your payroll, starting now."

Joe softly chuckled. "Well, that's definitely believable. Matt, while we waited on you, I told Steve how much we appreciated his coming in."

"You bet," I said. "We're depending on your help, Steve, to figure out exactly what happened here the other night."

Steve glanced down at his hands resting in his lap. He wore the typical college clothing, baggy jeans and an oversized sweatshirt that advertised his college of choice, St. Cloud State University. "I don't know what good I'm going to be to you. I already told Joe I didn't see anyone in the computer room or by the *filler* machine."

"Hey, I have my own special way of sorting things out. So, don't worry about what's helpful or not, okay?"

He ran a finger across his lower lip. "All right."

I reached into my shirt pocket, pulled out a pen and a folded piece of paper containing a list of questions I had prepared before leaving home, and laid them on Joe's desk.

Joe stood. "Well, if you don't need anything else, Matt, I think I'll take a walk around the plant."

"I didn't mean to shove you out, Joe. There's no reason you can't hear this."

Joe glanced at Steve. "How do you feel about my sitting in on this?"

Steve leaned his elbows on Joe's desk. "I'd rather you did."

"All right then, I'll stay," and he made himself comfortable in his chair again.

I crossed my legs and then faced the security guard. "Steve, I understand you come on duty at eleven and put in an eight-hour shift."

"Correct."

"How frequently do you make rounds during your shift?"

The college student fidgeted with his shirt collar. "Five times. That is unless something doesn't sit right with me."

"Like what for instance?"

"Well, if a driver shows up later than expected, I worry he may not have shut the loading dock doors properly."

"Did anyone pick up a late load last night?"

"Nope."

I had a feeling that was going to be his response, too bad. A lone truck driver showing up late for a load would've made this a slam dunk case, especially since I'm leaning more heavily towards Mrs. Welch and her partner in crime at the moment. *Maybe something will crop up yet to exonerate her.*

"Approximately what time did you discover the mess in the computer room and the bolts by the machinery?"

The young security guard's face drew serious. He shifted in his chair slightly. "Uh, the thing is I didn't notice both during the same walk around. I noticed the papers on the computer room floor around three-thirty, but didn't discover the bolts by the equipment till five-thirty."

I let Steve be for a second and threw out a question for Joe. "Has anyone checked the time cards to see if an employee clocked-in before their scheduled time?"

Joe slapped his hands on the table. "I didn't think of that, but I'll check into it when you're done."

"Good I appreciate your doing that." I focused on Steve again. "I assume bathrooms are checked throughout the night too."

The college student sucked in air. "Yeah, but not every walk around unless the plant's running full steam twenty-four hours."

"I guess that makes sense." I brushed my chin with the back of my hand, glancing at Joe as I did so. I couldn't read his face. Steve, how about hearing noises that might have been out of sync with the norm, were there any?"

The young security guard rubbed his firm forehead. "Sorry. I can't think of anything. The only sounds I heard were the ticking of the clock that hangs on the wall behind my desk and the occasional ping on my cell phone after a message has been left.

"I did see something else however, but I don't know if it's significant or not Mr. Malone."

"Let me be the judge, Steve. What was it?"

"There were tools sitting out on a table by the breakroom sink when I did my rounds at three-thirty. I didn't think much of it at the time. The lunch room faucet leaks a lot."

Joe nodded in agreement. "It does."

Steve continued. "But one of the guys always fixes the problem."

"So, you just assumed they forgot to put the tools away," I said.

"Right, except when I checked the building two hours later, they were gone."

I glanced at Joe for a second. "That could've been the tools used to loosen the bolts on the *filler* machine. "Steve, are you positive you didn't see anyone?"

"Absolutely. If I did, I'd tell you."

I tilted my wrist to expose the time on my watch. *I should be doing something more productive like taking care of my hunger pangs instead of questioning this kid.* I wasn't getting anywhere. "Okay, Steve, one last question. Then it's back to campus for you and hitting the books."

Steve displayed a lopsided grin. "Actually, I thought I'd hook up with a buddy of mine out this way and shoot pool since I don't have any classes today."

I folded my arms and leaned back in the chair. "That's cool. An occasional break from work or school can really help reenergize a person."

Steve immediately relaxed, dropping his hands to his side. "It sure can especially when I get stressed out about upcoming tests."

"I hear yeah. Being college age and finally living away from home doesn't make life a bed of roses. There's a lot more stress placed on you: classes, passing grades, work, bills, and little time to goof off." I straightened my back and drew serious again. "Speaking of work and classes, have you ever found yourself fighting sleep on the job after sitting through a full load of classes that day?"

Steve looked directly at Joe.

"I won't reprimand you for your honesty," Joe said. "It happens to all of us. But Matt needs to know what timeline he's working with in order to solve the break-in."

He rested his head on his hands. "That's a tough one. I'm not a hundred percent sure. No one else is here to tell me if I've been snoozing. But I can tell you that when my head starts to droop, I usually grab a pop or buy a snack."

"Did you leave your office to get a snack from the candy machine anytime during the night?"

"As a matter of fact, I did." Steve jumped in his seat. "Oh, crap. Do you think someone snuck in here then?"

"It's possible." I pulled out my wallet, took a business card from it, and handed it to Steve. "Sometimes the littlest detail helps crack a case. If you remember anything about the other night, call me, even if it seems insignificant to you."

Steve shoved the card in his pant pocket. "I will Mr. Malone," and then he got up to leave.

Joe hastened to the door and placed his hand on the security guard's shoulder. "Remember Steve, our meeting remains confidential. No sharing with anyone, including your roommate."

"Got it."

With the interrogation out of the way, I stood and moved the chair I had been using up against the wall facing the lobby where I remembered seeing it when I first arrived.

"What do you think, Matt? Is Steve covering up for someone?"

"I don't think so. You saw how upset he was when he realized someone might have pulled a fast one on him the other night."

"You're referring to leaving his post to get a snack. Couldn't he have faked his reaction?"

"Nope. I watched his facial expressions, Joe. He was sincere."

Delight's St. Cloud manager looked frustrated as he rubbed his deep-set eyes. "That means we're back at square one."

I raked my hair with my fingers. "Yup. Look I'll catch up with you later. I've got a few more things in the plant to check out, including the machine you told me about."

~26~

A man's voice suddenly startled me. At the time, I was kneeling next to the *filler* machine packing up the print lifting kit. When I turned in the direction of the speaker, I found a nerdy looking fifty-something guy hovering nearby. He wore thick black Cat-eye-shaped glasses, a white lab coat, and stiff black pants. "When you finish there," he said stiffly, "You're welcome to inspect my turf too," and then he positioned a pencil on the crook of his cauliflower ear.

Mistaking me for a safety inspector is probably better than knowing a real private investigator is prowling around. Taking full advantage of this chemist's ignorance I replied, "Actually, your department is next on my list." I quickly glanced at the name badge pinned to his lapel. "So, Mel, you ready to show me around?"

He flicked his hand in the air. "Sure. Come on."

I stepped behind him as he led us down one hall and then another until we reached his immaculate lab that smelled of sanitizer. "You know, I just told one of my co-workers it was about time for one of you safety guys to do a surprise visit." He slapped his thigh. "What a coincidence, huh? I just didn't expect it to be today."

"Well, actually I wasn't supposed to be here till next week."

"Really?"

"Yeah, I was lined up to do a safety inspection in Grand Rapids, but the snow storm spoiled the trip."

Mel Dobbs stretched out his hands like he was preparing to give me a blessing. "Well, welcome to my humble home away from home, Delight's quality control lab," he drew his hands inward and cupped them together. "Since you're here for such a short time, I won't bore you with every little detail.

"The big white barrels and small brown boxes sitting out in the hallway near the lab just arrived. They contain our corn syrup and concentrate supplies and get stored in the next room with the carbo cooler. The syrup gets mixed with water in a huge tank. I imagine you'll be inspecting the safety of that area after you've finished in here." I didn't offer a reply. "Anyway, once it's blended with water, it gets pumped into another tank and is mixed with the flavored concentrate and a powder consisting of citric or phosphoric acid."

I shook my head. "I still don't understand why scientists ever approved phosphoric acid for human consumption. It's extremely dangerous."

He adjusted the temples of his glasses. "It may not make sense, but the acid's necessary. It adds a tangy taste to the pop and it slows mold growth and bacteria."

"And, we all know how you can't afford for people to get sick," I said tongue in cheek. "So, walk me through what happens next, Mel."

"The finished syrup comes to our lab and we finally play with the stuff."

I pointed to all the items on the counters. "Using this elaborate equipment of course?"

"That's what it's sitting here for," Mel said gleefully. "At thirty minute intervals, one of us examines a sample of the finished syrup under a microscope, making sure no germs exist." He opened a spiral notebook and handed it to me. "As you can see, we've kept good records of our procedures, jotting down the time of day sampling took place, the batch number assigned the syrup, and who did it."

I flipped through the pages, pretending to check for proof of what he said but in reality, I was memorizing the names of the other chemists. "It looks like you guys stay on top of things like you should," I said, handing the notebook back to him.

"We strive for excellence at our plant."

"So, I've heard. After you give your stamp of approval to the tested syrup, I suppose it goes directly to the carbo cooler tanks."

"Yes, and then it gets piped into the filler machine where you were when I bumped into you."

Joe poked his head in the lab. He still looked frazzled. "Ah, there you are Mr. Malone. I hope Mel hasn't taken up too much of your time."

I offered a smile. "Not at all. He's been filling me in about the safety procedures for this department."

"Ah. So, are you finished, Mel?"

"I think so."

I snapped my fingers. "No, I believe there's one thing you've omitted, Mel."

He pressed his overly long fingers into his cheek. "What's that?"

"Who checks on the safety of the pop supply when it leaves the plant?"

Joe cut in, gently steering me to the door. "Mr. Malone, I'm sure Mel would like to get back to work. Why don't we get a cup of coffee and I'll share that information with you."

"Sounds good. I could use a caffeine pickup." I turned to Mel who already had his eye pressed against a microscope. "Thanks for explaining your safety department procedures with me, Mel. You did an excellent job."

"Come back anytime," he mumbled more to himself than me.

The instant the lab door closed behind us, I confided the following, "Great job of play acting, Joe."

"Yeah, I thought so too. Hey, maybe I should take a drama class so I can add more emotions to my repertoire. What do you think?"

I got serious. "Don't you have enough drama going on right here?"

"Leave it to a PI to burst my bubble." He jabbed me in the arm. "But, hey, I was serious about answering the last question you had for Mel if you really want to know."

"I learned so much about the process you might as well finish up the story."

"Believe me this part is very brief," he shared as we walked into his office and sat. "Probably take me all of five minutes."

I nodded. "That's good because I should get back to the cities and have someone take a look at the fingerprints I lifted."

Joe leaned back in his chair. "Once a month the pop inspectors hired by Delight travel to the stores we supply and randomly select different pop flavors from the shelves. If a particular flavor has been on the store shelf too long or if a later test at the lab shows something is wrong with a flavor, all of the batch will be pulled from the shelf."

"So, basically pop gets handled the same as food products sitting in a store."

"Exactly."

"Well, you made my day, Joe."

"How's that?"

"I may not have a clue to the break-in, but at least I know I won't get sick enjoying one of Delight's beverages."

"I'm glad you feel that way, Matt, because I lied about the cup of coffee." He backed his swivel chair away from his desk and leaned forward just enough to retrieve a cloth draped medium-sized object that had been hidden from view.

What the heck?

Before I could question what Joe was up to, he rounded his desk with the rectangular object, sauntered over to where I sat, and set whatever he was holding on his desk in front of me. "I hope you like pop," he said excitedly, finally whisking the cloth off to reveal what he had been hiding. "It's our new line of pop. And only a privileged few, like you, are getting to sample it beforehand."

"I don't know what I did to deserve being among the few, but thanks. From the articles I've read in the papers recently, it's been at least ten years since Delight has attempted to put a new beverage in the marketplace, isn't it?"

Joe rested his hands on his hips. "Yup. I just hope Bubble Gum blows the competition out of the water when it enters the market next Monday. Our employees have been looking forward to the extra revenue boosting their profit sharing since Limey Loon lost its momentum."

I'm surprised there hasn't been much mention of the pop on the radio or TV if the company's expecting to pull in the money."

"Our heaviest advertising's been concentrated in states where the Chinese population is the greatest: Boston, Colorado, California, and Seattle."

"But why would Delight gear an ad more to one particular group?" I asked in bit of a quandary. "Running an ad for such a small market is extremely risky." Rita had informed me of that fact one night when covering marketing issues. "Why would Delight suddenly change its business philosophy after all this time?"

"It was Welch's idea. For the past eight years he's been watching the steady arrival of Asians to the U.S. and felt it was time to market the group. Do you have any idea how many Chinese live here?"

I shook my head. "Nope. And I wouldn't even hazard a guess."

"7.3 million."

A sharp whistle escaped my lips. "Holy cow. That's a heck of a lot of people." I picked up the box of pop from Joe's desk and rested it in the crux of my arm. "So, what happens if this new pop is a flop?"

Joe frowned. "Word around here is the employees plan to let corporate know in a big way."

~27~

January 29

This morning when I awoke I had so much on my mind I wanted to get right to it. Of course, my stomach had other ideas and so did the mutt. So, after hastily chowing down on a piece of toast smothered with peanut butter and jam and a cup of day old coffee, I prepared myself and the dog for a robust morning jaunt.

As expected Gracie threw a conniption the second I tried to wrap a neon-striped doggie sweater around her midsection. She tore the sweater out of my hand and swung it from side to side like she was fighting an alligator.

I had no time for her nonsense this morning. Her stinker of an attitude needed to change pronto. If this master has to dress in a parka, wool stocking cap, and thermal-lined mittens for the blustery 25 below temp outside and scare the bejeebers out of the neighbors with the legendary Big Foot look, she can darn well put up with the warm covering I chose for her.

But no matter how much I tried to get the dog to drop her new play thing, she wouldn't budge. That is until I used the old bribery trick. I offered a Milkbone treat.

The minute we left the cozy comfort of the Foley behind the cold air tried invading every inch of my body. I resisted its advances the best I could by rehashing the many suspicious things I'd heard and observed regarding Neil Welch's business, starting with Frankfurt.

Gustav the plant manager and all the employees appeared to be above board except for Peter, the forklift driver. Although Gustav certainly displayed no loyalty to the owner of Delight when he decided to share with U.S. bottling plants what overseas papers were saying about Neil and his wife. And his huge indiscretion triggered not only talk among employees about walking off the job, but possibly opened the door for a competitor or disgruntled employee to create mayhem inside the plants.

What troubled me the most in Sao Paulo? The answer came swiftly. Sergio's demonstrative show for sure, when he swiped a finger across his neck to indicate how dangerous it could be for an international company who chose to ignore Sao Paulo's business climate. I took the act at face value. The warning seemed to be directed at Welch. "Don't mess with my plant." Could Sergio be secretly instigating problems here in the U.S.?

At least meeting George, Boston's plant manager, didn't trigger any undercurrents. But my gut instincts concerning Hu Ping, the head of the information technology department at the plant, suggested he was up to no good. When I visited his domain, I snuck a look at an incoming fax before he retrieved it. The fax left me completely stumped. It appeared to be written in a Chinese dialect, something I knew nothing about. Hu may have convinced George the fax was from his brother, but I didn't swallow his story. Could the welfare of this bottling plant be at stake?

Then there's Peter the forklift driver who surprises me with his appearance in the parking lot at the Boston plant. Who the heck was he connecting with and why?

And what about St. Cloud?

Gracie tugged on her leash several times. Apparently she thought I'd ignored her long enough and it was time to return to warm surroundings. Suspicions concerning the St. Cloud plant would have to wait.

The instant I broke away from the consuming thoughts swimming around in my head, the jarring cold I'd forgotten about smacked every inch of my body like a mad man. My stiff mouth barely moved, but the mutt got the message. "Okay, let's head home, girl."

***

As soon as we got in the door, the landline rang. Thinking it was Rita whom I hadn't spoken with since the trips to Boston and St. Cloud, I gave Gracie the *stay* command, kicked off my wet shoes, and rushed to catch the caller before they hung up.

"Hi, Matt," a deep husky voice said, "I've got the results you were waiting for."

"Great, Sam." Sam Sweeny, a retired cop, was my secret go-to person I've used for years to analyze fingerprints I've lifted. "Find anything interesting?"

"I hate to be the bearer of bad news."

"But...."

"But," Sam said, "The lifted fingerprints marked computer room only matched Wang Feng's, the department head."

"How about the *filler* machine, any prints that shouldn't have been there?"

"Sorry, I got the same results for the *filler* machine, no unknowns."

I ran my hand through my scalp. "Crap. I was afraid of that. Whoever messed around at the St. Cloud plant knew enough to wear gloves."

"Or the alternative, the employees working in those departments made it look like an outsider came in."

"Right, right. Well, thanks for your help, Sam. If you're around next week, give me a call and I'll buy you a couple beers at Shorty's on Fifth."

"I'll do that."

When I went back to the hallway by the entrance door, I found Gracie still patiently waiting for me. I unhooked her leash and she flew to the kitchen to scarf up a few bits of doggie food left in her bowl from last night.

While the mutt was busy entertaining herself, I stripped off my outdoor wear and dug out the number for Delight's corporate headquarters. Neil Welch expected me to report in as soon as I obtained information regarding my investigation. I wonder if having nothing to tell warrants a call. I'd much rather take care of things on the home front: call girlfriend, drop film off to be developed, dump suit off at cleaners, and pick up mail at the post office.

I strolled to the kitchen where the landline sat and glanced at the clock on the wall. 10:00 o'clock. Maybe I'll luck out and Welch won't be there. He could be in a board meeting. I stalled a while longer, warmed up a cup of coffee in the microwave and drank the cup dry. Then I bit the bullet. "Hi, Carol. Is your boss in?"

Her crisp, cheery voice replied, "Yes, Mr. Malone. I'll connect you straight away."

"Thanks."

"Hello, Matt." Hmm? Welch's voice sounded upbeat too. It surprised me considering all the turmoil in his life. Let's hope what I have to tell him doesn't sour his mood. "Well, how did it go in St. Cloud? Did you get a chance to speak with everyone you wanted to?"

Be cautious but optimistic, Matt. "Yeah, I had a good talk with Joe West, Wang Feng, Steve Mc Guire, and a chemist named Mel."

"Terrific. What did they have to say?"

I leaned against the kitchen counter and watched Gracie push her water bowl around the floor. Hopefully, she won't start whining. "Steve Mc Guire doesn't remember hearing or seeing anything unusual the night he was on duty, but promised to get back to me if he recalls something that didn't seem to fit."

Welch's voice dropped a couple notches. "That doesn't sound encouraging."

"Memories are a tricky thing Mr. Welch. Often times when a crime is committed, a person doesn't recall everything they saw or heard the day of the incident. But give them a few days to sleep on it, and you'd be surprised what they come up with."

"Well," he huffed, "Were you able to at least get some fingerprints?"

Gracie shoved her dish in front of my feet and gazed up at me. I ignored her. "Yeah, I got plenty and they've already been analyzed."

"So— don't leave me hanging, Malone."

"Sir, not a single unknown was found. The person or persons who created the havoc wore gloves, still leaving me with my three original suspects."

Neil Welch took a deep breath. "What does Joe think about your list of suspects?"

His question threw me off guard. I didn't plan to share Joe's thoughts yet. "He said I should dismiss your competitor, Big Top, as well as any disgruntled employee."

"I imagine he gave you a decent explanation for saying that. Although, you already heard what I had to say about Big Top being involved."

Gracie whined.

I covered the phone's mouthpiece. "Shhh. I'll fool with you later."

"Are you there, Matt?"

"Yeah, sorry. I should've known better than to call from home. The dog's being a pest. You asked what reason Joe gave for suggesting I eliminate two of the suspects. Here's what he told me. 'Someone familiar with a bottling plant could've easily destroyed the *filler* machine.'"

"Nothing wrong with his assumption," Welch said, "I strongly agree."

I cleared my throat. "Let me play devil's advocate for a minute, okay? What if a person knowledgeable with the pop business got scared off before they could do the damage? Or better yet, they plan to do something major and were testing the waters. You know finding out where the weak points are in your plant security."

"You could be right, Matt. Follow that train of thought and leave my wife off the suspect list for now."

"I'll try, Sir. But have you at least asked Mary where she was the night of the break-in?"

His harsh, "No," said it all.

~28~

When I came home from running all my errands, I ran into Margaret Grimshaw on the elevator. She had just returned from a late lunch, carrying the evidence in a small square white Styrofoam container. "Did you have a good lunch?" I inquired.

"*Si*, but too much on the plate as usual."

"Where did you go?"

"A new place a couple blocks south of here. Maybe you've heard of it, the Mandarin." I shook my head. "Well, you should take Rita there. They're really gearing up for the Chinese New Year."

"Chinese?" I clutched my stomach. My dumb curse had kicked in again.

Margaret's face drew serious. "Are you all right, Matt? You aren't coming down with the flu are you? I had my shot, but I heard it's supposed to be really nasty this year."

I flicked my hand in front of me. "I'm fine. It's my darn curse. It didn't bother me while I was overseas, but as soon as I started snooping around in Neil Welch's plants over here it's been aggravating the heck out of me."

The elevator dinged for the fourth floor. We stepped off and continued conversing as we made our way to our apartments. "Do you recall what you were doing when your curse felt the strongest?" the elderly woman asked in a quiet tone similar to a psychiatrist's prodding.

"Yeah, but it's going to sound crazy."

Margaret lightly tapped my hand. "Don't put the cart before the horse, dear. You're assuming I'm going to think one way when more likely than not, I won't. Now, tell me about it."

"Twice, when the curse flared up, I was in close quarters with computer technicians born and raised in China."

"Hmm? Do you have any idea how many of Delight's computer technicians are from China?"

We had reached our apartments now and I withdrew my apartment key from a jacket pocket. "Yes. I've been told the head computer technicians in the States come from China."

"But of course." Margaret struggled to get her key out of her purse while holding her leftovers, so I offered to hold the container until she got her door unlocked. "Thank you, Matt." She took the box back. "I think you need to find out who decided to hire all these Chinese employees and why. Once you know that, your curse probably won't bother you."

I shoved my apartment key in its keyhole. "I already know why. The computer equipment Delight uses is built in China and the head technicians have been heavily trained on it before stepping foot in the plants."

"Interesting. But if I were you, dear, I'd dig a little deeper," she suggested, stepping into her apartment. "Find the connection."

"Believe me I'm trying."

***

Gracie went bonkers the instant I strolled in. Something she didn't usually do when I followed a regimented routine. "Down, Gracie. Don't get yourself worn out. You've got me with you the whole rest of the day. Well, at least until suppertime, unless Rita's too busy to go out."

"Woof. Woof."

"Yes, you heard right. I said Rita."

She ran into the bedroom and brought out her ball. Rita loves to play fetch with Gracie when she comes over. "She's not here, girl but I'll play with you. Not for too long though. I've got to tackle my taxes."

Ten minutes later I opened the fridge and took out a can of Delight's Bubble Gum Pop and a recently purchased meat bone. The bone was for Gracie. As soon as she caught sight of the bone, she snapped it out of my hand and laid down to chew on it. *Yay.* That ought to keep her out of mischief for the rest of the day.

I studied the can of pop still in my hand. Its background color was solid pink. Superimposed over the pink were nine bubbles each containing a white letter used to spell out the flavor. Not a bad design. Would the huge ad blitzes on radio and TV for this pop prove worth it? I popped the can open. The fruity smelling fizz filled the air. I guess it could be a big hit with the right age group. Is that why someone tried to mess with the *filler* machine?

Distracted by the dogs loud gnawing and voices arguing in the apartment above me, I left the pop on the table instead of taking it with and eagerly headed down the hall to the quiet of the bedroom where all the important receipts for the past year are stored in the desk.

The second I stepped into the room the immediate plans I had were once again tossed out the window thanks to the answer machine. It was blinking like mad. Maybe Steve Mc Guire from the St. Cloud plant called. I pressed the PLAY button. It was Rita. I lifted the receiver off the phone and dialed. "Hey, I'm glad you called. How would you like to go out to supper tonight? Tomorrow night is better for you. Okay, I'll pick you up around seven."

"Are we dining at Fu Yu's?"

Since my curse seemed to be on red alert concerning anything Chinese lately, I decided to steer clear of Fu Yu's and Margaret's recommendation for the Mandarin and take Rita to a simple place in Minneapolis where they serve ethnic food of another culture I discovered while in Brazil. "No, not this time, but I know you'll like the place I've picked out."

"Okay. Well, I hate to cut this short, Matt, but..."

"I know. You gotta get back to work. *And so do I.* "Bye."

"Bye."

I trotted over to the desk, dug through the drawers, making sure I had all the receipts I'd filed away throughout the year, and then I carried it all to the bed where I sorted everything out according to business or personal expenses. When I finished, I clipped the stacks of receipts according to the month I received them and then sat at the desk to begin the tedious task of filling out tax forms, something I and ninety percent of the world dreaded doing. It's such a waste of time, but at least doing the taxes myself I can save what little money sat in my savings.

After two hours of number crunching, I'd had enough. My head felt like it had taken on the Mississippi River and was about to explode. The only thing that could relieve that kind of pressure was a good dose of caffeine in the form of an aspirin or pop. *Pop.* I glanced at the nightstand. "Where the heck did I put that can I opened?" I thought I brought it in here.

Remembering I'd left it in the kitchen; I retraced my steps and discovered a huge puddle on the floor. Shoot! Doggie pee. My hand flew to my forehead. Was I at fault? I sure don't remember hearing any whining. And Gracie didn't seek me out in the bedroom. I looked at the mess again and noticed how the trail of liquid thinned out under the table. The mutt had an accident all right, but not the type I thought. She'd knocked the opened can of Bubble Gum on the floor "Gracie, you naughty dog."

The mutt hates being scolded. She dropped her head to her chest and slinked over to the puddle to lick up the mess.

"What do you think you're doing?" I angrily questioned, stepping around her and the spill to collect cleaning materials from the cupboard under the sink."

Confused by the question I threw at her, Gracie stopped cleaning up and pranced back and forth, leaving a wide trail of messy paw prints behind.

"Stay," I ordered. While she remained frozen in place, I popped a much-needed aspirin in my mouth and then dampened a sheet of paper toweling to do battle with her feet.

The instant the mutt saw me coming at her with paper toweling, she knew the drill; she lifted her paws to be wiped. As soon as I finished with her, she marched off to the living room and the master of the house, me, dropped on hands and knees to scrub the floor.

By the time I dumped the dirty water out, the out of control headache still hadn't been tamed, so I gave up on the desk work, skipped plans for homemade meatloaf, and decided to hit the bed early.

I opened the corner cupboard and took out a can of Chicken Noodle soup. While it warmed on the stove, I filled Gracie's dish with Alpo. No matter how naughty the mutt had been she still needed to be fed.

When she didn't come running the second her food clinked against the metal bowl, I was a bit bewildered. That wasn't like her. She normally flies in here from where ever she is in the apartment. *Perhaps she thinks I'm still mad at her.* "Gracie, come and get it," I called in a soothing tone. No response. Huh?

I turned off the stove and paraded into the living room where she'd gone after her feet got cleaned. "Hey, sleepy head, aren't you hungry?"

Gracie attempted to lift her body off the couch but couldn't seem to do so. "Boy, that bone must've worn you out, huh? Just stay there, girl. I'm going to lie down soon too."

~29~

January 30

Around four-thirty a.m. a strange noise awakened me from deep sleep. Try as I might I couldn't place it at first. But after the incessant intrusion kept at it for a few more seconds, I finally concluded it was coming from the landline by my bed, not a giant mosquito as seen in an old horror flick.

I raised my head slightly off the pillow, stretched out my arm, plucked the phone receiver off its cradle, and placed it near my head. "Hello."

A youngish voice, I thinly recollected hearing not too long ago, traveled across the phone wires. "Mr. Malone."

"This is he."

"Sir, I'm sorry to bother you at such a strange hour, but you said I could call any time."

I almost jumped out of bed. The voice on the other end finally clicked in my head. "Is that you Steve?"

"Yup.

I flicked on the bedside lamp and grabbed paper and pen. "What have you got for me?"

"Sir, I've been thinking back about the night of the break-in like you suggested."

"And?"

"Cheng in packaging and Wang Feng look a lot alike."

Confused, I glided my fingers through my hair. "What are you saying, Steve?"

"Last night when I stood by the back door where the second shift employees clock out, I got a good look at Cheng. Why, he could pass as Wang's twin."

I yawned. *This is what he woke me up for?* So far he hadn't told me anything of consequence. "Please tell me your story is leading some place."

"I'm getting there. See, Cheng sometimes trades off with a guy in his department on first shift and arrives earlier than normal. Why? Because his wife uses the only car they have to drop him off and then drive to her job in the cities. But Wang frequently comes in early too. The morning of the break-in I thought Cheng had switched to the morning shift for the day, but it was actually Wang roaming around the building early."

I formed a fist. That kernel of information was worth waking even the dead. I lifted the paper and pen off my lap and set them on the nightstand. "You're positive it was Wang? According to Joe West no one clocked in early that morning."

"Yes, sir. I asked Cheng what time he showed up that morning. "Not until seven. He bummed a ride with a neighbor."

"Thanks Steve. If you remember anything else let me know immediately."

"I will."

So, Wang came in early. What time and why? I rubbed my bleary eyes. I could barely keep them open. The mysterious Wang would have to wait. Before I turned the lamp off, I glanced around the room. No mutt sleeping on the bedroom carpet. What gives? I tossed the blankets back, switched on the hall light, and headed for the living room where I last saw her before going to bed.

When I entered the room, I found Gracie's body still on the couch in a fetal position. I couldn't believe it. I leaned over and touched her nose. It felt dry. Thinking the worst, I ran to the phone and called Dad to get the emergency number for the veterinary medical clinic he'd used. At least he won't be jarred from slumber like me; he's used to rising early.

"Is she throwing up again?" Dad queried.

"No, not yet. But there's something terribly wrong with her."

A half hour later, I lowered Gracie on the icy steel exam table in Doctor Mallard's office and watched him gently probe her extremities. "How long has she been like this?" he kindly inquired.

I brushed my hand through my hair. "Geez, I'm not sure. She was tired at suppertime so I left her be."

The vet lifted Gracie's head and examined her eyes, ears and nose. "Has she been vomiting?"

"Just once on the way here."

His long piano fingers picked up a pen attached to a clipboard resting on a shelf and began to tick off a multitude of questions. "Do you remember what she ate yesterday?"

"She had a bit of dog food in the morning and a meat bone in the afternoon.

"And that's it?"

"I'm pretty sure."

"How old was the meat bone?" he inquired, tapping the clipboard with his pen while he waited for my reply.

I rubbed my bristly chin. "I bought it yesterday at a big chain grocery store. Do you think she got sick from that?"

Doctor Mallard shrugged his shoulders. "We won't know until we run blood tests." He checked another item off his medical list and then rested the clipboard on the steel table. "How about remodeling? Has there been any done in your home recently?"

"No. I'm an apartment dweller," I replied, and then something flashed through my mind. I flung out my hands. "Wait a minute. The hallway walls are being sanded and painted. Maybe Gracie ingested something when we walked through the halls."

Doctor Mallard's face remained neutral. "It's possible. How old is the building you live in?"

"I don't know. I'd say it was built around the late '60's. Is it important?"

The vet's brown eyes showed deep concern. "Very. Gracie's symptoms are similar to lead poisoning: lethargic and vomiting."

I felt like I'd been kicked in the teeth. "How could lead have gotten in her system, Dr. Mallard? I thought it had to be ingested."

"I'm afraid all a dog has to do is step in paint dust and lick their paws." Sensing how upset I was becoming, the doctor tried to calm me down. "I must tell you, Mr. Malone, that there are many other illnesses that mimic lead poisoning. That's why we'll check her blood, stools, and run a few other tests. But I need your permission to do so."

"Of course, do whatever you have to doctor. I can't lose her."

"I understand how you feel, Mr. Malone." Dr. Mallard lifted Gracie and gently placed her in a kennel. Then he and I strolled out to the lobby "What number can I reach you at when the tests results come back?" he asked.

I pulled out my wallet and handed him a business card. "Either number on there's fine."

On the drive back to the Foley, depression seeped in, but I didn't want to lay my burdens on my nonagenarian neighbor before sunrise. Would receiving a call this early frighten Rita too?

I opened the cell phone and pressed her number. She picked up on the fifth ring. "Hi, I'm sorry to disturb your slumber, but I couldn't wait till you were at work to call."

Rita's sleepy voice projected worry. "What is it, Matt?"

"I just left the vet's office."

"I didn't know they had office hours this early in the morning."

"Gracie didn't go for a check-up," I sniffed. "She's ill."

"Oh, my, gosh, what's wrong with her?"

Tears dripped down my cheeks. "Dr. Mallard said it could be lead poisoning—but he's not ruling out other possibilities."

"I'm so sorry. Is there anything I can do?"

"No, not at the moment."

"Honey, as hard as this is for you, you have to stay strong for Gracie's sake. She's a fighter. She'll get better."

"I hope so. Look, I know we planned to have dinner out tonight, but would you mind postponing it? I don't think I'd be very good company."

Rita kept silent for a couple seconds. "Sure, we can do it another time."

~30~

I tried to go back to sleep when I reached home at six-thirty but Gracie was on my mind. I'd nod off for a few short minutes and then boom I'd be awake again. Remembering that warm milk is supposed to help a person fall asleep, I got out of bed a half hour later and had a cup. It did the trick. Sleep won out, but it wasn't a peaceful one. A weird dream kept surfacing.

Life was spinning out of control. While Dad and my oldest brother were sitting at the kitchen table arguing about the stupid newspaper article, I found myself sitting in the living room hugging a curvaceous brunette until Rita showed up unexpectedly. She threw a hissy fit and stormed out. The other woman stomped off too, leaving me with a dying dog and Wang of all people.

Thankfully, a fifth go round of the same nightmare was interrupted by a light rap on the door. I jumped out of bed, tossed on jeans, and rushed to the door.

"Margaret! What brings you here this morning?"

The elderly woman ignored my bare chest. "Good morning, Matt. I won't keep you," she said, shoving a plate of caramel rolls in my hands. "I can see you're getting ready for work, so eat 'em while they're hot."

"Wait," I said, "I'm not going anywhere. Can you spare a few minutes?"

Margaret's olive green eyes studied my bare chest this time.

I had a feeling the little woman was uncomfortable seeing me without a shirt. She's been a widow a long time. "Would you come in if I made myself more presentable?"

Her cheeks turned rosy. "*Si.* That would help," she softly replied, shuffling across my apartment's threshold in her comfortable Isotoner slippers.

I closed the door and immediately ushered her to the kitchen. After setting the plate of rolls on the table, I pulled out a chair for her to sit. "I'll be back in a jiff," I said. Then I rushed to the bedroom, tossed on the shirt I wore yesterday, and returned to the kitchen fully clothed. "Would you like a cup of coffee, Margaret?"

"Is it already made?"

"Not yet."

"Don't bother then, unless you want some, Matt."

I pulled up a chair and sat. "I can make some later."

"Where's Gracie? I thought for sure she'd be romping around begging for a sweet treat. Have you got her kenneled up?"

I shook my head. "No, that's what I wanted to talk to you about."

"Oh, dear." The old woman's brows arched a bit higher. "Something serious has happened to Gracie, hasn't it? That's why you're in no hurry to get moving this morning. Where is she, Matt?"

"She spent the night at a veterinary facility with an emergency room." I ran my fingers across the new whisker growth on my chin, recalling last night's events as they occurred. "I wouldn't have known she was sick until I got out of bed this morning if the security guard from the St. Cloud plant hadn't called."

Margaret waved loose strands of limp hair off her cheek. "*Non capisco!* Sorry, I don't understand. How could a phone call alert you to Gracie's situation?"

"She wasn't in the bedroom where she usually sleeps, so I got up to check the other rooms."

"Ah." Margaret pushed the plate of rolls in front of me. "Well, what did the doctor have to say when you brought her in?"

"He asked a lot of questions. Said he'd run several tests, but wasn't about to rule out anything, including lead poisoning." I picked up a sticky caramel roll and took a bite. "Mmm. Delicious."

"*Grazie.* Exactly what kind of symptoms did Gracie have?"

"She was dehydrated and sick to her stomach."

Margaret slapped her petite arthritic hands on the table. "Sounds like a severe case of the flu to me."

I almost choked on what was left of the roll I had been chewing on. Margaret may be old and not have any college degrees, but her assessment of things we've discussed at various times throughout the years are usually on target. "I hadn't thought of that. Having the flu sounds better than being poisoned."

"It most certainly does. Do you remember when Petey turned ill last year?"

"Of course, you were scared he was going to die."

She nodded. "The silence in the apartment was unbearable. But Petey pulled through and Gracie will too. Our pets are tough like us."

A tear slid down my cheek. I reached for Margaret's hands. "I'm glad you came over. Thanks for listening."

"Anytime. Now, finish that roll you started eating," she ordered.

"Aye aye, *mon capitaine.*"

***

Margaret was the perfect catalyst to get me moving. As soon as she left, I put a pot of coffee on to brew and then made a quick call to Doctor Mallard's office to check on Gracie. Despite my hopes that she might be better I didn't receive encouraging news. The receptionist said she wished she had something positive to report but Gracie hadn't improved since I brought her in and tests results wouldn't be back till tomorrow or the next day. Surprisingly the gloomy information didn't make me sullen. Margaret's thoughts about the flu prevailed.

When I finished with the vet's office, the coffee was waiting but I didn't dare allow myself a taste of the caffeine yet. I needed to shower, shave, straighten the bedroom, and call Neil Welch.

A half hour later I found myself standing in the kitchen, phone in hand, eyeing the pot of coffee situated on the coffee maker. "Mr. Welch, I hope I'm not interrupting any family plans."

"Not at all. I'm sure whatever you're calling me about, Matt, must be pretty important to disturb me on a weekend."

"It is. Steve Mc Guire, the security guard I interviewed four days ago, called during the night and I thought you'd want to hear what he had to say as soon as possible."

"Hold on their, Matt. If he's told you he saw a woman at the plant while he was on duty, it wasn't Mary. I finally questioned my wife about her whereabouts."

"You did?"

"Yes. Mary doesn't need to be on your list of suspects anymore. She has a solid alibi. She definitely wasn't in St. Cloud the night of the break-in."

I twisted a finger around the phone cord, wondering if I should take what he said as the absolute truth, knowing how much he didn't want his wife to be tangled up in the break-in. "Do you mind telling me where she was?"

Welch delayed answering for a couple seconds. "Of course not," he replied brusquely. "My wife brought her sister to the Mayo Clinic and spent the whole night there."

Darn. Welch wouldn't dare spin a yarn like that. It's an alibi that can be easily verified. "I'm sorry I forced your hand, sir. I'm sure it wasn't easy for you to question your wife. But you were right. She wasn't involved. And thanks to yours and Steve's help my suspect list has been narrowed to one person."

"Who is it, Matt?" Welch sputtered. "I'll fire the creep immediately?"

"You may change your mind after you hear who it is, especially with your new pop being released on Monday."

"Cry'n out loud, man, just spit it out."

"Wang Feng."

"Wang! No, it can't be. That's impossible. Everyone likes him. He makes a great salary. Why would he want to create problems at the plant?"

"I don't know but I intend to find out."

"Matt, listen to me, tread lightly. I don't want a good employee to quit if he's not guilty."

~31~

February 1

It had been more than forty-eight hours since I brought Gracie to the vet's office and with still no upgrade on her condition I was beginning to wonder if she'd ever pull through. The only thing that kept me going was something I learned a long time ago. Being weighed down by misery never did any good. What a person needed to do was surround themselves with busyness. Mine included a late church service with my parents, finishing up the tax forms, washing dishes, and cleaning the apartment, something I had avoided doing since going overseas.

By late afternoon I was exhausted and ready for a much-needed break. I grabbed the now clean plate Margaret left behind with her homemade rolls and crossed the hall to her apartment.

Of course, as anticipated the elderly woman insisted I come in, so I did. Instead of directing me to her kitchen table though like she usually does when I stop by for a short chat, she threaded her way to the living room where she said she had been knitting and listening to the news. Noticing how loud the TV was, she offered to turn it off, but I told her not to bother.

"Are you sure, Matt?

"Yeah, it's fine."

Margaret picked up the remote and clicked the VOLUME button several times. "There, now we can at least hear each other." Then she stepped over to the rocking chair where she'd left her knitting, plucked it up, and sat. "How's Gracie doing? Have you heard from the vet yet?"

"She's not throwing up, but she's still pretty weak."

The elderly woman put her knitting needles into motion, adding another new row of blue and white yarn to those already completed. "I suppose the clinic hasn't hinted when she might come home."

"No, if they know they're sure not telling me." I studied the elderly woman's swift movements with the needles. "So, are you working on another gift for someone?"

"This one's for the nursing home. I'll let them decide who to give it to."

When I stopped focusing on the work Margaret's hands were doing, I caught a glimpse of a live news report on TV. Surprised by what I saw, I asked Margaret to turn up the volume. "There's something I'd like to hear if you don't mind."

"Why, isn't that Neil Welch being interviewed?" She grabbed the TV remote and raised the sound considerably.

"Yup. It looks like they caught him as he was leaving Delight's corporate headquarters."

"Mr. Welch," the meticulously groomed news reporter said, "there have been several negative articles in the newspapers recently in regards to your personal and business life. Care to respond?" Then he shoved a microphone in the man's face.

Welch cleared his throat. "Yes, I would Gunther. I don't know who is responsible for feeding false rumors to the press about my personal life, but it would be nice if it stopped. My wife and I have never discussed divorce. We've been married forty years and like all married couples have hit some rough spots along the way. But God willing, we'll be together many more years to come," and then he clamped his mouth shut.

"Sir, what about selling off some of your bottling plants, is there any truth to that?"

Neil Welch didn't flinch. "I don't usually air my business in public," he calmly replied. "But if you'd care to question me privately, make an appointment. I'm sure I can squeeze you in between meetings."

Margaret giggled. "Mr. Welch didn't let that news reporter get under his skin, did he?"

I rubbed my chin. "Nope. Welch must've been born with ice in his veins. I certainly can't remain that calm under pressure."

"Oh, I think you're doing pretty well considering what's going on with Gracie."

I rested my fingers on my chest. "I hide it in here."

"Well, I guess that's one way to handle it although it's not the healthiest." She pressed her fingers to her hollow cheeks. "Matt, what did you think about Mr. Welch's comment regarding his marriage?"

He probably denied the divorce rumors to keep the lid on strike talks, but I didn't dare tell Margaret that. "I think I'd take him at his word until he says otherwise. You know how easily rumors spread."

Margaret's head kept time with the rocker. "I most certainly do especially in an apartment complex the size of ours."

~32~

February 3

After supper last night, I called Joe West at home and told him I wanted to see Wang Feng the minute I arrived in St. Cloud. Joe immediately asked what excuse he should give. "Tell him a fax from China labeled *urgent* came in over the weekend and you can't decipher it. And Joe, whatever you do, don't tell him I'm going to be there."

"You going to tell me what's up, Matt, or do I have to figure it out for myself?"

"I think we've discovered who tried to tamper with the *filler* equipment."

"Oh? Wow! Has Neil Welch been notified yet?"

"Yes."

Of course, when Joe's and my conversation ended, I began to worry about the road conditions in the a.m. and if I'd even manage to get to St. Cloud at all. Like the general public, I hated being caught off guard. So, right before crawling into bed, I tuned into WCCO to get the next day's updated weather report. The well-coiffed meteorologist on duty dropped a bomb. According to him the Twin Cities is supposed to end up with a humdinger on its doorsteps due to a huge snow front moving in. Expecting the worst, I set the alarm clock accordingly, giving myself plenty of travel time.

Remembering the weather prediction from the night before when I awoke, I pulled back the bedroom curtains expecting to see mounds of snow flooding the streets, but I couldn't find one single speck of it to my delight. Apparently the white stuff had gone around us. That meant I could drive the Topaz to St. Cloud like a race car driver instead of a granny.

When I arrived at Joe West's office, I found him pouring over a pile of paperwork. He looked weary. "Looks like you could use some extra help. And maybe a cup of coffee," I teased.

Joe stopped what he was doing, rubbed his forehead, and looked up. "Is it eight already?"

"I'm afraid so." I turned to the two empty wooden chairs against the wall that closes Joe's office off from the lobby. "I see Wang's not here. Were you able to deliver your message?"

"I did. As a matter of fact he requested your phone number."

"Mine? I never received a call from him. Did he say what he wanted?"

"Nope. He just mentioned he needed to speak with you as soon as possible."

Wait. Remember that strange call you got last night right before turning off the lights. *No one spoke.* I just thought it was the same joker who's been shoving threatening notes under my door, but what if it wasn't. Wang didn't impress me as the kind of guy who'd keep his boss waiting. Concerned, I said, "Joe, buzz Wang's office and find out what the heck's keeping him."

Joe jammed the phone receiver to his ear, dialed Wang's number, and patiently waited for him to answer. After a few minutes passed, he quietly set the receiver back in its cradle. "No answer. Do you want me to see if I can find him?"

"How about we split up," I suggested. "You check the time cards and circle the plant clockwise. I'll go counter clockwise and meet you back here. There's no way we can miss Wang if he's in the building."

Twenty minutes later Joe and I caught up with each other. "He didn't clock in," the plant manager said, "and no one remembers seeing him."

"That's strange." I shoved my hands in the back pocket of my jeans. "Mel, your chemist, told me he saw Wang around seven-thirty, but maybe it was Cheng. Steve Mc Guire told me those two guys could pass for twins."

Joe sat in the swivel chair behind his desk and leaned forward. "Geez, to tell you the truth I've never given it a thought, but Steve's right. So, what's next? Should I try Wang at home? He could've come down with the flu. They say this year's strain is a killer."

I paced the floor. I didn't have the heart to tell Joe I thought something got to Wang and it wasn't the flu. But if he wanted to try him at home, let him. "Sure go ahead. Maybe he's been too sick to call in."

Joe turned on his computer, searched through files, and then dialed Wang's number. No luck.

"Do you still have Wang's personal information on your screen?" I asked, pulling up a chair to his desk.

"Yup. What do you need?"

"Does he live in a house or an apartment?"

Joe glanced at the screen. "There's an apartment number listed."

I picked up a Bic pen from Joe's pile and tapped it on the desk. "What about the apartment complex, is it listed?"

"Yup, the Shamrock in Waite Park. It's just down the road."

"Good." I let the pen slip through my fingers and fall. "Bring up info on the apartment complex. Shamrock's manager ought to be able to help us."

"Here it is. Do you want me to call?"

"No, I'll take over," I replied, setting his office phone in front of me. "What's the number?"

Joe studied the information on his computer screen. "1-800-777-5000. Do you want me to repeat it?"

"Nope. I've got it." The second I finished dialing I sat back in the chair and listened to the ring tone, hoping the manager would be available. I lucked out. After the fourth ring, the noise stopped.

"Shamrock apartments," a high-pitched female voice said. "How may I help you?"

I made the chit chat short and sweet, offering more honey than chat. Luckily, the women actually swallowed what I said. Which was great, otherwise she wouldn't have lifted a finger to check on Wang using her master key and we'd never know if he was home or not. After I got my small request out of the way, I thanked her profusely and got her to promise to call right back.

Joe was shaking his head when I put the phone down. "I can't believe you told the caretaker you were Wang's boss."

"I figured if I told her I was a PI she might not cooperate. Besides, you are worried about his welfare, aren't you?"

Joe took offense. "Of course, I am."

Fifteen minutes later Joe West's phone rang. He picked it up, listened to the person on the other end, and then hastily covered the mouth piece. "It's Wanda from Shamrock. She's extremely upset."

Crap. I hope Wang's not dead. I took the phone receiver from Joe. "Wanda, I appreciate your calling back so soon. You what? Found Wang slumped over his kitchen table. He's barely breathing. Yes, I'm sure it was very unsettling to see him like that." I lifted my eyes to Joe. Shock registered on his face. "You've already called 9-1-1 and first responders are on their way. Good. No, you don't need to call his emergency number. Our office will do that. Good-bye."

Joe pounded his fist on the desk. "That darn flu. I can't believe Wang's that bad off. My wife's been bugging me to get a flu shot ever since October and I keep ignoring her. I guess I'd better get one before I end up like Wang."

My gut tells me evil forces are at work here, not the flu. But what has China got to do with it?

I stepped out into the freezing cold and walked briskly to the car. Too much had happened within the past hour for this PI to even consider heading back to the cities just yet. Wang's welfare hung in the balance. Perhaps he hid a note of some sort for me in his apartment. Joe said he planned to call me.

I pulled out my cell phone and called Shamrock's caretaker back. After fabricating a story about Wang needing a few things for his stay in the hospital, she politely agreed to meet at his door in an hour, which worked out perfectly for me. The only place in town I could get straight answers about Wang at this juncture was the police department nearest Wang's residency since I wasn't a relative.

~33~

The second I parked the Topaz in an empty slot in front of the police station on Thirteenth Avenue, I began to have doubts about Wang's guilt.

Clearly someone wanted to cause problems. But who? I suppose a blackmailer could've forced Wang into faking the break-in. On the other hand, Welch could've paid Wang to set up the hoax simply to draw attention to Delight and the release of its new pop. I shook my head. No, I can't believe Neil Welch manipulated me. He definitely wanted those bottling plants to be examined as soon as possible. There's no way he would've pulled me off the other assignment if it wasn't necessary.

An officer near retirement age strolled out of the entrance to the station just as I stepped up to the building. He held the door open for me and I nodded in appreciation.

When I entered the building, I found a lone policeman sitting at the front desk and greeted him. "Good morning."

"Good morning."

I flashed my PI card in front of him. "I'd like to speak to the person in charge."

The young, neatly primed cop stared at the badge for a second. "Wait right there, Mr. Malone. I'll get someone," and then he scrambled off to a distant cubby hole. Within seconds he returned with a short plump fiftyish officer in tow. The man's gold rimmed glasses were perched askew on his nose. Telltale signs of having recently tasted something were apparent on his lips.

The officer quickly put out his hand to greet me. "Lieutenant Nelson. I understand you wanted to speak with me."

I shook his thick firm hand. "Yes," I said, then as a courtesy I presented my business card again.

"So, what brings you down here, Mr. Malone?"

At this point I didn't know how to proceed. The cop's attitude towards PI's wasn't registering with me. *Spit it out. What's the worst that could happen?* "I'm working on a case involving Delight Bottling in St. Cloud," I said in a noncommittal tone.

His eyes registered interest. He crossed his arms and leaned his overweight body against the front desk. "Oh, and which case is that? I don't recall any crimes being reported recently."

Seeing as my motto has always been *the more privacy one has the better,* I moved closer to him and quietly suggested we go to an enclosed room.

It became clear Lt. Nelson wanted to demonstrate to me who the big cheese was in this police station when he loudly proclaimed for all to hear, "Mr. Malone, I think we should go to a private area where we're not disturbed, don't you agree?"

I forced a smile. "That's a great idea."

It turned out the cubby hole Lt. Nelson had been dragged from in order to see me wasn't his work area at all. On the way to his glass enclosed office, I peeked inside. The room contained a couple chairs, a table, coffee pot, and snacks.

Lt. Nelson's work area reeked of disorganization, but he seemed like the type who could lay his hand on whatever he needed pronto. He stepped behind his coffee stained desk, shoved papers off to the side, and sat where his steel-blue eyes could scrutinize this PI from head to toe.

His staring tactics worked. Feeling like a kid who had been called to the principal's office for some infraction, I squirmed in my seat.

"Mr. Malone," he began in a *better listen to me* tone, "I don't rightly cotton to private investigators." He pointed two fingers at me as if he was aiming a gun. "Whatever you've come here to say better be worth it. Got it?"

The cop's finger-pistoling rattled my chain, but I caught myself before I screwed up and said something I'd regret. "Got it."

After I finished the tale, Lt. Nelson spun his chair to look outdoors. He sat frozen in this position; mouth tightly sewn shut for all of five minutes, contemplating God knows what.

His brooding behavior didn't sit well with me. It felt as though he didn't buy my story. I nervously tapped my fingers on the top of his desk. Perhaps the noise would remind him that I hadn't disappeared.

Thankfully, he got the message and turned to face me. His speech was curt and to the point. "Mr. Malone, if you think for one minute I believe your story you're sadly mistaken. Delight Bottling Company and our police department have a good relationship. They would never cover up a break-in."

Even though my innards had the energy to blow a gasket, anyone looking at me would've thought I was as cool as a cucumber. I folded my hands. "For the record Lt. I did tell Mr. Welch to call you when a certain problem arose at his plant on January twenty-eighth. I don't believe in overstepping boundaries. I'm the type of person who likes to keep things above board and professional: military police experience and such. Unfortunately, Mr. Welch preferred not to ask for police assistance. But I'm sure he'd be happy to share his reasons for that with you."

"I understand your reluctance to accept what I'm telling you, sir. I work out of the cities and you've never heard of me. Look, why don't you call Joe West, the plant manager. He'll verify my story." I whipped Joe's business card out and handed it to the Lt.

The officer fumbled with the card like he had a book of matches in his hand, trying to decide whether to light up or not. If he kept it up too much longer, there wouldn't be anything left to read. He finally dropped the card and picked up the phone. "Mr. West, I'm calling in regards to a PI named Mr. Malone. Do you know him? I see. He was at the plant earlier. Ah, huh. What time did you say he arrived? Is Mr. Malone employed at your plant?" He reached for a pen and paper to jot down a note.

"What kind of project would that be? The officer's grayish-brown eyebrows knotted. "Look, Mr. West, I realize your boss doesn't want anyone to know, but Wang Feng's situation has drastically changed all that." He scribbled more info down. "Thank you. You've been most helpful."

Lt. Nelson reread the notes he'd taken. When he spoke, his face looked like it had been trampled on by an opponent. "It would appear your story rings true, Mr. Malone. Sorry I gave you a hard time, but as I said earlier I don't care for PI's. So, have you figured out who tampered with the equipment yet?"

I propped my elbows on his desk and rested my head. "I thought I had, but it's a little tough to prove when the person I need to question has been hauled off to the hospital."

"You think this guy Wang is responsible?"

"Yes, I do. Now if you don't mind, I have a few questions for you."

Lt. Nelson glanced out the inner window he kept watch on his men from. "I'll answer if I feel it's appropriate," he replied curtly.

Better than nothing I guess. "What's Wang's condition?"

The Lt. dropped his hands to his lap. "Unconscious."

"He doesn't have the flu, does he?"

"Nope."

"Did he have any noticeable wounds?"

The cop shared a blank expression. "I haven't heard."

"How about off the record," I asked. Oops. That phrase got some big-time news reporter in deep water. Maybe I should reword that. Ah, heck. I have nothing to worry about. I'm not taping our conversation.

Luckily, under Lt. Nelson's rough exterior a teddy bear lurked. He rolled his chair around the desk to where I sat and whispered, "Off the record, we found no visible wounds or marks on him." Then he gazed out his inner window again.

I glanced over my shoulder to see which officer he had selected to home in on. There were several men milling about, but only one was fast approaching his door, the young one working at the front desk when I arrived. "Well, I'd appreciate it if you could keep me in the loop, Lieutenant. My gut instinct tells me someone attempted to knock off Wang Feng permanently."

Apparently Lieutenant Nelson didn't want the cop to see how much he had cozied up to me within the last few minutes. He shoved his chair as far from me as possible and raised his voice. "Malone, didn't I tell you I don't like PI's. Get the heck out of my precinct," he said pointing to the door.

~34~

The minute I got back to the Foley, I called Delight's corporate office to bring Neil Welch up to speed. "Hi Carol. It's Matt Malone. Is your boss available?"

"Ah-choo. Sorry, Mr. Malone," Carol sniffed, "I'm not at my best today. Ah-choo."

"Sounds like it. Well, I hope you feel better soon."

She sniffed again. "Thanks, I do too. Ah-choo. Okay, he's off his phone, I'll put you through."

"Matt, I didn't expect to hear from you this soon. How did it go with Wang? You treated him fairly I hope."

"I never got the chance,"

"What do you mean? Didn't you drive up to St. Cloud this morning?"

"Yes." I stared at the matted carpet by the foot of my bed. It seemed strange not to find Gracie there. "Wang was asked to meet with Joe this morning, but he never showed up at his office. And when we questioned the employees about Wang, all we got were blank stares. Apparently no one had noticed his absence at the plant. So, I decided to ask Wang's apartment manager to check on him."

"Well, did the person find him?"

"Yeah, but he wasn't in any shape to be questioned," I explained. Before I could continue, Welch was interrupted on his end.

"Hold on a minute, Matt, Carol needs me. Yes, Carol, what is it?"

"I'm feeling worse, sir," I heard her say. "I think I should go home. Ah-choo. Ah-choo."

"That's probably a good idea," Welch said with a fatherly tone. "Get a good night's sleep, Carol. Hopefully you'll feel better in the morning."

"Yes, sir. Ah-choo."

"Sorry, about the interruption, Matt," Welch said. "This latest flu seems to have hit us all off guard, especially our corporate office. A quarter of the people who fill this building are out sick."

"Wow, that's a big chunk of your work force, but it fits with the recent report put out by the Center for Disease Control. Their spokesperson said the late start of the flu season caused the delay in reported cases." When I finished sharing the CDC info with Welch, I heard a rapping noise off in the distance. Apparently it was coming from Welch's side of the phone. "Sounds like someone else needs your attention, sir. Perhaps I should call you back."

The president of Delight let loose with a chuckle. "I assure you no one's trying to see me. That was me you heard. You know the old superstition *Knock on Wood* to keep bad luck at bay. I'm hoping the flu stays away from me. So, is Wang down with the flu too? You mentioned he was in no shape to be questioned."

I ignored Welch's first inquiry and replied to the second. "That's right. He was so bad off he had to be taken to the hospital."

"No kidding. I wonder if he skipped getting a flu shot like so many of our other employees. Well, put a lid on talking to him for a while, Matt, until he's better."

"Sir, his condition's worse than you're picturing. Wang's unconscious. No one knows when he'll wake up. But when I spoke with Lt. Nelson from the Waite Park Police Department, he told me the doctors don't think his condition was caused by the flu."

A heavy sigh came across the line. "Matt, are you telling me someone may have had it in for Wang?"

"Quite possibly," I said, letting it go at that.

"Matt…"

"Yes?"

"I'm depending on you to come through for me. Don't let me down. Watch your back and stay healthy."

The second I hung up with Neil Welch, the landline rang. No one knew I was home, not even Margaret. Since I didn't have Caller ID to inform me who was on the other end, I put off answering in case it was a long-winded salesman. A couple seconds later the answering machine kicked in. "Hello, Mr. Malone, this is the Vet Tech from Doctor Mallard's office."

I snapped the phone out of its cradle. "Yes, I'm here." Fearing the worst, I said, "What's happened to Gracie?"

"Why, she's much better," the young woman on the other end politely explained.

"Does that mean she doesn't have lead poisoning?"

"As far as we know. The tests we ran were inconclusive."

I took a deep breath. *Thank God.* Doctor Mallard had warned me about the dangerous effects of lead poisoning and they weren't pretty. It could cause brain damage and blindness. "So when can I bring her home?"

"Dr. Mallard said you can get Gracie this evening if you're in town."

"Phew." I ran a hand across my eyes. Tears had welled up in their sockets. It couldn't be helped. At least Rod Thompson, the FBI agent neighbor of mine, wasn't around to see me coming unglued. He'd call me a sissy. "This evening is fine." Good news finally. Now, if I could figure out what's behind the break-in at Welch's St. Cloud plant, life would be perfect.

***

I reached for Rita's black leather-gloved hand as she slid into the Topaz. "I'm so glad you could squeeze in supper with your heavy schedule."

"Me too," she cooed. "I still can't believe it's been a month since we've seen each other."

"I know. I've missed you terribly. That's why I want this evening to be extra special." I released her hand. "And we have something to celebrate."

"What's that? This isn't the anniversary of the day we met."

"Gracie can come home tonight."

Rita patted my knee. "Oh, Matt, that's wonderful news."

"Ah, huh. So, how about going with me after supper to get her?"

"Sure, I'd love to. I've missed seeing that mutt too."

I turned on the car's blinkers giving fair warning to drivers coming up on Lavender Street from behind that I planned to move away from the curb in front of Rita's building. When the rearview mirror showed the coast was clear, I swung out, drove to the corner, and took a left on Third Avenue.

Once the car had warmed up sufficiently, Rita took off her gloves and red wool knit neck scarf. Then she unbuttoned her black ankle-length coat and pulled down the mirrored visor so she could fluff her shoulder length hair just so. "Matt, I know you said we weren't going to Fu Yu's, but we're still having Chinese cuisine, right?

"Nope. I'm taking you to a totally different restaurant I've heard about. It just opened in Dinkytown. But since you mentioned Chinese, did you catch a news report last week regarding a big meeting top officials in China were supposed to take part in?" Oh, boy. Bad timing. Those gut-wrenching feelings stabbed my stomach. I gritted my teeth and pretended to be fit as a fiddle for Rita's sake.

"Sorry," Rita said, "I only heard some sort of a meeting took place on January sixteenth. But I'm sure there's tons of information out on the Internet if someone really wanted to dig a little."

"You're right. When I find time, I'll do just that."

Rita's well-proportioned body pressed tightly against mine as we made our way through the dark walnut door of the Rio Restaurant. The small intimate dining space was jammed with diners. I'm glad I decided to make reservations. While patiently waiting for someone to notice our arrival, I helped Rita slip out of her coat and draped it over my arm.

A friendly hostess, in her early twenties, quietly emerged from the far corner of the restaurant finally and asked my name before shuffling us off to a table for two towards the back where she had just been. Once we were comfortably situated, she handed us menus and said someone would be with us shortly.

Having been given no specific time for the waiter to show up, Rita and I immediately scanned the enticing meals listed on our menus. "It all sounds so appealing," I said, "and it's authentic to boot. The owners were both raised in Brazil and just recently moved here."

Rita continued to stare at the mind-boggling menu. "There are so many choices, Matt; I can't decide what to order." She set aside her menu for a moment and checked out the restaurant instead.

"Look there at one o'clock," I said. I frequently refer to the hands on a clock when I want a person to notice something in particular.

My lovely date quickly turned her head in the opposite direction. "Which party?"

"The two standing by the table near the front. I bet it's the owners." Rita and I watched as the couple in their mid-thirties proceeded to the next table. "They must be making the rounds."

"Yup. Looks like it." Rita opened her menu again and then took a breadstick from a basket on our table. Knowing how busy she is at work she probably skipped lunch again. Hopefully, she'll allow herself a big meal tonight and we can both finish eating at the same time for once.

My stomach growled as I watched her swiftly devour the snack.

Rita glanced at me and laughed. "I think your stomach's in worse shape than mine. She grabbed a breadstick and offered it to me.

"Thanks. At least I know my stomach's complaint isn't due to the flu."

"Did you get a shot this past fall?"

I shook my head. "Nope. How about you?"

"Ditto. But I'm beginning to think I should. I can't believe how many people are out sick in my department. The work load just keeps piling up." She picked up a fork and waved it at me. "You know you're darn lucky I was able to get away this evening."

She doesn't know how lucky. With all the hours I've been putting in for Neil Welch, I don't know when I would've gotten around to giving her the ring I purchased for her while in Brazil. Just as I swallowed the last of the breadstick Rita had given me, the restaurant owners approached our table. I greeted them warmly with words from their home country, *"Boa Noite."*

The tannish-skinned couple seemed surprised but responded in like manner. *"Boa Noite."* Then the husband attempted to further engage me in his native tongue.

Feeling like an idiot, I hurriedly cut the fellow off. "Sorry, *nao falo Portuguese,"* I said, pinching the thumb and forefinger together and adding, *"Falo um pouco Portuguese.* I recently vacationed in Brazil."

"Ahh," his dark-haired gorgeous wife replied and then she shared my words with her husband. He smiled politely, nodded, and quietly commented. "My husband asked what cities?"

"Rio and Sao Paulo."

She glanced over her shoulder. "Well, I see your waiter is anxious to take your order, we'd better move on. Enjoy your meal."

"Thank you."

"Good evening," the suave waiter said as he swooped in and made immediate eye contact with Rita. "What can I get for you, Ma'am?"

"I'd like to try the Galinhade."

He smiled. "Ah, the chicken dish."

"Yes," Rita replied, handing him her menu.

"That's a fine choice," he said, tucking the menu under his arm. "And do you care for anything to drink?"

Rita glanced across the table indicating it was my decision. "Yes," I said, "we would like a bottle of Pinot noir and I'd like the Feiljoada."

The waiter grinned. "Another good choice," he said, taking my menu. "Our black bean stew happens to be my favorite dish. All right then, if there's nothing else, I'll be back shortly."

"The owners of this restaurant sure seemed nice," Rita whispered, "but I have to admit I was uneasy when you greeted them in their language and then couldn't converse more with them. You've got more guts than I do."

"I couldn't help myself. I wanted them to feel at home here. It's so hard for immigrants to make a new life in a strange land."

"Coming from a caring person, that was well put, Mr. Malone. That's what attracted me to you."

"Huh, and all this time I thought it was my good looks."

"Don't be silly, although you're a handsome devil. It's what's inside you that counts."

"Oh, what's that?"

She rested her hand on her heart. "Your caring attitude of course."

I cleared my throat. "Ah, well, don't award a halo to me quite yet. I've been a little negligent in showing you exactly how much I care about you lately. But that's about to change." With that said I slipped a hand into a coat pocket, pulled out a white ring-sized box, and plopped it in front of her.

Totally forgetting about the people around us, Rita squealed. "Is this what I think it is?"

"Of course not," I bluntly stated. She was referring to an engagement ring which we both agreed we weren't ready for yet. At least I thought we had. But one never knows about women they're so fickle.

Rita's petite hands trembled as she lifted the box lid. "My God, Matt, where did you ever find such a beautiful blue ring? It's a Topaz, isn't it?" I nodded in agreement. Her hands continued to shake when she plucked up the ring and slid it on her finger.

"Does it fit?" I asked, curious to know if I selected the right size.

Tears trickled down Rita's face keeping her from speaking.

"Here," I offered her my cotton hankie and filled in the silence. "I found the stone at the Praca da Repiblica in Sao Paulo. According to Yang Quing, who steered me there, the place has one of the best stone selections."

"Yang's the computer guy who wants to transfer to the States, right?"

"Yup. When I first mentioned jewelry to him, I was thinking more along the lines of a pendant necklace with your birthstone attached. But, as you can see I selected a stone for a ring setting instead."

Rita stopped crying and gave me back my hankie. "The ring fits perfectly."

"Well, do you like it?"

"Like is such a weak word," she teased. "I'd rather use love." She leaned across the table, giving me the impression her luscious lips were about to plant a kiss on mine but then the darn waiter arrived with our wine and interrupted her plans. Disappointed, I leaned back in my chair.

"Your wine, Sir," he said, showing me the bottle before opening it and pouring a glass for each of us.

When he finished his duties, another waiter took over and set our food in front of us. "Do either of you wish for additional seasoning?"

"No, thank you," Rita and I kindly replied in unison.

Alone at last, I raised my wine glass to my gorgeous girlfriend and offered a cheer. "To the two of us and our perfect evening together."

"And, to Gracie's return to good…"

"To what Rita? Please finish what you were about to say."

She shook her head. "I will later. I think I heard your cell phone. Didn't you turn it off, Matt?"

I heard ringing now too. "Shoot. I must've forgot to put it on vibrate." I set the glass on the table and hunted in my coat pockets for the dumb phone. When I finally had it in hand, I glanced at the screen to see if I recognized the caller. "Honey, I'm so sorry, I have to take this call. It's Neil Welch." What could be so dang important the man couldn't wait a couple hours to bother me? I wondered. I glanced around the restaurant, found an out of the way spot to talk, and headed towards it.

~35~

Rita couldn't resist making herself comfortable on my nice leather couch as soon as we returned with the mutt. "Matt, you should've seen your face when Doctor Mallard reassured you Gracie had no serious health issues. I thought for sure you were going to pass out."

I shrugged. "Well, I kept thinking if her diagnosis wasn't lead poisoning then she probably had stomach cancer." I rubbed Gracie's noggin. "But all you had girl was a terrible case of the flu like Margaret suspected, didn't you?"

"Woof. Woof." Gracie spun this way and that near my feet and then circled the full width of the room.

Rita kept an eye on Gracie as she sniffed everything within reach. "She's sure happy to be home in her own digs after being penned up a couple days. Thanks for inviting me to ride along to pick her up."

"I'm just glad you didn't change your mind after Neil Welch's call spoiled the evening."

She flapped her hand at me. "Nonsense. No one's spoiled our evening. It hasn't ended yet, has it?" Rita focused on Gracie again and attempted to get her on the couch with her, but the mutt wasn't ready to settle down yet. "What was Welch's call about anyway? You never did say."

"That's because I didn't want to ruin what little time we had left at the restaurant."

"Care to share now?"

"Sure, if you're really interested."

Rita fluffed the hair at the base of her neck. "I'm always interested in what you're doing. You should know that."

"Glad to hear it. How about we go into the kitchen to talk, that way we can eat the dessert we brought home from the restaurant too?"

Rita licked her lips. "Mmmm, sounds good." She got off the couch and patted her knee. "Come on, Gracie your master has a treat for you."

"Woof. Woof."

I went to the cupboard to get a Milkbone snack for Gracie and then I grabbed a can of Bubble Gum Pop from the fridge for Rita, thinking she might like something to wash down the dessert with.

Rita noticed the can in my hand. "If that pop is for me," she said, "you can put it away. I'd prefer a glass of water. I don't think pop goes too well with custard."

"You're probably right. I'll make sure to have you try it another time. But I'd love to have your thoughts on this can's design before I put it away though, how about it?"

"Sure."

I set it on the table in front of her.

"It's very clever. I really like the way they made use of the eye-catching bubble design and bold colors."

I got bowls and spoons out for us and brought them to the table. "See. I figured a person with your type of marketing background would appreciate the new can design Delight's come out with." I lifted the pop off the table and stashed it back in the fridge. Then I retrieved a glass from the cupboard, filled it with ice cubes and water, and handed it to Rita. "Here you go."

Rita opened the dessert box with her free hand and stared at its contents before taking the two portions out and placing them in our bowls. "Matt, what did the waiter say this baked sweet is called again?"

I pulled out a chair and sat. "Quindim. It's made up of egg yolk, ground coconut, and sugar." I took a bowl from Rita, plopped it in front of me, and sniffed it. It smelled too good to devour in two bites, which was fine because my girlfriend was patiently waiting for me to open up about my conversation with Welch.

I took a quick taste of the custard and then set down the spoon. "I'm sure I've mentioned how Mr. Welch always seems to have it all together no matter what comes his way. Well, not tonight. He sounded like he was at his wit's end."

"I suppose he's still frustrated with the break-in at the St. Cloud plant. Did you ever figure out who was responsible?"

"I think so," I replied, squeezing in another teeny bite of custard. "But the guy's in the hospital and it doesn't look like I'll have a chance to talk to him any time soon."

Rita tilted her head. "So, is it something new that's troubling Mr. Welch?"

I jerked my head up and down. "Believe me the break-in issue is minor compared to his most recent problem."

Rita's emerald-green eyes seemed to grow in intensity. "Does this mean you're going to have to leave town again, Matt?"

"I don't think so. But with Welch one never knows. For now, I'm at his beck and call till all is resolved."

Rita placed her hand over mine and pleaded for information. "Can you at least tell me what's going on?"

"I suppose. It'll be on the news soon enough. One of Welch's employees from the Boston plant died."

My girlfriend's oval face turned ashen. "Oh? Sorry to hear that. Did he die on the job?"

"No, at his home. A neighbor reported smelling smoke coming from his apartment. By the time the fire department arrived, the smoke had gotten so thick the men could barely see a foot in front of them. Apparently Hu's body was discovered when one of the men stumbled over it. Welch said the paramedics suspect Hu's unexpected death was heart related. I told him that call was too simple. The guy was young, under-weight and Oriental's rarely have heart problems.

"I can't believe Mr. Welch is taking the guy's death so hard, Matt. Hu's not the first person to die suddenly. Look at all the young athletes who have died while playing sports. When our time is up, it's up."

"The thing is I don't think he died unexpectedly."

Rita crossed her arms. "Matt, if you're suggesting he was murdered, you need to pull away from whatever you're doing for Neil Welch this instant. The job isn't worth whatever he's paying you. It's not safe anymore. At least tell me you didn't meet Hu when you were in Boston."

I dug into the custard again. "Unfortunately, I did. Hu Peng was in charge of the computer department."

She eyed her custard. "What did you think of him?"

"I didn't like him much. I felt he was hiding something, but I wasn't able to uncover what it was. Maybe if I had extended my visit there I might have been able to find out something, I don't know."

"Did you share your thoughts about Hu possibly being murdered with Mr. Welch?"

I nodded.

"What did Mr. Welch say?"

"He wasn't convinced even after I mentioned Wang, St. Cloud's head computer guy who almost died the other day from causes unknown. So, I strongly recommended Hu's family order an autopsy. Mr. Welch doubted the uncle who raised Hu would request one. He lives in Singapore."

"Doesn't Hu have any family in the U.S.?" Rita inquired, pushing her empty dish out of the way so she could rest her hands on the table.

I ran my hand through my hair. "Apparently not. But thanks to all the pertinent and not so pertinent stuff my brain absorbs daily, I swiftly relayed info to Welch he had obviously forgotten."

"And what was that?"

"Hu has a brother. I learned about him when a particular fax came through while I was in Boston's computer control center. Being a PI of course, I attempted to read what it said before anyone else realized a message had come over the wires."

A loud yawn escaped from Rita. "So, were you able to make out what it said?"

"No, it wasn't in English. But I remember the minute Hu noticed the fax, he examined it rather quickly and then explained aloud that it was from his brother who worked at the Hong Kong plant. Supposedly the brother wanted Hu to meet him in Las Vegas for the Chinese New Year. Hu said he'd reply to him later."

My girlfriend stared at me wide-eyed, eagerly anticipating the rest of my story to unfold. "Go on. Don't stop now."

"Mr. Welch told me I must've heard wrong. As far as he knew Hu didn't have any relatives working in Hong Kong."

"Knowing you honey, you've got the facts straight."

I winked at her. "Thanks for your undying support."

"Your welcome, sweetie. So, Matt, what's your thoughts on why Hu would tell an outright lie to someone he barely knows."

"That's just it I can't think of any plausible explanation that makes sense," I replied. Then I drew silent, remaining lost in my thoughts for a few seconds. "Of course," I slapped my forehead, "I'm such an idiot. I forgot about the video pictures in my mini-camera. I haven't had a chance to download them on the computer yet. If one of the items I videoed in Hu's computer control room is decent enough, maybe Rod Thompson wouldn't mind taking a look at it."

"That means you probably what to download the video tonight, huh?"

"What? Ah, yeah, but I'll take you home before I get involved with that. It's getting late."

Rita pushed her chair back. "Oh, no. You're not getting rid of me that easily, Matt. I'm tired of waiting in the wings to hear second hand what you've been up to. Go fetch your laptop and mini camera," she ordered, "I want to see what you uncover."

~36~

February 4

A copy of the fax photo I downloaded onto my computer last night was still burning a hole in my hand in the wee hours of the morning when it should've already been in the hands of someone knowledgeable in Chinese languages at the Minneapolis FBI headquarters. Clearly the blame fell on Rod Thompson's shoulders not mine since I am only privy to his landline number and he never picked up. Knowing him he purposely ignored his phone when he noticed the caller wasn't a gal he'd recently met at a party. All I could do now was wait till the clock struck seven and pound on his apartment door before he left for work.

The fingers that held onto the printout all night felt numb. I let the paper drift to the coffee table and shook my hand until the guilty fingers began to tingle. Once they came to life, I tossed back the purple and gold knitted afghan, a gift from Margaret last Christmas, and got off the couch.

Gracie lifted her head off the carpet for a second and then dropped it. Apparently she wasn't about to give up on her beauty rest yet.

"Don't feel guilty," I told her. "You deserve to sleep a little longer after being cooped up in a kennel for several days."

The mutt responded with a half-hearted "Woof," and then shut her eyes.

I plucked my wristwatch off the coffee table. It read 6:30. Good. There's plenty of time to have breakfast and get presentable before bugging Rod. I turned my back on the dog and treaded lightly towards the kitchen, trying to be considerate of the renters below in case they were still sleeping. Not having met them I didn't know what kind of work or sleep habits they had.

After I filled the coffee pot and pulled out the cereal I planned to eat, I strolled down the hall with thoughts of a nice warm shower. Unfortunately, a loud knock at the door put the kibosh on getting in the shower.

Thoughts of the other day when Margaret came by unexpectedly and found me half-dressed flashed before my eyes. At least my visitor this morning wouldn't be embarrassed to see me. I had fallen asleep with my clothes on.

"It's about time. I knocked three times," Rod said with a flippant tone, dressed in a navy blue pinstriped suit with a long winter coat thrown over his arm. "What were you doing, taking a shower?"

"Not yet." I didn't owe Rod an explanation and I didn't plan to present one.

Rod stared at my rumpled clothes. "I hope you're not planning to step out of the apartment looking like that."

"Why not," I snapped, "I heard it's the most fashionable look these days."

"Okay, okay. I deserved that." Rod raised his hand. "Mind if we call a truce."

As much as Rod gets under my skin, I needed his help so I said, "Sure. So, what brings you to my door this early? I thought you didn't leave for work until seven."

"Normally that's the case, but today's different. Anyway, when I got home late last night my caller ID showed you called so I thought I'd stop by and find out what you needed."

"I have something written in Chinese that needs to be deciphered and was hoping one of your guys could do the job."

Rod threw back his head. "Are you crazy? Do you think the FBI goes around doing jobs for simply anyone who calls us?"

"Look, this is serious. If I was asking for myself I'd understand, but I'm not I've been doing work for Neil Welch since the beginning of January."

"Neil Welch, holy cow. I didn't realize the really wealthy dudes call on you."

What a snob. I ignored his remark. "The work I've been doing for the man was going fine until a break-in at his St. Cloud plant. After that, all hell broke loose. One of Welch's computer technicians, a Chinese fellow, is lying unconscious in a St. Cloud Hospital and another with a similar background is in a Boston morgue."

Rod ran his hand through his perfectly combed thick blond hair. "What the heck have you gotten yourself into this time? Haven't I warned you about taking on jobs the police should handle?"

I inhaled deeply. "I wasn't anywhere near those guys when things went haywire. But I do have a copy of a strange fax the dead guy received. And I think it's a key to my case. You need to see it." I rushed to the table where I'd left a copy of the photo, returned to Rod, and shoved it in his hand. "Please take this with you. I need it translated as soon as possible."

Rod studied what I'd given him. "Okay, I'll have someone look at it. But you owe me big time, Matt, and don't forget it."

"Believe me I won't. Thanks." I slapped Rod on the back and then opened the door to let him out. "Remember to call me the minute you know anything."

~37~

After Rod left, I took a quick shower and enjoyed a bowl of Cheerios with a cup of brewed coffee before giving any thought to going out in the freezing cold to take a long walk with Gracie. It would be her first stroll around the neighborhood since returning from her extended stay at the vet's, and I must admit I wondered how she'd react.

As soon as Gracie scarfed down her last Milkbone for the morning, I slid her bright-red knit sweater on her. Of course she put up a fuss. She hates having anything wrapped around her. "Settle down. You do want to go for a walk, don't you?"

"Woof. Woof."

"Okay," I pointed to the hallway leading to the door, "go get your leash."

The mutt immediately flew off to search for it. A few seconds later she came back to the kitchen and dropped it at my feet. "Nice job." I patted her on the head and hooked the leash to her collar. "I see your stay with the vet didn't mess up your memory."

The minute I opened the door to leave, I ran smack into Mr. Edwards, the caretaker. He was just stepping on a ladder to change out a lightbulb in the hallway. "Oh, Matt, I'm glad you're still here. A man with a very pointy nose and a bald head handed me a note just as I was opening the ladder. He pointed to your apartment and said to make sure you got it." Mr. Edward's scratched his head. "He was a strange sort of fella," he shared. "Never seen him at the Foley before." He thrust his hand in a jean pocket. "Here you go. I didn't read it in case you're wondering."

Gracie sniffed the note. Then she sniffed the bottom of Mr. Edward's jeans and sneezed. The strong cleaning agents he uses probably bothered her nose.

I yanked Gracie away from the man's pants and took the note. "I know you wouldn't, Mr. Edwards," I said, showing no disgust for the familiar looking notepaper as I shoved it in my jacket. "Thanks for picking it up before someone else did." *Like Rod Thompson.* I can't imagine what he would've done with it if he'd found it. At least I knew the notes weren't from Rita's Uncle Arnie. He has a totally different look, a mop on his head as long as a horse's mane and a bulbous nose.

Gracie tugged on her leash, demanding to go.

I glanced down at her. "All right, mutt. We're going. See you around Mr. Edwards."

"Yup. Take care."

I lead Gracie to the not so well-lit stairwell and zipped down the steps with her as fast as I could. By the time we reached the ground floor, I'd come up with another person who might be having fun at my expense, Rod. As you know he loves getting under my skin. Maybe he asked a buddy to deliver the message. Well, two can play this game. I'll get him back but after he's helped me, not before.

Before I entered the lobby, I cracked the stairway door open a smidgen to allow sufficient light for me to read the note in private. Maybe I could pick up a few clues this time. "You scum bag," it began. "I told you to stay away from her. No more warnings. The minute you show your ugly face to me its lights out." Hmm? If these notes are from Rod, I'm not picking up any of his normal jive.

I tucked the note back in my jacket and waltzed into the lobby with Gracie, ready to tear through the Foley's doors and freeze my butt off. Fortunately for me, Margaret Grimshaw pulled me aside before I had a chance to follow through. "Matt, you have to come quick. There's a lunatic loose in the laundry room."

"He's not brandishing a weapon, is he?"

Her frail hands clutched my thickly covered arm. "I... I didn't see a knife or gun. He just keeps saying he's going to bash a guy's head in. Why would he want to do that?"

I had a feeling I knew why, girlfriend problems. But what possessed him to go to the Foley's laundry room? "Margaret, did he mention who he was mad at?"

"Dick Lenson," she mumbled. "I assume he lives somewhere in the building."

I thought about the name she tossed out. It didn't ring any bells. "Look, stay here with Gracie. I'll try to calm the man down. And if Mr. Edwards shows up, tell him to come to the laundry room, I may need his assistance." I probably could handle the guy alone, but I had no idea if he was high on drugs and didn't want to take any unnecessary risks. If I got injured, I wouldn't be able to wrap up Neil Welch's problems and I'd be deeper in debt than I already am.

The ninety-year-old woman's hands shook uncontrollably as she took Gracie's leash from me. I've never seen her like this. The man in the laundry room had done a good job on her.

I opened the door to the laundry area and peeked inside. A bald-headed man sat hunched over in one of the two rickety chairs next to the utility tub. Either he was revving up to lash out again or was worn out from yelling. I assumed the latter. "Sir, do you need help?" I asked in a non-threatening tone.

The man slowly raised his head, exposing a pointy nose like Mr. Edwards described. "Huh? Oh! You're not the police."

I ran a hand through my hair. "No, I'm not. Why would you think that?"

"There was an old lady in here a couple minutes ago. I thought maybe she'd called them."

"She told me you were looking for a man by the name of Dick Lenson. Does he live on the fourth floor?"

He rubbed his watermelon stomach. "Yup. Do you know the scum bag?"

"Nope, afraid I don't." I whipped out the folded note he had given Mr. Edwards to pass on to me and waved it in his face. "But you've been slipping your threatening notes meant for him under my door for over a month, and I don't appreciate it one bit. I should have you arrested."

Apparently the threat of arrest didn't mean a thing to the guy. Instead of apologizing he said, "Well, that's where my ex-girlfriend told me he lived."

"I'm sorry, sir, but I've lived in the same apartment for many years and I don't recognize the name."

"You mean she lied to me. How could she?" He sputtered, pressing his bulky hands to his forehead. "I've gotta get out of here. Do you know where the old lady is who heard me ranting?"

I leaned against one of the washing machines. "I do, but first tell me why you want to know. You've already scared her plenty."

"Crap. I didn't mean to. Honest." He crossed his legs and leaned back in his chair. "When I left the fourth floor, I saw a guy who looked like Dick entering a room near the end of the hall. I thought he'd gone in here but I was mistaken. He must've entered the garbage chute room instead. Anyway, by the time I walked into the laundry room I was so wound up I couldn't think straight."

"So, I heard."

"I swear if I'd noticed the old woman by the dryer, I would've never blurted out my thoughts."

I took the guy by the arm and led him to the lobby where I'd left Margaret and Gracie. "Margaret, I believe this man has something he wants to say to you before he leaves." I withdrew my hand from his thick arm and waited for him to undo his mess.

"Ma'am, I'm so sorry I scared you. I was extremely upset and should've never hollered like that."

Still visibly frightened, Margaret backed up a bit. "You aren't still planning to harm this Dick Lenson are you?"

The furrows on his forehead deepened. He shook his head. "No, ma'am. I've learned my lesson. I won't be threatening anyone anymore."

Margaret straightened her five-foot frame. Then she crossed her hands, and pressed them against her stomach. "Good. I abhor violence in any form."

"I understand," he said, and then he fled the building.

Margaret turned to me and hugged me like a mother would a son. "Oh, Matt, I'm so glad you were here. I don't know what I would've done if you hadn't shown up. That man scared me to death. I thought if he didn't find Dick he might beat me up instead."

I rubbed my neighbor's back. "Everything's all right now. He won't be back. His ex-girlfriend lied to him about where her new beau lives."

"Smart girl," Margaret said, dropping her arms to her sides. "That man has serious issues he needs to resolve."

"That's for sure." I took ahold of Gracie again. "Say good-bye to Margaret." The mutt obeyed and licked the elderly woman's tiny hand.

Margaret laughed. "Good-bye Gracie. Enjoy your walk."

"Woof. Woof."

***

When I got back from my walk with Gracie, I grabbed a can of Bubble Gum Pop and took off for my hole-in-the-wall office on Lowry Avenue. After the little episode in the laundry room it became quite clear that I needed a place away from all the distractions at the Foley to get my mind back on track concerning the two Delight guys who were harmed.

Sure Rod was having someone decipher the fax I took a picture of, but what if it proves to be nothing of significance. And what about Wang? How did he fit into all of this? I glanced up at the grayish patched-plastered ceiling hanging over my head in the office half expecting the answers to suddenly come crashing down on me before anyone else was harmed. Luckily, the ceiling remained solid and nothing fell on my head.

My gut told me Hu and Wang were only the first of many computer department managers to be harmed. They needed to be protected, but from whom? Neil Welch may be one of America's wealthiest guys, but he certainly can't afford to have around the clock security just for the men who run his computer control room.

The phone intruded on my thoughts. Maybe it wasn't such a good idea to come to the office for solitude. I picked up on the second ring. "Hello, Matt Malone speaking."

"I hope you're sitting down, Matt." It was Neil Welch.

I didn't like the way he sounded. "Are you calling about Wang? Did he die?"

"No," Neil snapped sharply, "I haven't received any updates on him. But this morning our security guard at the plant in Colorado Springs found their computer manager propped against one of the company dumpsters."

"Let me guess. He wasn't sleeping one off."

"You got it,"

I inhaled deeply. "I imagine the police have been notified."

"Yes."

I felt a gnawing in the pit of my stomach. Whatever tales Hu's fax uncovers it's too late for this guy too. "Could the guard tell how he died?"

"No," he reverently responded, "But he did report no weapon had been found near the body."

I cleared my throat. "Just like Hu and Wang," I whispered into the phone. You're not expecting me to fly to Colorado are you, Mr. Welch?" I was hoping he'd say he didn't, I had enough on my plate right here.

"I wasn't expecting anything, Matt. I just thought you'd like to know about Dai Guowei's death since you met him."

"But I didn't meet him." My arms jerked as another spasm hit me like a tidal wave. "That was one of the trips you aborted."

"What's that?"

"You aborted my trip there."

"Oh, yes. You're right. Sorry, I've had so much on my mind lately I don't know if I'm coming or going. I don't understand why someone would want to harm Dai. He was a nice fellow. Everyone at the plant respected him."

"Is his family in Colorado?"

"Singapore. According to his fellow workers at the plant he's been saving all his money to bring them to the States where it's safer."

"How ironic." I spun my office chair around and looked out the window, light snow was falling. "Look, I have a pal on the police force there. I'll call him and try to shake his tree."

"Thanks. Call me if you find out anything useful."

"I will. By the way, how's Carol doing? Is she any better?"

"She says she's planning to come back to work tomorrow, so we'll see. Her cough still sounds bad though. Oops, looks like I'm late for a meeting. I'd better get going."

The second I hung up the phone I reached for the Ferris wheel like card index I owned. Not much on it. I bet Neil Welch had over two hundred on his if not more. For some dumb reason a quote by Hildaur Neilsen, the inventor of the Rolodex system suddenly came to mind, "The bigger the Rolodex, the bigger the man." I guess he knew what he was talking about. I flipped through my meager card stack, found the number I needed, and picked up the phone again.

"Hello, may I speak with Lieutenant Jones in Homicide." I couldn't believe it had been over two years since I'd last seen Lou? But that's got to be right. Irene's cancer was in remission so we decided to go skiing with Lou in Aspen. I'd actually met the cop seven years earlier in Vail when we were both waiting for a ski lift to take us to the top of the China Bowl region.

"This is Lt. Jones," a stern but steady voice said, "How may I help you?"

"Hey, Lou, are you ready for some ski action?"

"Matt? Well, son of a gun. I don't believe it. I thought for sure you'd dropped off the face of the earth. So, are you finally planning to come down here to do some skiing this winter?"

"Maybe if I can get this case resolved I'm working on."

"So, what the heck you been doing with yourself?"

I pulled out a scratch pad from the desk drawer and began to doodle. "Trying to keep out of trouble like my cop friends suggest. I've been doing undercover work since December. As a matter of fact, the company I'm working for has a plant right there in Colorado Springs."

"Oh, yeah? What does the company do?

"They bottle a well-known brand of pop."

"Which company, Pepsi or Coca Cola?"

"Neither. It's called Delight Bottling. Perhaps you've heard of it."

"Sure. I drive by that place on the way home," is all Lou offered. Obviously, he was trying to be discreet. I guess I'll have to be the one to open up first.

"Look. Lou, I heard about a death at the plant down there. Can you verify that for me?"

Lt. Jones laughed. "I should've known you weren't calling about coming down here to ski, Matt. How did you hear about the death so fast? Nothing's been passed on to news reporters yet?"

"I just got off the phone with Neil Welch, the president and owner of Delight Bottling. I told him I had a friend on the police force down there and offered to find out what I could. Is there anything you can share with me? Do you have a list of suspects?"

"Not yet," Lt. Jones said in a subdued tone. "At the moment we're thinking he overdid the partying and ended up in the wrong neighborhood, if you get my drift."

I scribbled some more. "But if his body was dumped by rift raff like you're suggesting, why not dump him in the river or near his apartment? It doesn't make sense to leave his body where he works."

It sounded like Jones slapped his leg. "To be honest that bothers us too. His apartment is on the other side of town. We spoke with the landlord. Dai never had guests as far as he knew. He seemed to be a loner."

"Have your guys talked to the neighbors yet?"

"No. They're busy questioning the employees at Delight. Don't worry, if I hear anything worth passing on I'll call."

"Lou, I think you should know within the past week two other managers from Delight have met similar fates. One guy's dead and the other is in a coma. I definitely don't consider what's happened to them freak accidents. Whoever wants these guys out of the way knows them pretty well."

"Thanks for the tip. Listen, if you can get away this winter, bring your mutt with, the one you've written about in your Christmas cards."

"How about I bring a girlfriend instead?"

"What? How long have you two been dating?"

"A year."

"Good for you, Matt. Sure bring her out here. But I want you to know the dog's still welcome too."

~38~

I hung up the phone and continued scribbling on the writing pad. How many more of Welch's computer managers are going to be harmed? If Rod doesn't come through for me, I don't know what to look at next. I dropped the pen, rested my feet on the desk, and leaned back in my chair. Two seconds later the radio came on. I'd forgotten that I'd set it to AUTO the last time I was here.

A husky male announcer's voice sliced through the silence. "The latest news report just in, a spokesperson for the Center for Disease Control confirms this year's flu outbreak is the worst they've ever seen. The vaccine created for the flu season this year doesn't seem to be working on this latest strain attacking our populace. It hits a person like a ton of bricks. And when you presume you're getting better, you're knocked flat on your back again."

I turned the radio off. It's hard to believe the guys who make big bucks can't figure out a simple strain of flu. How many flu samples do they need to make a match, anyhow? *Wait a second, Matt.* Maybe they do know what's affecting us this season but don't want to cause a panic.

I stared at the can of Bubble Gum Pop I'd brought with. I couldn't believe I still hadn't sampled the stuff. I did try once. That was the night Gracie managed to knock an open can on the floor before I got to it. Well, there's no dog lurking here today. She's at home napping.

Looking forward to tasting the pop, I pulled the can's tab and raised the can to my lips. I'm sure you can guess what happened next. The darn phone rang. In the rush to answer it, I set the can down too hard and spilled most of the contents. With one hand I picked up the phone, while the other searched the drawers of the desk for Kleenex or paper toweling to sop up the mess. Finding nothing to clean up with, I ran my flannel shirt sleeve across the wet surface. "Hello, this is Matt Malone, private investigator."

"Matt, it's Rod. Sorry, I couldn't call you sooner."

I lifted my wet arm off the desk and swung my feet to the floor. *Oh, man, I hope he's got something for me.* "I understand. You're kept fairly busy at the headquarters. So, did you find someone who could translate the fax?"

"I did, but he wasn't available until a half hour ago."

"The main thing is you got someone to do it for me today, not tomorrow." I paced the worn carpet in front of the mammoth desk. "I haven't had a chance to tell you this yet, Rod, but another Delight employee has been found dead."

"Another death? Unbelievable. Did he work in a computer department too?"

"Yup."

"What the heck is going on with that company, Matt?"

"I don't know. But whatever it is, it's deadly serious. Tell me what your translator said about the fax? Was it simply a friendly message from a relative or something more sinister?"

"As much as I hate to admit it, your gut instinct was right on. The fax turned out to be a warning. I'll read you the translation I was given. 'Follow through on what you've been assigned to do or you and those you love will suffer the consequences.'"

I scratched my head. "My God, what could Hu have been forced to do? Who was threatening him?"

"I wish I had the answers for you. When the fax revealed the guy's life had been threatened, I tried to find out who sent it but I hit a dead end."

"That figures the way things are going," I said, "but thanks, Rod, for going beyond what I requested of you. Say, would you mind dropping off a copy of the translation tonight or tomorrow."

"Sure. No problem."

~39~

February 5

I stared out the bedroom window, not liking what I saw. Darn! At least two feet of new snow covered the streets this morning, a total surprise to me. That's what happens when I get too wrapped up in solving a case to take note of weather reports broadcast throughout the previous day. A drive to St. Cloud to ferret out more info from employees who worked with Wang would have to be scrapped for another day.

Disappointed, I shook my head. Surely the guy shared his problem with someone. You'd have to be a hermit not to. But who would he have spilled his guts to? I wonder if the hospital has come up with any conclusions on his condition. I had planned to check on that too. There's no way the hospital staff would release updates about Wang over the phone especially since I'm not a relative.

The dog tagged closely behind as I made my way from the bedroom to the bathroom. She'd been sticking to me like a newborn pup ever since she got back from her stay at the vet's. Worried I might trip over her if I have to rush to the phone, I pointed down the hall. "Go get your snack. I left it in the kitchen for you."

The word *snack* didn't do anything for the mutt. She didn't budge. I got aggressive. I took ahold of her collar, tugged her out of the bathroom, and shut the door. I hate to be mean, but there are certain places in this apartment where I need my privacy, the bathroom being one of them.

The water in the shower was ice cold. The early risers must've used it all up. Total time spent in the shower approximately three minutes, a new world record for me. I grabbed the bath towel from the rack and swiftly dried off. I might not like the person I saw in the mirror as I dressed, but there were things I could do about it: go on a diet, get a haircut, and exercise more.

That wasn't the case for Neil Welch's situation. A communist country, namely China, was at the root of his problems and until I can pinpoint all the bits and pieces to complete the crazy puzzle I'm stuck in a darn holding pattern using up precious fuel.

My nonagenarian neighbor Margaret came to mind at the thought of puzzles. She's good at figuring out crossword puzzles printed in the daily newspaper and magazines. I've never asked her what she does when she runs into a brick wall. But in all the years I've known her, I never seen her act irritated when she can't figure something out.

Heck, as long as I'm snowbound, I might as well invite her over for a cup of tea and get some advice.

Maybe she'll even reciprocate and share a meal. Now, that's a win-win if I ever heard one.

As soon as I dressed and shaved, I called Margaret and asked if she'd like to come over. She gladly accepted my invitation. With that out of the way, I collected the mutt and got boots, stocking cap, and a jacket from the hall closet. I may not be able to get on the road due to the weather, but that doesn't mean Gracie can be ignored. She needed to do doggie duty whether there was one foot of snow or ten.

The instant I stooped to put the old-fashioned rubber buckled overshoes on I noticed a folded piece of paper on the carpet. It had to be from Rod. The jerk who scared Margaret to death didn't dare return to our building. I dropped the paper on the hallway table and took off.

Gracie and I got back just seconds before Margaret was expected to show up. I immediately flew around the apartment like a mad scientist, drying off the mutt's legs, putting on the teakettle, hunting for teacups, digging out a half-empty package of Oreos, and searching for teabags. I never found the teabags and couldn't remember when I last used any. I wonder if Margaret would mind drinking plain water. I know she never drinks pop.

Knock. Knock.

"That's her, Gracie. We'd better get the door."

"Woof. Woof."

I raced to the door and swung it open. "Come on in, Margaret. Let's sit in the living room. It's more comfortable than the kitchen."

"I don't mind sitting at your kitchen table," the elderly woman said, making herself comfortable on the couch.

"I'm sure you don't, but I thought if I get longwinded your back won't get sore. By the way, do you mind having a glass of water instead of tea; I can't seem to find the teabags?"

Margaret pulled her apartment keys from her solid-blue ruffled apron and handed them to me. "Here. I can give Gracie attention while you get the teabags. You'll find them in the canister by the stove labeled TEA."

Three seconds later I came back. "I found the teabags," I said, setting them on the coffee table. Then I went to the kitchen to fill the cups with hot water and brought them back to the living room. "One more item to get, Margaret, and I'll be right with you."

"Do what you have to do, Matt. I'm not going anywhere, am I, Gracie." The mutt snuggled up closer to her and licked her face. "Nor is Gracie for that matter."

I hurried to the kitchen and returned with the plate of cookies. "I want you to know I got up early this morning just to bake these for you."

Margaret smiled. "I hope Rita appreciates your baking skills."

I took a cookie and put a teabag in a cup of steaming water for myself. "I have no idea. She's never here long enough to discover what's in my cupboards."

"You know," Margaret said, picking up her teacup, "I just realized I never asked what conclusion the doctor came to concerning Gracie's illness."

I slapped my knee. "And I've had so much on my mind I forgot to tell you. Apparently she had the flu like you thought."

"Oh, I'm so glad to hear that. I know how worried you were. Are you still doing a project for Mr. Welch or have you finished it?"

"It's not finished yet. There are too many loose ends and I don't know what to do next, Margaret. I thought since you're such a great listener and an expert at solving puzzles perhaps I should share what's happened with this case and go from there."

"Why, Matt, I'm always happy to help you," the elderly woman said. "Is that why you invited me over?"

What do I say? I don't want Margaret to feel insulted. "Ah, well, I wanted to see you too. You don't mind mixing business with regular chit chat over tea and cookies do you?"

Margaret's eyes twinkled. "Absolutely not. To be honest I was hoping you might share what you've been doing lately, but I didn't want to force the issue. Shall we get started?"

"Of course. But first, would you like more hot water; I see your cup is empty?"

"No, thank you. Not yet."

"Okay." I shoved my hands in my jean pockets. "Since I'm not really sure what tidbits are important, Margaret, I'll tell you as much as I can recall. Mr. Welch hired me to check out various bottling plants. He thought he might have to sell a couple of them. I think I already told you when I was overseas I discovered only people trained on specific equipment designed in China were hired for the Delight Bottling plants computer departments."

The woman on the couch nodded. "Yes, and I told you to find the connection. Have you?"

"Partly. Rod managed to get a co-worker to translate a fax I had taken a photo of while at the Boston plant." I showed her the note.

The minute she read it her rosy-rouged cheeks turned ashen. "It sounds like this fellow is in grave danger. Can you get protection for him?"

"Nope. It's too late for him as well as another guy in Colorado Springs. They're dead. But I'm hoping Wang pulls through. He's in a coma in a St. Cloud hospital. I had planned to drive up there this morning to find out how he's doing, but as you know the weather didn't cooperate."

"Did you ever meet the man in the coma?"

I braced a hand on my hip. "Yes, not too long ago due to a break-in at the St. Cloud plant. I wish the scheduled inspection had taken place before that though. If I had been able to do it, I feel I might have learned some important facts."

Margaret pointed her arthritic fingers at me. "Second guessing yourself is a waste of time, Matt. You of all people should know that."

She's right but I still find myself doing it a lot. I moved away from the couch and dropped my body in the comfy La-Z-Boy chair. The second I pulled the lever on the chair to pop the footrest out, the landline rang. I tried to ignore it, but Margaret insisted I get it.

"Hello. Yes, this is Matt Malone. When? I see. Well, thank you for contacting me. I appreciate it."

The elderly woman visiting me studied my face when I rejoined her in the living room. "What is it, Matt? You look like you received bad news."

I pressed the palm of my hand against my forehead. "I did. That was an officer from the Waite Park Police Department. He wanted to inform me that Wang from the St. Cloud plant died a few minutes ago."

"Oh, dear. Three men are dead. Why were they snuffed out? For being Chinese, ignoring a threat, or knowing too much?"

"Maybe all three. What if the government of China wanted to cause turmoil in the U.S. and ordered these men to cause major damage to one of our businesses that sells its products worldwide?" The question created a stabbing pain in my stomach. Huh? Was I finally on to something?

"What kind of damage could a person running a computer department at a bottling plant do?" Margaret timidly asked, adjusting her wire-framed glasses.

"Those guys create programs that help the machines operate properly. Wait a second."

Margaret scooted to the edge of the couch. "What is it?"

"The other day I wanted to question Wang about the break-in, but he didn't show up for work. You see I'd finally come to the conclusion he was the one who had messed with the bolts and screws on a *filler* machine."

"Why would he need to do that? You just said he ran the programs. He could shut down a machine simply with his computers."

"Yes, but what if the thing he had been ordered to do actually required hands-on work with a machine, something he knew nothing about."

"Matt, have you ever considered the possibility that Wang may have purposely messed with the machine to lead everyone astray?"

I mulled over what Margaret asked. "No, it never crossed my mind. I wish it had. When Welch told me about the break-in, I'd assumed it was some sort of setup by an insider or someone outside the company to stir up trouble since there had been talks of a possible strike. So, when I narrowed the possible suspects down to an employee, I expected the person to say he messed with the *filler* because he was angry with the company he worked for.

"I like your line of thinking, Margaret. The break-in definitely made the *filler* machine the focus of everyone's attention, leaving the door wide open for a person to do damage elsewhere in the plant. Maybe we should go sit in the kitchen after all. I can heat up more water for another cup of tea and we can look at photos I took at a Delight bottling plant. Four eyes are better than two, don't you agree?"

The tiny woman smiled. "I do indeed."

~40~

"What's this, Matt?" Margaret asked, poking a finger at a piece of paper laying underneath the pile of developed photos sitting in the valise I'd just opened. "It looks like directions for putting something together, except it's not in English." She pushed her glasses closer to the bridge of her nose to inspect it better. "Were you helping your brother put toys together for his kids at Christmas?"

"Are you kidding? I don't know the first thing about connecting Part A to Part B, including an artificial Christmas tree. If anything needed to be put together, Irene did it."

I finished pouring hot water in our teacups and placed them in the center of the table. "Here, let me see what you're looking at. Maybe I picked up something by accident when I toured the plants overseas. "Oh, oh. Where the heck did I pick this up? It's a fax written in Chinese like the one I gave Rod to have translated."

Margaret wrapped her hands around her teacup. "I'm too old to have you explain how a fax is sent from one place to another, but isn't it possible you handled some when you inspected the three plants?"

"I suppose." I pulled out a chair and sat. "I sent Rita an e-mail from the Frankfurt location. Everyone had already gone home for the night so I had the computer control room to myself. It had been tidied up though. No paperwork or manuals had been left out on the computer desks."

"What about when you were in Sao Paulo? Margaret inquired.

I examined the fax again. "I'm sure I didn't pick this up there. Yang, the manager, was with me the whole time. I wonder if it got in my valise by accident when I helped Wang clean up his office after the supposed break-in?" I snapped my fingers. "Of course, that's got to be it. Maybe that's why Wang asked the plant manager for my phone number. He just wanted the fax back. Not to come clean about what he'd done."

Margaret ran her hand across Gracie's back. "My goodness you definitely need help sorting things out. Three computer technicians died within days of each other. Originally from China, the men traveled to the States alone and at some point were ordered to do damage within the Delight plants, probably not in their area of expertise though. Before the men died, faxes were sent to at least two of the men, one of which we know was a threat message. Is there anything else you haven't shared yet?"

"Well, there was this one young guy, Peter, in Frankfurt who almost forced my driver off the road the first day we came to the plant. Later the same day he almost killed me with a forklift. The really weird thing is I spotted him when I headed to my rental car at the Boston plant. He was cruising through the parking lot looking for someone. I never did figure out how he happened to be in Boston the same time I was."

"Did you consider the possibility that Peter worked for someone who didn't want you poking your nose around the plants."

I rubbed my forehead. "Do you remember when I came over to your place early December, all excited about Neil Welch wanting to meet with me, and you mentioned he was having marital problems?"

The elderly woman lightly nodded her head.

"Well, that tidbit stuck in my head. I mean who else was there to blame at that time besides Welch's wife. I figured she hired Peter to be her eyes and ears and scare off anyone who came poking around, including me."

Gracie begged for attention. Margaret leaned over, patted the mutt's head, and then straightened her tiny frame. "If I were you Matt, I wouldn't discount the wife quite yet."

I gave her a questioning look. "You're not seriously thinking she had something to do with the death of the men, are you?"

She patted my arm. "No, dear. If a woman wants to make sure she gets her fair share in a divorce settlement, she certainly wouldn't cause drastic problems at her husband's plants. Being a PI you should know that. But she would want someone she trusted to evaluate the seven plants on the QT."

"Of course, and one can easily check that with her privately when and if the need arises. I hate to admit this but I actually thought she might've been the one behind the break-in at the St. Cloud plant."

"How did Mr. Welch take the news?"

"Not too good. I thought he might can me."

Margaret turned her head towards the living room. "I know my hearing is not as good as it used to be, but I hear knocking."

I rested my hands on the table and listened. "Hmm? I wonder who it could be." I shoved my chair away from the table. "Excuse me, Margaret, I'll be right back."

"I hope I'm not disturbing you, Matt."

"Not at all, Rod. Margaret and I are having a cup of tea in the kitchen. Why don't you come in and join us, there's something important I'd like to show you."

Rod stepped inside and followed me to the kitchen. "I can't stay too long. Hi, Margaret. How are you doing?"

Margaret gave Rod a quick smile. "Fine, thank you for asking."

Rod pulled out a chair. "Matt, did you get the copy of the fax I shoved under your door?"

"Yup." I picked up the paper he was referring to and waved it in the air. "I got it right here." Then I quickly closed the valise and moved it to the counter. Rod didn't need to find about the photos I'd taken at the various bottling plants. He knows enough about my business as it is.

"And," Margaret said excitedly, "We have another fax for you. Matt found it tucked away in his valise a few minutes ago." She slid it across the table to Rod.

Rod's Nordic face turned stern. "You've got Margaret caught up in your PI work too? What's wrong with you? You'd better not be putting this elderly woman in any danger."

Whoa. Does a heart of gold really beat under Rod's stiff exterior? For someone who has admitted he doesn't know much about the nonagenarian living on our floor, I can't believe he secretly cares what happens to her. More than likely he's talking like a tough guy because he wants to belittle me in front of her. I clamped my teeth together, like a bull dog defending its turf.

Rod plucked the fax off the table and studied it. "Where did you get this one from, Matt? I hope you didn't trespass the home of one of the dead men."

"Calm down, Rod. First of all I'd never dream of putting Margaret in any danger. Second, I didn't find this in anyone's home." Which is true, I may have illegally trespassed on Wang's premises, but that's not where the fax came from. "Do you think your guy at work would be willing to translate this too?"

"I think so, but it depends when he can get around to it. Today's Friday and he usually doesn't work weekends. So, if he made it into work, he's probably trying to tie up loose ends."

~41~

February 8

The translator at the FBI headquarters hadn't made it into work last Friday so Rod Thompson is hoping to catch him today. In the meantime, I got a call from an old college chum, Stanley Walker, asking me to track down the whereabouts of a sister of his.

According to Stanley, his parents recently died and left a great deal of money to all five of their children, but in order to settle the estate the kids needed to track down their youngest sister, whom no one has spoken to in five long years. Stanley told me he used to be very close to Susan, the troubled sister he'd lost touch with, and hoped she hadn't died of an overdose or been murdered.

After being given Susan's last known residence, I decided to check all Susan Walker's listed on the Internet as residing in Minnesota before I began digging. I came up with a handful, but at least it was a start.

I grabbed my coat and hat and rounded up Gracie. "Come on we're going for a short ride." Since I was batting zero with the Delight case, I felt it wasn't necessary to stay glued to the La-Z-Boy all day. I'd give the Susan Walker case a shot. Her last known residence the family had was a couple miles from the Foley.

A few minutes later I pulled up in front of a Victorian style house, circa 1910, that had seen better days. The faded green paint on the front of the house was past blister stage. The picture window and smaller one protected by the porch weren't much better. Besides needing a decent paint job they looked like they required a quick reinforcement before they popped out.

After I pressed my thumb about seven times in the indent where the plastic cover for a doorbell should be, someone finally responded. I immediately flashed my PI badge. The woman who appeared at the door to check things out backed away. "You don't have to be afraid," I said, "I'm not the police. Ms. Walker's family asked me to get in touch with her."

"Why?" the emaciated young woman with nicotine stained nails asked.

I wasn't obligated to share my real purpose for being there and I didn't plan to. This notorious neighborhood was on the fringes of the downtown safe zone. If someone around here found out Susan had tons of money coming to her, who knew what they might do to her. So, I lied. "They thought she'd like to know her parents died."

She threw her scraggly hair over her ears. "Well, in that case, she left this halfway house about two years ago."

I rested my hand on the siding of the house, hoping I wouldn't get any wood splinters stuck in my fingers in the process. "Do you have any idea where Susan might have moved to?"

She shook her head. "I don't know and I don't care. All I remember is her telling us she found religion and she wasn't coming back," and then she slammed the door in my face.

Found a religion. I wonder which one. I thought Stanley was raised Catholic, but I didn't recall him attending services at the Newman Center during our college days. Of course, that doesn't mean anything. Most of us let church fall by the wayside when we were in college.

Gracie jumped all over me the second I climbed in the car. "Yes, I'm back. Settle down you crazy mutt." She ignored my command and kept right on parading over my legs and kissing me. Frustrated, I applied gentle pressure to her butt. Message received, she scrambled to the passenger seat. Not knowing how long she'd remain there, I wrote a note to myself concerning Susan Walker's involvement with religion and then started up the car. "Ready to go home, girl?"

Gracie stood and faced the passenger window. "Woof. Woof."

The second I squeezed the Topaz into the Foley's underground parking slot assigned me, the cell phone rang. I unzipped my jacket, pulled the phone out of an inside pocket I had tucked it in, and looked to see if I recognized the number before accepting the call. "Well, this is a pleasant surprise, Rita. You must be on break. Oh, you took the day off. I wish I would've known sooner we could've planned something."

"Well, if you let me in we can still do something together," she cooed.

Surprised by her comment, I said, "You're here at the Foley?"

Rita laughed. "Is that all right?"

"Why, of course it is. I'm not upstairs though. Gracie and I just got back from a car ride so I'll meet you in the lobby by the elevator. Remember, don't talk to any strangers while you're waiting," I teased, making sure to press the right number to unlock the Foley's front door for visitors before jumping out of the car with Gracie.

Rita took off her boots, mittens and coat as soon as we entered the apartment and handed them to me. I stashed them in the hall closet and then proceeded to stick my outerwear in there too.

"I hate wearing stocking caps," Rita said, waving her hand over the top of her head. "Look at all the static it creates."

"It's okay. I love you no matter how charged up you get."

"Oh, boy. When you tell me that, I know I look pretty scary. Where's the nearest mirror?"

I pointed down the hall. "In the bathroom. Hopefully you can ignore the mess."

A couple seconds ticked by before Rita joined Gracie and me in the living room. Her hair looked about the same but I didn't dare tell her. She'd probably walk out the door and never come back. "Honey, why don't you take the La-Z-Boy," I said, "I never seem to park on the couch anymore."

Rita strolled over to the chair and sat. "I don't blame you. Once you treat yourself to this comfy chair, you don't want to sit anywhere else."

I stared at my girlfriend for a few seconds, enjoying her presence on a weekday, early afternoon no less. "You must've done something really good at work to merit a day off."

"Yup. I convinced a new client that an ad I designed was perfect for them."

"All right. Keep doing that so we can have more time together."

Rita beamed, "So, where did you just come back from? Did it have to do with your case for Delight?"

"No, I'm working on something new while the Delight thing is on hold."

"Rita acted surprised. "What about the fax you wanted Rod to get translated? Did it get done?"

I nodded. "Yes, it didn't help. But I'm hoping another fax I gave Rod last Friday proves useful."

"Where did that one come from?"

"The St. Cloud plant."

Rita fanned herself.

"I can adjust the thermostat if you're too hot," I said, walking towards the small device mounted on the living room wall before Rita had a chance to respond.

She pushed her sweater sleeves up. "Don't turn down the heat on my account. I'll just drink something cold. Have you got anything in the fridge?"

"Sure," I pivoted towards the kitchen, "would you like pop or a beer? I've got both."

"If you still have Bubble Gum Pop on hand, I'll try that."

Since I hadn't sampled the pop yet either, I brought two opened cans to the living room, handed one to Rita and set mine on the coffee table by the couch.

"How much do you think Delight shelled out for this concept, Matt?"

With the little time we spend together, did Rita really have to discuss marketing costs when there are so many other things we could talk about? *What about you, Matt? You're no better. You haven't exactly told Rita you don't want to speak about work.* "I don't know," I said with a slightly grumpy attitude, "I never asked anyone."

Rita didn't pick up on my irritation, thank goodness. She was too busy examining the pop can and smoothing out imaginary pant wrinkles. "Did I tell you I thought the design for Delight's new pop was clever?"

I released a heavy sigh. "Yes, the last time you were here."

"Oh, sorry." She lowered the can of pop to her lap and wrapped both hands around it. For someone who just admitted she needed something cold to cool off with, she sure wasn't rushing to drink it. Although holding on to something chilled is known to help too.

I stared at the can of pop sitting in front of me and thought back to the night Gracie got sick. She had licked up a considerable amount of this syrupy stuff from the floor before I managed to stop her. I suddenly had a crazy thought. Maybe the ingredients in the pop made her sick. If too much chocolate can kill a dog, what about pop?

While I had been dwelling on the night Gracie got sick, Rita had finally gotten around to putting the Bubble Gum can near her lips. I watched as she allowed her nostrils to take in the aroma. When the pop fizz hit her nose, she giggled and quickly wiped it off. "Umm, this does smell like the bubble gum we chewed as kids. Should I try to chew it or drink it, Matt?"

"Can't help you there, I haven't touched my can yet."

She puckered her luscious pink-coated lips and pressed the can against them.

"Don't drink that," I suddenly shouted as I leaped off the couch and yanked the can from Rita's grasp, spilling a small amount of beverage on her sweater as I did so.

"Are you crazy? You just ruined a very expensive cashmere sweater."

"I'd rather ruin a sweater than your health," I stated, setting her pop next to mine.

Rita pressed the palms of her hands against her forehead. "What are you talking about?"

I positioned myself on an arm of the La-Z-Boy before attempting to explain my behavior. "Gracie licked up a considerable amount of Bubble Gum Pop from the kitchen floor the day she got sick."

"How did the pop end up on the floor?" Rita quizzed.

"I'd opened a can and then forgot it on the kitchen table. Gracie must've become curious about the new aroma wafting through the air and knocked it over."

Rita acted skeptical. "You actually think pop made her sick? Come on, Matt, be sensible. You're mutt's a human vacuum. With all the stuff she's scarfed up since I've met you, she should've gotten sick long before this."

"That's right, but she's never tasted pop before. And don't forget Doctor Mallard admitted he never succeeded in pinpointing her illness. Obviously, it was triggered by something he'd never witnessed before, a reaction to Bubble Gum Pop."

"I don't buy it, Matt. It wouldn't fly with my boss either, but it's a cute ad idea. Dog hovers over a glass of pop waiting for the master to leave the kitchen. As soon as his master walks away, the dog tastes the beverage."

My voice almost reached soprano level. "I expected you of all people to take me serious, Rita. Not turn what I said into a marketing idea."

Rita reached for my hand. "I'm sorry if I upset you. I didn't mean to. But what else do you have to prove your theory? Gracie can't speak."

I stood and began to circle the room. "Ah, but I know what her symptoms were. And they happen to be the same as the newest flu strain hitting humans."

Apparently Gracie didn't like being left alone. She jumped off the couch and steadfastly followed my trail like Watson did with Sherlock Holmes.

"Matt, that's just a crazy coincidence."

"I think not." I rubbed my arms like one does when they have the chills. "Bubble Gum Pop got released at the same time people began complaining of an unknown strain of flu."

Rita rested her head against the back of the La-Z-Boy and let what I said sink in a few seconds before sharing her thoughts. "My God, Sherlock! You could be on to a monstrous scheme. But who would mastermind such a sinister plot?"

~42~

"Who, is what's bugging me. Putting a virus in a pop to make citizens of the U.S. ill smacks of an outside source, someone powerful enough to undermine our country, but I don't think the government of China had anything to do with it. With all their intelligence, they could've concocted a sneakier plan of attack long before this."

Rita stretched her arms above her head. "Well, whoever instigated the dirty deed planned it well. They found out personal stuff about the men in charge of Delight's computer departments and held it over them so they'd cooperate."

I scratched my head. "Then the guys of course had to figure out where along the bottling process it was possible to introduce the virus without getting caught. I suppose they could've gotten a chemist at each plant involved. But surely someone in that department would've noticed things out of whack. The chemists keep tight track of every little thing in an official binder."

"You're saying a virus was introduced into the pop. Couldn't it have been bacteria?"

"Nope. Bacteria is definitely not the culprit."

"How can you be so certain?"

I plopped down on the couch again and folded my hands. "A chemist at the St. Cloud plant explained about the chemicals used in the pop process. Carbon dioxide serves many purposes. It creates the fizz which keeps pop from going flat. I'm sure you've put plenty of cans back in the fridge after opening them only to discover, a couple days later, the pop tasted flat."

Rita's curled hair bounced in agreement.

"Carbon dioxide is also used in the pop industry to kill bacteria, giving pop a long shelf life."

"Hmm?" Rita tapped her pink-painted finely manicured nails on the arm of the La-Z-Boy. "Do you think all of the Delight plants have produced contaminated pop?"

"I don't know. I certainly haven't heard anything on the news about people overseas being hit by this new strain of flu. You know, maybe I've been too critical of Wang. What if he faked the break-in to warrant a tighter security in the building?"

Rita continued. "Yes, that makes sense. With more eyes on everything, it would be impossible to do what he was being forced to do. Matt, what if other flavors of pop besides Bubble Gum have been tampered with too? You said pop has a long shelf life, so people could be getting sick way down the road."

"Let's not jump the gun quite yet," I suggested. If Delight needed to check pop already sitting on store shelves, they could easily do that. But was the pop can

Gracie knocked over still in my recycle bin? Without saying a word to Rita, I got off the couch and headed for the kitchen.

The moment I left the room, Rita scrambled after me. "What are you up to?"

"Give me a minute and I'll tell you," I said, ducking down and pulling out the recycling bin from under the sink. Eureka! The pop can wasn't tossed yet. I took it out of the bin and showed it to Rita. "This is the can Gracie spilled. I'm going to give it to Rod. He can request the pop be analyzed by the Center for Disease Control."

"Do you want me to get the ones left in the other room?"

"Yeah." While Rita was busy with that, I took out the rest of the Bubble Gum Pop sitting in the fridge, which included the carton of free stuff I got in Boston too, and then I looked up Rod's home number and left him a message. "Hey, Rod, it's Matt. Please don't disregard this call. I got more stuff pertaining to the case I'm working on. You really need to take a look at it as soon as you can. It's time sensitive."

Rita waltzed into the kitchen as I hung up. "Who were you talking to?"

"I left a message on Rod's landline. Hopefully he hasn't been sent out of town. These cans need to be tested right away."

"Why don't you call his cell phone?"

I threw my hands in the air. "I can't. I'm not privy to that number."

"Your next door neighbors and he's never given it to you. Whoa. I guess you meant it when you said the two of you don't get along that well. Maybe you should try reaching him at the FBI headquarters. Or isn't that a good idea?"

"No. It's a great suggestion. I'll tell whoever answers I'm calling about a family emergency. Rod will be mad at me, but he always seems to be ticked off with me for some reason or other."

Rita's face brightened as she paged through the phone book. "Have you ever thought it might be because you have a steady girl and he doesn't?"

Could Rita be right? "No. Never. But now that you've brought it to my attention, it's possible I guess."

"Here, Matt, I found the number," she set the open phone book by the landline, crossed her fingers, and watched while I dialed.

A woman with a deep-monotone voice answered. She sounded like she was bored with her job. "I'm sorry Mr. Malone, but Mr. Thompson isn't in the building. He's out in the field. Would you like us to get the message to him?"

When I told the gal it was an emergency, I didn't figure on Rod being out of the building. If he heard about the emergency through a second-hand source, he definitely would never speak to me again. I guess that wouldn't be too bad, unless I needed his help later down the road. "No, that's all right. But could you tell me if his field work is in town or out of state?"

"He's in town."

"Thank you."

"You're welcome."

~43~

The love of my life had gone home and I was just wrapping up the leftover pizza for tomorrow's lunch when there was a loud rap at the door. I wiped off my hands on my jeans and went to see who it was. "Rod! Well, it's about time. I was worried you'd be working through the night."

"I lucked out. After the receptionist mentioned the emergency call I received while out of the office, the boss said I should go straight home. But before I left, I decided to call the apartment and check my messages. It didn't take long to put two and two together. Good thing you didn't tell her a relative died. I wouldn't be standing here."

"That's why I decided not to leave a message with the gal."

"So, what have you got for me?" he asked, stepping into the living room with a spring to his step.

I rubbed my chapped hands together. "Lots of things."

"All right. Lay it on me." Rod wandered over to my beefy-easy chair and sat. His tall fine-tuned body fit perfectly. "That is if the stuff is here in your apartment."

"Don't worry. It is." I paraded to the kitchen and carried the empty pop cans and full cans into the living room.

"What this? You want me to try that new pop. No thanks. I'd much prefer a cold beer if you have one."

I refrained from laughing. This geek clearly isn't on the same wavelength as me. "These aren't for you. Nor are they for anyone's consumption. I want them to be tested by the CDC." I set the pop on the coffee table. "This pop is endangering our citizens."

Rod looked me up one side and down the other, trying to decide if I had a screw loose I suppose. "Care to explain how?"

"You've heard about the unknown strain of flu going around, right?"

"Of course, I don't live in a vacuum. I know what's going on in the world around us."

That's a matter of opinion. "Well, I think the virus got into Delight's new line of pop, Bubble Gum."

"You can't be serious?" Rod harshly quipped, leaving my favorite chair behind and standing. "Over the years you've come up with some wild notions, but this goes to the top of the list. Suggesting a virus has been introduced into a pop and having CDC waste their precious resources to test your theory. Were you dropped on your head when you were a baby?"

I balled my hands into fists and grinded my teeth. If there was going to be a battle here, I was prepared. "No.

But I most certainly am serious. This new brand was released to the public just a couple days ago."

"I'm aware of that. I saw an ad on TV. So, exactly how does the safety of our nation come into play here?"

I shook my head. "If you wipe that smirk off your face, I'd be happy to explain."

Rod's facial expression changed dramatically. "Okay, fine. Whatever you have to say next better be darn good or I'm splitting."

"I've received your message," I said sarcastically, "And, it's coming in loud and clear. The timing of the pop release and the first outbreak of the new flu coincide perfectly."

"That could be a fluke," Rod snorted. "What if your theory is wrong, what then?" He didn't wait for a response as per his personality. "I'll tell you. A major company like Delight could lose millions. Plus, you more than likely would find yourself on the other end of a lawsuit something I'm sure you can't afford."

He always has to squeeze in a dig about my income. One of these days the tables will be turned and then look out, buddy. "Look, I have no desire to drop a bombshell on anyone, a monetary one at that, or be sued for that matter. "But, I can definitely get a second verification on the pops release date from Delight's corporate office if that's what you want."

I could tell Rod wasn't happy about the way things were going. His stance completely changed to a closed off one. Crossing his arms in front of him, he said, "Fine. Now what other proof do you have that the pop's to blame for everyone coming down with this strange virus? Don't tell me you've experimented on yourself?"

"No, I'm not that foolish," I mumbled.

Gracie got up from where she was curled up on the carpet and started circling Rod. "What's this crazy dog of yours trying to tell me, Matt? Does she have to go out?"

I chuckled. "Nope. Her next trip outside isn't until after supper."

Look, Matt, I know we don't always see eye to eye, but if I told the home office what you told me, I'd be drummed out of the FBI. I need solid evidence to back up your claim." The dog kept circling Rod's lanky legs. "What is with Gracie?"

I might live with the simple gift of sixth sense bestowed on me by Great Aunt Fiona, but the mutt I saved has gifts beyond my realm of understanding. I swear she's trying to share her story with Rod in doggie language.

I tapped a couch cushion. "Jump up there, Gracie, out of the way." She did as I bid. "Good dog," I said before turning my attention to Rod again. "The dog wasn't trying to be a pest, Rod; she simply wanted to let you know she got terribly sick after licking more than a half a cup of liquid from one of these cans she happened to knock on the floor."

"You're in and out of the building so much you probably didn't even notice Gracie's absence. She was under a vet's care for several days."

Rod leaned over, rubbed Gracie's noggin, and then smoothed his own hair out. "You're right. I miss most of what happens around here, including fire alarms going off in the middle of the night for no reason. What did the vet think caused Gracie's illness?"

"He was stumped after receiving inconclusive test results and passed it off as some sort of flu. The good news is the can Gracie messed with is one of the open ones I tossed in a plastic bag."

Rod gave me a blank stare. Had I given him enough info now to warrant the FBI's and CDC's involvement? I tried to take a stab at what the Nordic neighbor was thinking, but I came up empty handed. "I'll tell you what," he suddenly said, "I'm going to put my job on the line here. All CDC can say is, 'No.'"

I couldn't believe what I was hearing. "So how many cans do you think they'll need?"

"I'd say at least a couple cans from both boxes." Rod headed towards the door. "Why don't you get them out for me, Matt, and I'll go get a couple shipping containers."

"How long will that take, Rod, an hour?" Assuming he'd have to drive to headquarters to pick them up, I allowed extra time for rush hour traffic.

Rod rested his hand on the door handle. "Two seconds. I keep a few in my apartment. By the way, when I come back you'd better be prepared to tell me who all was involved in this scheme."

~44~

February 9

This morning started out awful. I rolled out of bed with a severe headache and a bad case of the sniffles. Had I caught a cold despite trying not to? I searched high and low for a box of Kleenex and a bottle of aspirin, finding neither I chose strong coffee and toilet paper as substitutes.

As soon as I padded down the carpeted hall to the worn-linoleum floor in the kitchen to prepare java, the landline rang. I expected it to be Rod with great news about my case. It wasn't.

"Matt, I haven't heard from you in days," Neil Welch said, sounding rough around the edges, "What are you doing to earn all my money?"

I cradled the landline's receiver on my shoulder, allowing my fingers the freedom to massage my forehead while talking. Without the ammunition needed from CDC, there was no reason at this juncture to imply the man needed to pull Bubble Gum Pop off the shelves. What little info I had for the present would have to suffice. "I've been hitting so many brick walls, Mr. Welch, but I'm slowly making headway. I've discovered two faxes from your plants, one of which has been already translated. It turns out it was a threat to Hu and his family."

Welch exploded. "Who in their right mind would do such a thing, Matt?"

My head felt like it was ready to take off for parts unknown. "I haven't been able to uncover that yet, sir. But, I'm positive your other two department managers received similar threats if they didn't follow orders to cause a major problem at your plants."

"I've been in business for fifty years and have never experienced anything like this. I don't understand it. Where are these threats coming from?"

"Somewhere in China I believe."

"China? But that's where the heads of the computer departments are from. Look, the minute you find out anything else, Matt, call me. I don't care what time of day it is. Do you understand?"

"Yes, sir." Unfortunately, I understood too well what he was implying. If I didn't comply with his wishes, I'd be out the door.

When I hung up the phone, I gave serious thought to how I was going to handle the rest of the day in my condition. There's no denying it's imperative I dig deeper into the family history of the three dead men, see if there was a secret connection between them. But with this horrendous headache, speaking to anyone especially over the phone was out of the question.

I put the coffee on and dug in the fridge for something to eat. Pizza from a couple nights ago caught my eye. It would have to do. My nose began to drip. I took the pizza out and padded back down the hall to the bathroom and tore off several squares of toilet paper. By the time I marched into the kitchen again, the smell of fresh brewed coffee filled the air. I grabbed a paper plate off the counter, set the pizza on it, and nuked it.

After my so-called breakfast, I carried a second cup of coffee to the desk in my bedroom where I planned to sketch a rough draft of an internal layout of a Delight Bottling plant. I figured a drawing might help me pinpoint where a virus could be introduced without anyone being the wiser. "Pictures of the setup would help," I murmured, dabbing my nose with a Kleenex again.

I jumped out of the chair, opened the closet, and tore things off the overhead shelf until I found what I was looking for, three manila envelopes. Each was labeled with a different plant location and contained the developed photos from those plant tours. Since Hu worked at the Boston plant, I selected that envelope first, emptied its contents on the bed, flipped the photos face up one at a time, and examined them as I did so.

My crazy dog thought I was playing a game with her and took a running leap for the bed. Luckily I caught her mid-air and put her on the floor. I couldn't afford to have the photos damaged. Neil Welch hadn't seen them yet. "Stay on the floor, girl. There's nothing up there for you." The mutt whined and headed for the nearest corner.

With the dog taken care of, I finished sorting through the Boston photos and lined them up according to the bottling process. Then I stacked them in a pile and carried them to the desk to use for reference.

I took a piece of computer paper out of the desk drawer and drew the different areas of the plant on it according to the photos. "Where could a person infuse a virus into pop without drawing attention?" Dumbfounded, I scratched my head. There are too many people around when the depalletizer places bottles and cans on the conveyor belt. Not only that, there's a huge mirror suspended on the ceiling directly over where the process takes place and workers eye-ball it frequently to make certain nothing is amiss.

I moved on to the next grouping pertaining to the rinser. No one would waste their time trying to insert a virus before the washing occurs. The rinse would wash the contamination away.

The next photos I examined were for the *filler* machine process. Wang messed with it, but I think he did it to throw us off or to tighten security. Whatever his reason was it doesn't really matter anymore. I counted the men shown working in this section and remembered being told that four employees mix and fill the stainless steel tanks at all times. That means if someone introduced a virus at this juncture, more than one person would've been involved.

I lifted my head to glance out the window and dizziness hit me as hard as the heavy snow bending the boughs on the pine trees below. I shoved the chair away from the desk, strolled to the bed, and collapsed.

When I was awakened three hours later by a whining dog, the dizziness and headache had subsided, not so for the drippy nose. Realizing Gracie hadn't done her duty yet this morning, I stuffed toilet paper in my jacket pocket and off we went.

The minute we got back I pounded on Margaret's door to beg for a couple aspirin tablets.

Margaret's wardrobe was half hidden by one of her fancy aprons when she greeted me at the door holding a paper towel between her hands. The smell of freshly baked chocolate chip cookies soon wafted to the doorway as well. "You poor boy. Why didn't you call me earlier? When the cookies in the oven are done, I'm going to whip you up chicken noodle soup and bring it over. Just leave your door unlocked."

"That's not necessary. I only came by to get something to deaden the pain in my head."

"You hush. When a person doesn't feel good they need a little pampering."

"Does that include throwing in a cookie too?"

Margaret's old eyes twinkled. "*Si*. Now go take that aspirin and see if it helps."

When my neighbor came by with the soup twenty minutes later, I was looking through the photos from the capper machine area. Since I didn't want to stop what I was doing, I brought them to the kitchen.

"What do you have there, Matt?"

"Photos I took of a capper machine used at Delight's bottling plant." I set the pictures down, took the pot of soup from her, and put it on the table. Then I got a bowl and spoon out and sat.

Margaret pulled a plastic bag from the pocket of her ruffled apron. *What a saint.* She had filled it with about a dozen cookies. "Here's your dessert. Do you mind if I take a peek at your pictures?"

"Sure, go ahead," I said as I filled my bowl with soup.

She picked up the photos and went through them one by one. "How does this machine work?"

I swallowed what was left in my mouth. "The filled cans move along a conveyor belt to the capper machine. When they get in the right position, caps roll down a chute and the machine presses them in place and folds down the sides."

"Oh, my, goodness. That's amazing." The elderly woman pulled out a chair and joined me at the table. "May I ask what you plan to do with these pictures?"

"Nothing at the moment, other than to see where in the bottling process it might be possible for someone to insert something in the pop that shouldn't be there."

"Sounds like something a good PI would be hired to figure out. "Does mechanical equipment also place the caps in the chute?"

I shook my head. "An employee actually feeds the packaged lids into the capper machine as needed."

Margaret steepled her hands. "I imagine the machine runs constantly in the warmer months of the year."

I stirred my soup. "Yup. Unless the lids jam in the chute or someone forgets to add more lids." With that said, a thought suddenly ripped across my brain. Packaged lids! I should've thought of that sooner. The person posted at the capper machine only leaves his position when he goes on break or to get more supplies. If Hu or Wang had studied the person's habits long enough, they could do something in this area. "That's it!" Margaret if I didn't feel lousy, I'd kiss you."

Margaret looked at me like I had completely lost it. "Whatever for?"

"You just helped me figure out how something could get into the pop without anyone else noticing." Wait until I tell Rod. He'll be impressed. But the FBI still needs to verify a virus has been put in the pop."

~45~

February 12

"Carol," I sniffled, "Put me through to Neil Welch please."

"I'm sorry Mr. Welch is in a meeting. May I ask who is calling and what your call pertains to?"

Colds seem to make most people irritable, including myself. I don't know why. Not getting a decent night's sleep could be to blame I suppose. "Carol, this is Matt Malone, I really don't have time for this malarkey," I groused. "Put me through to your boss, pronto."

"Of course," Carol blubbered. "I'm so sorry, Matt. I ah didn't recognize your voice."

"I've got a cold."

"Oh? I hope you don't have what I had."

Welch's phone buzzed a couple times before being picked up. "This is Neil Welch. How may I help you?"

I cleared my throat. "Neil, this is Matt Malone. I have something extremely important to share with you."

"Oh? Don't tell me you've obtained more information regarding the three men who died?"

"Forget about the men for a moment," I said in a feverish voice. "You need to pull Bubble Gum Pop off the market immediately."

"Have you lost your mind?" he screamed. "Why would I pull the plug on Delight's newest beverage?"

"The men in charge of your computer departments, here in the States, contaminated the new pop with a virus. You know, the new strain the CDC couldn't figure out."

"You've got to be joking."

Cold or no cold I was prepared for Welch's reaction. If I was in his shoes, I'd be raking the guy over the coals who delivered such bad news too. "Believe me, I wish I were."

Delight's president stammered. "Wha...t? That's impossible. How could they do it? The chemists check the pop after it's mixed and before it's fed into the cans or bottles."

I blew my nose. "That's what I kept asking myself. It wasn't until I studied all the photos I took at the Boston plant that I finally figured it out. The men tampered with the pop lids."

"Preposterous! The caps are sealed inside plastic bags and no one touches them until they're released into the capper chutes."

"Right. That's exactly what I was told when I toured your plants. But there are two ways a virus could be spread using caps. Either someone opened the cap packages and dusted them with a virus before setting them in the capper chute or someone prepared the lids before they arrived at your locations. At this point I don't know which theory is correct.

"Look, I'm aware of the enormous consequences to your business if you do what I ask, but I take your problem seriously. As a matter of fact, I've dragged the FBI into this too. And we both know they don't joke around. Sir, the action I'm requesting of you boils down to a simple word you like to use, 'trust.' Do you trust me or not?"

Welch remained silent. I'd just thrown him the worst curveball for a man in his industry. When he finally spoke, it was with a reedy voice. "I don't know what to do, Matt. It's hard accepting such radical advice from someone younger than me, and a PI at that. This business I've fought so hard to keep going could be destroyed in an instant by an order mandated by me. I shudder to think of the number of people who'd become unemployed overnight. It's staggering." He inhaled deeply. "Matt, I'll consider what you want me to do, but only if you swear there is absolutely no other available solution."

"Believe me there isn't. CDC said the only solution was to get the pop off the market as soon as possible."

"All right. I'll call all my managers and ask them to work out the details at their end."

"Mr. Welch, before you hang up I need to ask you one more thing. Did your company recently switch lid suppliers?"

He exploded. "Hell, I don't know. Those details are taken care of at the plant level."

"Ah choo. Well, find out," I fired off, "And let me know."

~46~

February 13

I finally resigned myself to the fact that the terrible cold I'd caught would hang around for at least another week and loafing on the couch wouldn't change the time table. Besides that I'd grown tired of being glued to the phone waiting to hear from Rod Thompson and Neil Welch. If they wanted to get ahold of me, let them call my cell phone.

So, around ten o'clock armed with only a small package of Kleenex stuffed in an inner pocket of my winter jacket and a huge insulated mug of coffee for fortification, I hopped in the Topaz with my crazy mutt, who's wild about car rides, and went in search of Susan Walker again, using the short list I'd compiled of women with the same name, five to be exact, living in the suburbs surrounding Minneapolis.

I drove to Bloomington first. "Sorry, hon," the mid-fifties woman with a Texas twang said, batting her overly caked eyelashes every few seconds as she spoke. "I just moved here two years ago. Walker was my married name."

"Thanks," I sniffed and returned to the car with Gracie who was getting antsy.

As we drove up to the next address, a cozy-looking rambler in Golden Valley, I glanced at Gracie. She was shaking something awful. Only two things made her do that, the thought of getting a bath and a trip to the vet's. "Don't worry, girl. You don't have to get out this time. I'll talk to the lady by myself, okay?"

"Woof. Woof."

"I figured you'd like that plan," I commented, rubbing her noggin for good measure right before stepping out of the car.

The double-wide walkway leading to the front door of this particular property was unusually long compared to the rest of the neighbors on the block, but it didn't bother me in the least even with a crummy cold. How can one complain when it's sunny out and the temperature reads mid-twenties?

The second I stepped up to the stoop of the house I searched for a doorbell. Finally finding one, I pressed it and patiently waited for someone to answer.

A woman in her mid-thirties with light-brown hair severely tied back and bound in a ponytail soon appeared and gave me a blank stare through the worn screen door. Her wardrobe consisted of white and black cleaning garb similar to what I'd seen in the Sparkling Maids' TV ads. "Yes, can I help you?"

"Hi. I'm here to see Susan Walker. Is she home?"

"Just a minute I'll get her," she replied curtly, closing the storm door and marching back into the interior of the house.

Five minutes later, a wheelchair bound woman in her seventies came to the door and offered a pleasant smile. "Hello. I understand you're looking for me. How can I help you?"

This woman wasn't Susan either. She was too old. I apologized profusely for disturbing her and hurriedly explained why I'd showed up at her house. The kind woman was so gracious. She invited me in for coffee and cookies. Imagine that. Hungry as I felt though I kindly declined, explaining I'd left my dog in the car and couldn't neglect her that long.

After checking out three more Susan Walkers residences, and coming up empty-handed again, I decided to go back to the halfway house and squeeze more info out of the gal I had spoken with before. She said Susan got religion. Maybe she knew what church Wanda had been attending at the time.

As I rounded the corner on the block where the halfway house is situated, Gracie attempted to get on my lap. Using a firm, but gentle tone, I told her nothing doing. Apparently her ears were full of wax, she tried again. Luckily, I didn't need more words to enforce how I felt. My nose did it for me. I let loose with a couple earsplitting sneezes. Shocked senseless, the dog stayed put.

When I finally pulled up alongside the curbing in front of the house, I seriously began to consider safety in numbers and cajoled Gracie into accompanying me to the doorsteps of the Victorian house, which hadn't been magically transformed from dilapidated to majestic since my last visit on the eighth.

While I waited for a resident of the house to check out who was so persistent in bringing them to their front door, I crossed my fingers, hoping the gal with scraggly hair and wasted body hadn't departed the premises to run errands.

"Yes. Oh, it's you," she said, pushing her long hair off her face. "I don't know why you've come back. I told you Susan's been long gone."

I raked my fingers through my hair. "I know. But I'm wondering if you might remember where around here she might've found religion."

The woman's nicotine-stained fingers slid up and down her turkey-sized neck as if she'd discover the answer in that region of her body. "Yup," she sputtered, "That I do recall. Father Kevin, the pastor over at St. Luke's down the road a bit, used to come by and chat from time to time. I don't know if he's still there. He may have gotten transferred by now."

"Thanks. I appreciate the info." I tugged on Gracie's leash letting her know we were leaving. Then I turned my back on the woman, dug out a Kleenex, and walked off.

"Hey," she yelled, "If you find Susan, tell her I'm still waiting for that money she owes me."

***

A few minutes later as I pulled up in front of a small brick building labeled St. Luke's Rectory, I found myself hoping the priest Patty Rose mentioned hadn't moved on yet. When I was growing up, the priest assigned as pastor of a parish remained there till he retired or died. But as soon as the Church found themselves with a shortage of men entering the seminary, things changed. Now, a priest stays at one church roughly five to ten years and then the bishop transfers him to another community.

An elderly man dressed in black shirt, pants, and highly-polished shoes opened the door to let me in. "What can I do for you young man?" he inquired while rubbing his thick gray beard.

"I'm on a mission, Father. Is Father Kevin still working for this parish?"

The priest didn't say one way or another if he was the man I was looking for. He merely straightened his thin wire-framed glasses that were about to slip off his long nose." That depends. What kind of mission are you speaking of?"

"I've been hired to find a missing person." To put the priest at ease I hastily added, "In case you're wondering, the person's not wanted by the police."

"That's good to know." Then the man of cloth wrapped his arm around my shoulder like he was welcoming back a long lost sinner. "Mr. Malone, if you're as good at your job as I suspect, I'm sure you've already surmised that I'm Father Kevin, so why don't we stop wasting time and take ourselves into my parlor where there's more privacy and a couple chairs."

I followed the priest into the tiny room opposite the doorway as he suggested and immediately made myself comfortable in the plumpest chair available. "Father, according to Patty Rose at the halfway house down the road you used to stop in to visit the gals from time to time. Is that correct?"

He nodded. "Yes, I did. But that was a couple years back, before I got bogged down with health complications."

"The woman I happen to be looking for left the halfway house roughly two years ago. Does the name Susan Walker sound familiar to you?"

The priest brightened considerably. "Why, of course."

Pleased with his answer I relaxed, allowing my folded hands to rest on my lap. "Patty Rose also told me Ms. Walker left after getting religion. So, I thought perhaps she might have shared with you where she planned to go."

Father Kevin looked me straight in the eye and asked, "Why would a private eye care where Susan went? You said your search for her had nothing to do with the police."

"It doesn't. Stanley Walker, Ms. Walker's brother, hired me to track her down. Both parents are deceased now and the estate needs to be settled. But in order to do so all the children need to be present at the meeting."

"I see." The priest's brow furrowed slightly while he pinched his beard. "Well, you're in luck young fella. I know exactly what Susan has been up to and I don't think she'd mind my telling you one bit. You see she's decided to devote her life to Christ."

I was taken aback. "Really? In what capacity? Is she doing volunteer work for the church in Central America?" If she was working out of the country somewhere, that would certainly explain no contact with the family.

"No. She's about to become a novice."

My jaw dropped. "What? You mean like in a nunnery?"

Father Kevin chuckled softly. "Yes. I bet you never suspected that did you, Mr. Malone. Ms. Walker is at the Mother House of Our Lady of Perpetual Help in Hudson, Wisconsin," he happily shared.

Concerned the woman I'd been hired to find may have joined an order which didn't permit her to leave the premises and only allowed contact with family once a year, I questioned the priest further. "Is that a cloistered order she joined?

The elderly pastor of St. Luke's shook his head. "No. No. I steered her away from that. She'd already made so many major changes in her life I thought it might be hard for her to be so confined."

I stood. "I'm sure Susan's family will be most appreciative of the path you directed her on, Father."

"I hope so." Father Kevin uncrossed his legs and pushed himself off the rocking chair he'd been sitting in. "Well, I suppose you'd like the number of the convent before you leave so Ms. Walker's brother can contact her."

"Most definitely."

"Stay right there. It'll just take me a second to get it."

The instant Father Kevin stepped out of the parlor my cell phone rang. Neil Welch's name popped up. I picked up. "Mr. Welch, I'm just finishing up with someone. Can I call you back?"

"Don't bother. This will be brief. You asked if our lid supplier had been changed recently."

"Yes."

"It had."

~47~

February 20

"Matt, we're going to be late," Rita gently chided.

"Okay, just a sec," I called from the bathroom, adjusting my tie in front of the mirror one last time. "Yup, you look fine you handsome devil. And if you want to continue to look this way, you'd better join the girlfriend in the living room right away." I snapped the light off and closed the door, hiding the mess behind.

"Well, what do you think?" I said, finally standing in front of Rita and Gracie. When nothing was said, I twirled so Rita could view me from every angle. "Do I look spiffed up enough for you?"

Rita rested her petite hand on her hip and stomped her size-seven foot on the carpet. "You don't know the first thing about dressing up, Matt. He can't go like that, can he, Gracie?"

Gracie's head bopped up and down. "Arooo."

I flung my arms in the air. "What? Really?" What's wrong with the way I look?" I scrutinized my ensemble from head to toe. Suitcoat, pants and shoes all matched. No food or toothpaste had marred them. Quite honestly I had no idea what Rita thought was wrong. "Can you give me a clue at least?"

Rita curled her slim index finger and gave me the come hither sign. I accepted the invitation. "Closer," she said. I inched a bit closer. "There that's perfect. Your tie needs to be straightened."

"What? But I just fixed it in the mirror," I grumbled.

"Calm down. I'm just going to fix it a little better." Rita put her hands around the tie and tugged on the knot I had made. "There it looks great."

"Good. I'm glad I meet your Good Housekeeping stamp of approval because a few seconds ago a certain someone said I needed to get moving."

"And we do."

I went to the closet, took out Rita's black wool coat, and helped her put it on. As she buttoned up, I gripped the door handle to leave.

"Aren't you forgetting someone?" Rita said, jabbing me in the elbow.

"Who?" I glanced over my shoulder. There sat Gracie patiently waiting for her master to attach the leash to her collar. "Sorry, girl, I've got too much on my mind tonight." I grabbed her leash off the hall table and hooked it up. "Okay, gals, let's trot over to Margaret's."

"Woof. Woof."

"Nope, there's no time for visiting Petey," I explained while standing in the middle of the hallway. "We're taking Margaret out to a fancy restaurant tonight."

Before I even had a chance to announce our presence at her door, Margaret cracked the door open a smidgen. She must've heard Rita and I talking. "Oh, it's you. *Ciao*, Rita. *Ciao*, Matt. Hello, Gracie." She quickly unchained her door and shuffled out of our way. "Please come in. I thought I'd better check to see who was in the hallway before unlocking the door. I worried that crazy man might be loose in the building again."

Rita's neatly plucked eyebrows reached new heights, seeking an explanation from me.

"I'll tell you another time," I whispered in her ear. "Just mention your Cousin Arnie."

"Margaret, would you like Matt to help you with your coat?"

"Not yet, dear," came the sweet as honey elderly woman's reply. "I'm having a hard time deciding which coat to wear. Perhaps you can help me. Should I wear a heavier coat or a lighter one?"

I'm glad she didn't ask me for advice. This guy generally grabs the wrong coat no matter what the outdoor temperature reads.

"It'll be toasty in the car, perfect for a light coat," Rita replied, "but it's not like that outside. It only got up to minus 15 today."

"Hmm. I guess that's settled. The wool coat it is."

"Okay, lady, just turn this way and I'll help you slip it on," I said.

"*Grazie.*" After the elderly woman buttoned her knee length coat and slipped on leather gloves, she locked her arm in mine. "I hope your girlfriend won't be upset I took you away from her, Matt?"

I gave Rita a quick wink. "Nah. You've got nothing to worry about."

One more person on the fourth floor would be joining us at supper tonight. After Margaret turned the key in her lock, the four of us headed to his door next.

"Well, it's about time," Rod Thompson said in a teasing tone.

"You know how women are, always making us men late."

A resounding, "Thanks a lot," from the two women caused my ears to ring.

While waiting for Rod to secure his apartment door, I examined the bright blue suit he had on. *Hmm. Not bad. I wonder what Rita thinks of his suit.* I rested my eyes on the lovely woman standing next to me. Yup, looks like she's impressed. Perhaps I should purchase an outfit similar to Rod's. I definitely can afford it with the handsome compensation package Neil Welch recently gave me.

Rod pocketed his key and then we strolled down the narrow hallway to the elevator. "Matt, I'm not carrying much in my wallet at the moment. Are you positive this guy is paying for everything?"

"How many times do I have to confirm that the guy is picking up the tab. Don't the words, 'dinner on him,' mean anything to you?"

"Yeah, sure. I just don't want to be caught off guard."

"Believe me you won't be."

The elevator dinged. We had reached the garage floor. The second I stepped out onto the basement level I noticed snow puddles everywhere. The gals didn't need to tromp through that. I handed Gracie's leash over to Rita. "Honey, you and Margaret stay put. Rod and I'll get the car."

Rita glanced at the clumps of snow directly ahead of her then she looked down at the heels she had on. "Great idea. Thanks."

When Rod saw the car, he immediately made fun of it. "Matt, were on the cusp of the twenty-first century. Is this clunker the best you can do for your mode of transportation? You'd better give me proof that it's safe to ride in."

"Chill out Rod. Tonight we're calling a truce, okay? The ladies are looking forward to a pleasant night on the town and that's what they're going to get. Save the bickering for another time."

Rod ran his hand through his thick hair. "I'll try, but you're such fair game."

~48~

My fellow companions and I may not have known what to expect of our host this evening, but thanks to Rita's kind words about Kincaid's exceptional dining experience, having eaten there twice before, we knew we wouldn't go home hungry.

When we checked in with Kincaid's hostess fifteen minutes later, she informed us we'd be eating in the private dining section at the back of the restaurant. Since there was no set path to get there, we were forced to meander past enormous clay pots overflowing with arranged flowers, empty dining tables decked out with linen tablecloths and umpteen pieces of fine silverware, and a mirrored wall built to showcase Kincaid's ample supply of top quality liquor for quenching even the fussiest person's thirst.

The minute Neil Welch caught sight of us entering the reserved room; he stood, wrapped his arm around his wife's tiny waist and led her over to us.

I find it interesting to note what people with megabucks wear at these types of functions since I rarely receive invites to swanky shindigs. So, I examined the couple from head to toe like a professional reporter who was expected to turn in an article at evening's end.

The owner of Delight Bottling, who was dressed to the nines, had donned a black suit, tie, and shoes which made him look like he'd just stepped off a Paris runway. Although the crisp white shirt he wore could've been borrowed from a Knights Formal Wear down the street.

The man's refined wife, who appeared to be ten years younger than him, wore a two-piece rose colored suit, matching shoes, and earrings. Of course, one couldn't miss her French manicured nails if one tried. The four expensive gemstone rings on her fingers helped flatter them even more.

I did the introductions — oldest to youngest. Mrs. Grimshaw, this is Mr. and Mrs. Welch."

She smiled meekly. "Hello, Mr. and Mrs. Welch. It's so nice of you to invite me."

"It's a pleasure to have you here tonight, Mrs. Grimshaw."

After Margaret stepped aside, I linked my arm with Rita's. "This is Rita Sinclair, my girlfriend."

Rita nodded and offered a hand. "Hello."

"Hello," the Welch's said in unison.

Now, I motioned for Rod to move in closer. "And, this is Rod Thompson from the FBI," I continued.

"Oh, yes," Welch said, "The young fellow who helped you." He pumped Rod's hand vigorously.

"Thanks for inviting me," Rod said keeping his hand in gear with Welch's, "I've never had a chance to eat here before."

"Let me assure you, you won't be disappointed," Mary Welch said.

Once Rod moved by Margaret, Rita passed off Gracie's leash to me. "This is my faithful mutt, Gracie. If it weren't for her, I would've never figured out what was going on at your plant."

Mrs. Welch leaned over and padded Gracie on the head. "Such a gorgeous dog you have, Matt."

"Thank you. She was primped special for this party."

She continued to shower attention on the dog. "So, Gracie I understand you're our hero."

"Woof. Woof."

"Okay, Gracie," I said, "That's enough. We don't want to get tossed out of this swanky restaurant. We haven't eaten yet."

Done with the introductions, Neil Welch pointed to the long table reserved for us. "Shall we sit down so the waiter can begin his duties?"

The second we were all seated at the table I noticed two extra place settings, but nothing was mentioned concerning them. Perhaps Neil Welch felt there wasn't any need to explain the absence of the other guests, especially if they were board members.

After a few minutes of light chatter with others at the table, I noticed motion by the doorway. Thinking it was our waiter finally, I glanced up. To my surprise it wasn't the waiter who had waltzed in, but Welch's secretary. What's Carol doing here? Surely there's no need for notetaking tonight. This is meant to be a leisurely evening.

Neil Welch stopped chatting when he saw his secretary enter the room. "Everyone, I'd like to introduce my daughter Carol who also serves as my secretary."

My jaw almost unhinged. "What?" I can't believe their relationship slipped past me. That's why Mr. Welch didn't have the heart to can her.

Evidently, Margaret caught the deer-in-the headlights look on my face. Her charming little grin quietly let me know she enjoyed the fact something actually slipped past this PI.

I cleared my throat. "Nice to see you again, Carol."

"You too, Mr. Malone."

As soon as she got situated at the table, Neil Welch said, "I'm sure you've all noticed we're still missing one guest. Unfortunately, the person has been delayed at the airport. So, Matt and Rod, why don't you two share what the FBI and CDC uncovered while we enjoy drinks and hors d' oeuvres."

I studied Rod's face. He didn't appear to be any more anxious to speak than I.

Welch grew impatient, "Well, who's going to begin?"

Since I appreciated the tremendous work opportunity Neil Welch had already given me and hoped to be invited to work for him in the future, I figured I'd better get the ball rolling. But before I could, two waiters interrupted us.

After the short chubby waiter placed a couple bottles of chilled Dom Pérignon champagne on the table, he opened one and poured a sample for our host to taste. Welch did so, and then quickly nodded his approval so the waiter could fill the rest of our wine glasses.

When the shorter waiter finished his duties, the taller slimmer one swooped in with huge plates of appetizers for our table. Then he passed out small cold empty white plates to each of us.

Wouldn't you know my stomach loudly proclaimed it required food the instant I received my plate. Embarrassed, I pressed my hands to quash anymore weird sounds that tried to come forth.

Luckily, I didn't need to be concerned about my stomach for the moment. Neil Welch lifted his glass of champagne, indicating a toast. *I hope it's a long one.* "Here's to Matt Malone, a first-rate PI."

The others raised their glasses. "To Matt."

After I was saluted, Welch offered another toast. "Here's to Rod Thompson's gracious assistance."

"Woof. Woof."

"Of course, we can't forget Gracie," Neil Welch said, raising his glass again. "Without her, my business could've gone in the tanker."

"Arooo."

Margaret interpreted Gracie's message. "She agrees with you Mr. Welch."

He grinned. "Of course she does. Gracie's a very intelligent dog."

I patted the mutt on the head, said, "Good girl," and then I dug out a few Milkbones from a suitcoat pocket and offered them to her. The treats should keep her quiet while her master explained about the case.

"I'm sure by now all of you have heard about the break-in at the Saint Cloud plant and about the death of three department managers. But what you might not know is the unknown influenza outbreak was caused by contaminated Bubble Gum Pop."

"What?" Mary and Carol said with one voice.

I repeated myself. "The new influenza outbreak was caused by the pop. When I figured it out, I got the FBI involved. Rod immediately sent samples of Bubble Gum to

CDC to test my theory. Their lab came to the same conclusion."

Rod cut in. "The new virus strain is actually a mutation of two already existing types. Because it can withstand cold, it actually gets stronger the colder the exposure."

"Excuse me," Rita said, holding a slice of salmon and cracker in her hand. "Can you tell us a little more about this particular virus and who is to blame?"

I ran a hand through my hair. "The new strain is a mixture of Type A, a respiratory health issue, and the Norwalk, which is gastrointestinal."

"The Type A used in this particular virus has been recently classified under a new heading by the CDC," Rod added. "It's called Hong Kong Duck. They said it was only a matter of time before it surfaced with so much human and duck contact."

Margaret Grimshaw dabbed her lips with a cloth napkin. "Matt, with Type A and Norwalk merged which symptoms should one look for?"

I took a sip of champagne. "That's an excellent question, Margaret.

When a consumer opened Bubble Gum Pop, Type A was released in the form of a mist and entered their nasal passages, giving them a terrible respiratory cold. The Norwalk doesn't actually kick in until the person drinks the pop."

"Which I did," Carol piped up. "Believe me you don't want to be the recipient of that double whammy. I thought I'd never get better."

Mrs. Welch, who had been listening on the sidelines, finally entered the discussion. "Mr. Malone, I mean Matt; I don't understand how general practitioners failed to recognize this new virus."

I leaned my head in the direction of Mrs. Welch. "Dick's doctor wouldn't have detected a new virus if Dick only complained of gastrointestinal problems, which are normally associated with the 'winter disease' called Norwalk.

"Sally, on the other hand, complains about upper respiratory problems to her doctor and he treats her for a cold. Then there's George who comes into his doctor with both symptoms, gastrointestinal and upper respiratory. His complaints are heard by an over-burdened doctor who rushes through the exam. 'Just influenza,' he states, which in layman terms means go home, drink plenty of liquids, and get lots of rest. Unfortunately, George's condition will be reported to CDC as simply another person struck by this year's known virus, not the new unknown one."

"It's a well-known fact," Rod said, "that overworked doctors rely heavily on available explanations so they don't have to waste time searching for other answers."

Mary Welch set down her empty wine glass. "It sounds to me like the creation and implementation of this new virus was well thought out."

"It's too scary to even think about," my lovely girlfriend interjected.

My stomach growled again. I eyed what was left of the appetizers sitting on a platter in front of me that I hadn't had a chance to try yet, and decided Rod could pick up where I left off. "Rod, why don't you take over."

"Sure."

Mary Welch suddenly stood and excused herself. "Neil, make sure to tell me what I missed when I get back," she said, walking off in the direction of the restrooms.

"Of course, dear."

What luck! I've been waiting for the perfect opportunity to have a private chat with Mary Welch. In my mind there was still a small piece of the puzzle that hadn't been resolved yet, namely a German guy by the name of Peter. "You know, Rod, why don't you hold off a bit. It seems I need to use the facilities too," I lied.

I caught Mary by the arm as she was about to step into the women's restroom. "Excuse me, Mary, but I need to talk to you."

"About what? she questioned with a hostile tone. "We certainly don't travel in the same circles, Mr. Malone."

"That's true. But this is in regards with my travels to Germany and Boston for your husband."

"I can assure you I know nothing about the goings on at Delight. I keep myself very busy with charity work."

"Ah, but that's where your wrong. If I'm not mistaken, you know quite a bit. After all, you do have a daughter living with you who works very closely with Neil. I can't believe she's never shared any work related info with you."

Mary Welch put her hand on her hip. "Exactly what are you insinuating, Mr. Malone?"

"When you and your husband were having marital problems, I'm sure you thought about how much money you'd get in a divorce settlement."

"So, what if I did? Is that a crime?"

I shook my head. "Of course not. But I think when you learned Neil was selling off plants without your knowledge, specifically the ones I was hired to tour; you hired someone on the inside to be your eyes and ears, a man named Peter."

Her face grew ashen. "But... how? When?"

"Ah, I see your husband never revealed what my real line of work is."

"And, what pray tell is that?"

"Why, I'm a private investigator."

Mary pressed her hand against her cheek. "Oh, no. Have you told Neil about Peter yet?"

"No, and I don't plan to. I have nothing to gain by telling him."

"Thank you, Mr. Malone. Thank you. You know we are getting along much better now."

"So, I see."

***

As soon as Mary and I rejoined the group in the private dining room, Rod shoved his empty appetizer plate out of the way and rested his elbows where the plate had just been. "Rita," he began, "I believe you wanted to know who was responsible for placing the virus in the Bubble Gum Pop, right."

"Yes," she murmured.

"Well, I've spent many hours digging through the computer system at the St. Cloud plant and discovered the faxes Matt obtained from U.S. locations originated at Delight's Hong Kong bottling factory. The faxes were written in an old cryptic Chinese code. When I handed the first fax Matt gave me to a translator here in the Twin Cities, all he noted was a threat to Neil's Boston computer department manager and the family he left behind in China. But after I brought in the second fax from the St. Cloud plant, another FBI agent took a look at it and decoded the hidden message."

Margaret tilted her tiny head. "Oh, my! What did it say?"

"The computer department managers were told they'd be receiving a shipment of contaminated lids and what date to use them."

Margaret frowned. "Why didn't the managers report what was going on? What's happened to company loyalty?" She shook her hand as if she was reprimanding school kids. "This would've never happened years ago with people in my age bracket. Someone would've blown the whistle."

Neil Welch cleared his throat, preparing to explain, but Rod replied instead. "I'm sure the men wanted to squeal, but their hands were tied so to speak."

"How so?" Carol asked.

Having quieted my stomach with sufficient food, I took over for Rod. "The managers living here in the U.S. were all brought into the country illegally."

Mary Welch flashed her husband a look of contempt. "How could you?"

Neil tossed his hands upward, pleading innocence. "I had no idea."

She seemed unsure of his words so I helped defend him. "He's telling the truth, Mary. Illegal trafficking of humans is widespread in third world countries. Those smuggled to a new destination may be leaving their old life behind, but they never get to cut their ties with the traffickers. In order to receive legitimate looking documents, the people smuggled in here to infiltrate Delight were forced to swear allegiance to the traffickers."

"But those guys were highly-educated men," Rita said, "Why would they get involved with traffickers?"

"They wanted a better life," I said, "just like people from other Third World countries. Little did they know they'd be used as pawns in a sinister plot at some point in their careers."

Chills ran up and down my spine when I reflected on the three managers, especially Hu and Wang, and their fatal China Connection. If they hadn't wanted to escape the harsh realities of their country, they'd probably be alive today.

Margaret bit down on her lip. "I can't help wondering why some Chinese group chose to have a virus inserted in a particular brand of pop. What did they hope to accomplish besides spreading a new virus around?"

Carol turned to face her father. "Dad, do you think they were mad at our company for some reason?"

Neil Welch shrugged his shoulders.

I quickly dispelled her concerns. "This had nothing to do with revenge, Carol," I softly replied. "This Chinese faction simply wanted to find out how easy it would be to overthrow the United States. If their little experiment worked, our water supply would've been next, making the virus more potent and deadly."

I glanced around the table after I delivered my frightening information. Everyone's bodies had stiffened.

"My God," Rita whispered.

Carol ran a hand across her forehead. "I'm swearing off water. I don't care if drinking eight glasses of water a day is good for my health or not."

My elderly neighbor rubbed her arms. "Did you ever find out how the three men died, Matt?"

I shook my head. "Yes, a tiny pinprick near their earlobes transferred poison into their bloodstream."

Margaret's eyes displayed sadness. "Those poor men."

Neil Welch gently squeezed his wife's hand for support. "They were hard workers," he said with a solemn tone to his baritone voice, "and will be hard to replace."

This morgue like atmosphere I'd created was becoming unbearable. We came here to celebrate. Where were the waiters? I sure could use a mixed drink.

~49~

A familiar voice outside of our little group suddenly burst forth from behind me. "Hey, what's going on here? I thought you invited me to a celebration, Mr. Welch. It looks like I'm attending a funeral, unless this is how you Americans party."

I glanced over my shoulder. "I don't believe it," I said under my breath, "He finally did it."

"What are you talking about, Matt," Rita quizzed.

Margaret turned to me. "Do you know this man, Matt?"

"Yeah," I replied excitedly, "I sure do." I pushed my chair back, rushed over to Welch's last guest to arrive, and patted him on the back. He grabbed my hand and shook it. "Good to see you again," I said, "I hope you had a comfortable flight. So, you've officially moved to the United States to work. Do you know which plant you will you be assigned to yet?"

"I believe I'm going to St. Cloud," Yang Qing answered in his thick Portuguese accent, grinning from ear to ear. "Is it located in a nice community?"

I smiled. "Of course it is. I spent four years of college there."

Yang released my hand and turned his attention to the people at the table. "Hello, I'm Yang Qing. I'm sorry I'm so late, but my departure from Sao Paulo, Brazil last night was delayed due to poor weather. From the looks on your faces I'm sure most of you are wondering why a complete stranger has been included in this little party. Well, blame it on Matt." He pointed to me. "This fellow shared such exciting tales of Paul Bunyan, Native American Indians, and the environment; I couldn't resist requesting a transfer to the land of 10,000 lakes."

"*Bem Vinda*, welcome Yang. As you can see we're all pleased to have you here. So, quit yammering," Neil Welch teased, "and take the empty seat by my daughter. I think we Minnesotans have waited long enough to eat, don't you?"

66746046R00167

Made in the USA
Lexington, KY
23 August 2017